COMPOSER

ANONYMOUS

C. ASH

1. The Renaissance 1

2. Underwater Labyrinth 6

3. The Katrin Show 19

4. Candy Opera 26

5. Secret Passages 37

6. Princess Falls From the Sky 47

7. Championship Run 59

8. Candlelit Rain 73

9. Birthday Cake Castle 82

10. Something New 93

11. Performed Live 104

12. Holo Music 113

13. Star Sparkler 123

14. Candy Palace 137

15. Surpassed 148

16. Waltzes and Sketches 165

17. Tower Fireworks   180

18. Tea With Frenemies   196

19. 0.000001   210

20. Identity Crisis   223

21. The Truth Matters   234

22. Royal Hacker   248

23. The Imperfect Replica   258

24. Stakeholders of the Future   276

25. By Colin Burke   289

Meet the Author   303

Meet the Press   304

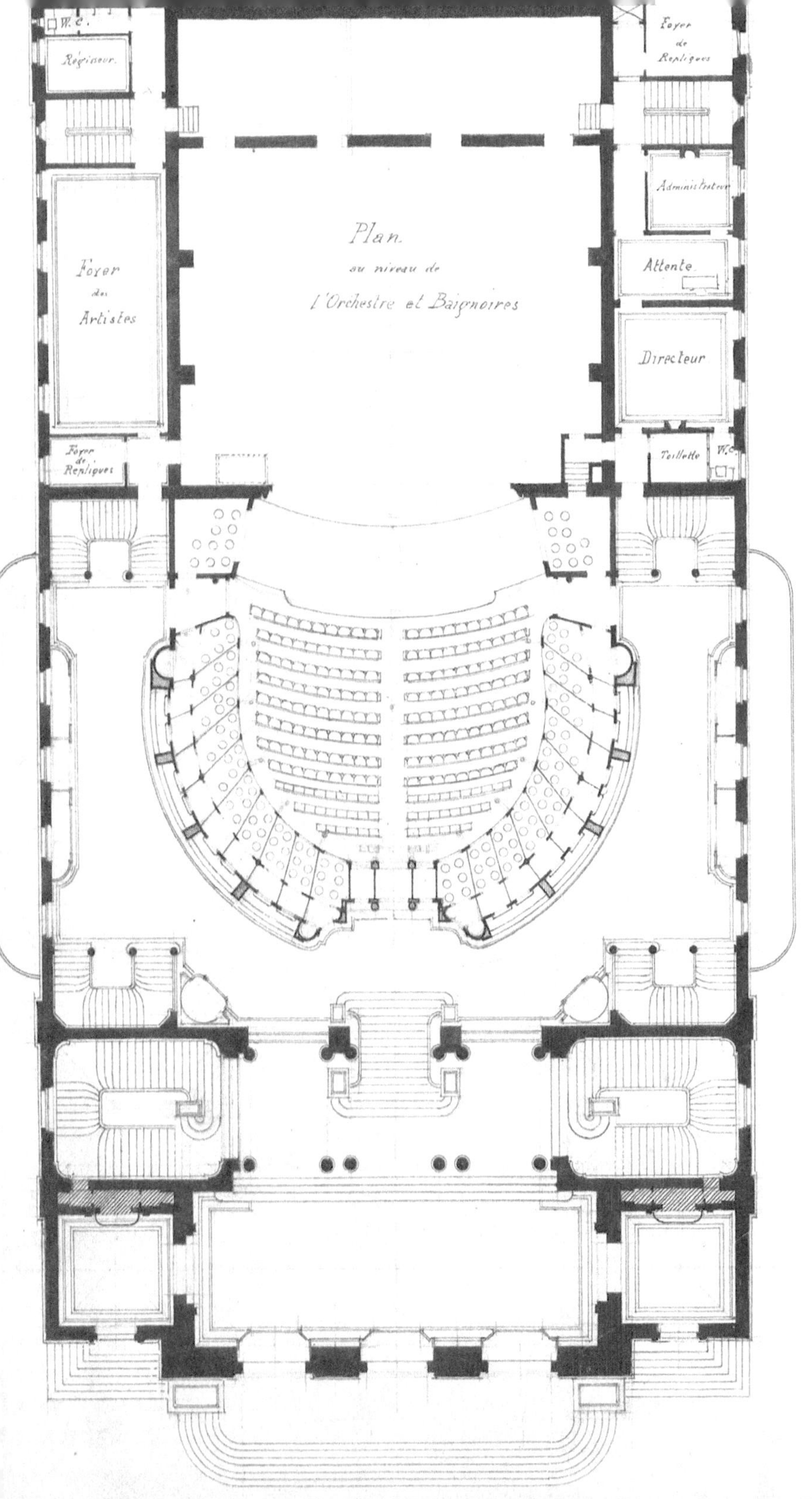
W.C.
Régisseur.
Foyer de Répliques
Administrateur
Attente
Directeur
Plan
au niveau de
l'Orchestre et Baignoires
Foyer des Artistes
Foyer de Répliques
Toilette
W.C.
Régisseur
Foyer de Répliques

"God is our refuge and strength,
a very present help in trouble."

Psalm 46:1

Chapter One

The Renaissance

Kaelum City (formerly Paris), 2437

Train stations and anxiety are made for each other. The maglev whizzes by, too fast for him to see anything but a blur of black. It darkens the lounge behind glass panels and leaves behind an instantly brighter room. Colin Burke squints at the windows, then presses the music note bead on his bracelet between his thumb and index finger. He'd worn off the black paint with his rhythm of constant twirling until the bead turned white. It gives his hands something to do, his brain a singular object to focus on.

Another departure announcement crackles from the speaker in the ceiling. Colin moves his hands to grip the straps of his backpack and begins to hum out of habit. His steps pause. *Too bright, too loud, too much.* Royal Station is *always* too much. The new building is named after an ancient theater in London. Although it opened a year ago, the station has wooden floors and counters. Cases display old tickets and passport pages. It smells deceptively like sawdust and smoke, though neither has ever contaminated the purified air. People rush up and down moving sidewalks, in and out of automatic glass doors, and the ceaseless voices from hidden speakers overlay the station with a torrent of information.

Colin's stepbrother Josiah shoves him from behind. "Keep moving. You can't just stand in traffic," he snaps.

Colin's other stepbrother, Davin, watches from a few paces ahead. His stepfather, Lance, halts last, the expression on his face customarily exasperated, before motioning them forward. Lance is the perfect government executive. Always stressed. Worships his schedule. If he didn't have such advanced genetics, Colin would wonder why he didn't already have gray hair. But he was designed to look perfect, and his two sons were designed to mirror him with their black hair and silver-black eyes.

Colin is clearly the odd one out of the set.

Lance makes a left turn for the platform. Colin hurries a few steps, his eyes darting between his stepfather and a businessman rushing by on a video call. A girl behind Colin pushes past, her contacts glowing blue as they translate the signs above her in two languages aloud. His attention snaps back when Lance grasps his arm and pulls.

"We don't have time for your attacks or episodes or whatever you call them today. The boys have to get to the stadium for practice or their coach will not forgive me this time."

Josiah laughs. "He didn't forgive you last time."

"Exactly." Lance doesn't crack a smile. "Just keep up and don't say anything. If you make a scene, your time with that tablet is going to be over."

Colin nods, ignoring the instant frustration that burns in his chest.

Lance will always treat him like he's seven instead of seventeen. Still, Lance knows Colin's weakness: composing music on his tablet. *Just get on the maglev as quickly as possible. Sit down.* As he hurries along, Colin focuses on the *Canopy Crown* song he's composing a melody for. He mentally rehearses the harmonics of the violin section. The graceful pizzicato over the next few measures. It'll contrast nicely with the—

Colin crashes into Davin. "I'm sorry," he sputters, glancing up. *Not Davin.* The stranger's contacts glow, his acknowledgement of Colin's presence minimal before he continues across the platform. Colin's head swivels. Where is his family? His breathing quickens. He turns a desperate circle, the noise around him suddenly dialed up. He nearly claps his hands over his ears to focus.

Why am I so stupid? Thinking about music instead of—

"Colin!" A familiar voice slices through the cacophony.

He catches sight of Lance. He's already on the maglev, waving both hands in frustration. Colin dashes across the platform and slips onto the train just as the lights flash. The doors hiss shut behind him. So close. Too close.

He drops into a seat, shoulders hunching and pulse still racing. He could have been stranded at the station. Everything happened so fast. Lance sits beside him. The boys are sitting behind them in paired seats. Colin's eyes betray him and drift up from his lap. Lance glares at him.

"Are you incapable of functioning in any public space without causing some kind of disaster? It's very simple. You keep up. You get on the train. You sit—" His gaze pierces into Colin's until he abruptly gives up, shifting in the seat and holding out an arm. "Just hand me the tablet. I know you can understand that much."

Ouch. That last barb is a new generation of insult to his intelligence.

Colin digs his fingers into the grooves of his bracelet. How is he going to finish the song drifting through his head without access? What will he do on this trip without TIRA? She keeps him sane when everything is unfamiliar. Even if she is only an AI system.

Colin slides the case out of his backpack and hands over the silver-lined tablet, watching out of the corner of his eye as Lance opens the display and presses his finger down, receiving a single tone as the program recognizes him as a legal guardian. His digital education program allows parents to restrict their children's access, so students can be locked out of anything or everything. Education, society, activities, music. Gone.

When the tablet is dropped back into his lap, Colin touches the screen once and realizes that he's locked out of everything *except* for his music software. Huge mercy. He fishes his noise-canceling headphones out of his backpack but looks up at Lance. Colin hasn't apologized yet—although he feels like he apologizes every hour, every day of his existence for being the way he is. Still, it doesn't hurt to keep repeating it.

"I'm sorry."

Lance's expression doesn't waver. "If you were, you'd change."

Colin settles the headphones on his ears until they feel right, then connects to his tablet, playing back the electronic bars of the measures he's composed on his song so far.

He'll compose. He'll do the only thing he knows he can do right.

He doesn't know why he has melodies always forming in his head. He doesn't know why he always seems to function on a different wavelength than others. He can't fix it. He doesn't know how.

He *does* know that two hundred years ago, advancements in genetic code allowed geneticists to purge so-called "neurodivergence."

It might be easier to be autistic if he wasn't the only anomaly in the year 2437.

Chapter Two

Underwater Labyrinth

The stadium is built in a spiral on the inside, seats winding down after it. The dome is massive like the ancient arenas but has better holographic technology and paneling than they did. Within the glass spiral is an underwater racing labyrinth. The place smells both like chemicals and the commercial air fresheners used to mask the chemicals. Colin's stomach knots just thinking about swimming inside glass, even though each section opens back up to a pool with air at the surface. The course is illuminated with colorful lights on the inside too, but somehow that only makes it look more intimidating.

Colin circles his way down empty bleacher seats until he gets to seat 100. He composes in this exact seat every practice. Cold air is blowing down into the bowl of the immense stadium, so he twists in the seat to tug his coat back on. It's a little short at the sleeves, but he doesn't call any attention to it. Maybe Lance hasn't noticed. New clothes are still the bane of his existence. That and an angry Lance.

Unfortunately for Colin, the domed city is in the height of a Victorian Renaissance. Kaelum is busy unearthing the thick fabrics and hand-sewn embroidery and lace from the past. The elites started it, picking up fashion trends inspired by the 1800s.

Colin mourns the day this Renaissance caught fire. It was one of the ways his mom had first realized that he was different. When he was three, Mom had finally saved enough money to buy him a new outfit. There was a shirt, waistcoat, and scarf combination. Colin was not pleased. He tugged at the scratchy fabrics, crying in the shopping center, then screaming until the clothes were removed—which took forever with all the buttons.

He didn't have a lot of words back then, but the root of the problem was such an extinct disorder that Mom spent hours looking it up on digital archives. *Sensory Processing Disorder*. One of his less delightful qualities.

The alternative was to wear the simple platinum-colored shirts that were made available for free to struggling families in the city and were now only worn by customer assistance androids at shopping centers. But Colin liked the way they felt, so his long-suffering mother let him wear them. When he was six, Mom once left him alone for a moment in the corner of a tech shop, and a woman stopped to ask him questions. He had just stared. It didn't help that his family had no money to customize his genetics. His eyes were solid gray and his hair ash brown. The woman gave him several standard instructions, then reached out and tapped his forehead in confusion when he didn't respond. His mom swept in and pulled him away. "He's a real child!" he remembers her exclaiming. Several people in their dresses and hats and wool coats stopped to gawk.

Footage of the incident was leaked onto the internet by an anonymous source. Colin was famous for nearly a week as the kid mistaken for an android.

Then he discovered music.

Colin turns his attention to his tablet. "Hello, TIRA."

TIRA responds automatically. Her voice is warm; it's a comfort he's known since childhood. *"Hello, Colin."* The AI pauses in an almost humanlike way, then continues, *"What are we working on today?"*

"Canopy Crown," he says, a satisfied smile teasing his lips. Now he must compose a song worthy of the name. He wants it to sound like raindrops filtering through leafy trees to the forest floor. He's never seen a forest—at least nothing beyond the immersive experiences that technology has to offer—but the sounds of the raindrops' calming, ceaseless patter in the simulation stuck with him.

Above him, the boys' coach is running along the narrow, floating walkway outside the glass labyrinth, watching each swimmer navigate the coils of the underwater course. He talks to himself and mutters constantly. At the pace he's currently muttering, it looks like he'll have a lot of pointers for the boys later.

Colin glances back as Davin executes a perfect dive into the silver water at the starting pool, working his way determinedly through the turns of the labyrinth. His stepbrother second-guesses himself a few times, reaching dead-end tunnels in the water and back-tracking until he solves the puzzle. After he surfaces at the top pool and the hydraulic maze reshapes itself, Josiah follows. He dives into the labyrinth and weaves his way expertly through a glass coil to the top. He's the last leg of the team, finishing out the relay event. Josiah has always been the strongest swimmer and the most naturally athletic. Colin admires how much

Davin works and spends countless extra hours learning to keep up and perform well. It doesn't come easily for Davin, which might be the one thing he and Colin have in common. Not that Davin would be the one to mention it.

"You are not looking at the song," TIRA informs him. Now that the tablet is running, her location updates. *"You are at the stadium. You are watching the practice instead?"* When he doesn't reply immediately, she adds, *"Would you like to try swimming in Labyrinth?"*

Colin doesn't know how her program gets these ideas. "Absolutely not. I don't like swimming underwater, or in glass obstacle courses, or getting yelled at by a coach, or holding my breath for that long. It sounds terrible."

"It sounds fun to me," she says, some sort of humor matrix kicking in, as always.

Colin replies evenly, "Okay, I can drop my tablet in the water later."

His eyes finally shift down to the music software, and he begins setting the key signature for his song. TIRA doesn't reply to his suggestion, not that she'd be worried. His tablet is waterproof.

Colin blocks out the splashing echoing through the stadium by putting on his headphones and focusing on the tedious task of adding dynamic markings. He adds them quickly, innately knowing where to place each one. He's jolted out of his zone by the vibration of boots on metal stairs. Peeking over his shoulder, he watches three boys find seats together. He recognizes two of them as the younger brothers of one of Davin and Josiah's teammates. The third is a stranger to him. They sit nearby. Not too close, but close enough that, if he wants to, Colin can talk to them without raising his voice.

The sound of the races above them has quieted as the coach gathers the boys to review their upcoming schedule.

Colin should say something. Competing thoughts cause his pulse to quicken. He wants to have someone to talk to, to meet someone new. To possibly make new friends. But if he tries to act normal, he'll slip up somewhere. He will say something they don't expect, start a conversation the wrong way, or not respond quickly enough. Even worse, he might offer information they don't care about—that no one cares about. No normal person anyway.

Alternatively, he could tell them the truth. Then he'd watch as they'd glance at each other, they'd commence as short a conversation as their almost telepathic, neurotypical brains deemed socially acceptable, and then they'd leave.

He thinks through all this before realizing he's been staring at them. They've started to stare back, awaiting the start of a casual conversation.

A game? *Win*. A speech? *Listen*. Casual conversation? *No idea*. He tries to recall the latest article TIRA read to him about exchanging pleasantries.

Conversation tip: Don't ask prying questions. Ask them about their job, their hobbies, or where they've lived. Don't ask questions about their health, finances, whether anyone in their family has died recently, or why they've chosen their haircut.

TIRA has said that human conversation is a lot like a program. There are predetermined responses for any greeting or reply. He just has to memorize them. He tries to take some solace from this and removes the headphones to start the conversation with a greeting TIRA deems safe.

"Hey."

One of the boys tips his chin up. "Hey."

The three of them have matching twill waistcoats. Ironic, since the goal of the Victorian Renaissance was to explore distinctive, handmade styles.

The blond one in the middle gestures to the swimming course. "Are you going to try out next year?"

Colin thinks about this for a moment. He knows why he doesn't enjoy the sport. He can explain this well enough. "I find swimming enjoyable, but to be competitive at this level requires lung capacity training to complete a majority of the course in one breath. There are methods to get your body accustomed to it, but the training schedule the team requires is extensive. I also find the experience uncomfortable and not worth the continued effort of maintaining the scores eligible to swim in the event itself. I have other endeavors that make better use of my time."

He pauses there, gradually realizing that the response should have been shorter. A lot shorter.

Confound it.

The boy raises an eyebrow, then fires back, "Well, I'll be trying out. I consider this competitive, uncomfortable lung capacity endeavor worth my time."

The other two boys shake with laughter, and only one tries to hide his grin behind his hand.

Colin nods once. "Right. Well. Have fun." Colin chalks the conversation up as a catastrophic failure. He should have known that these boys were interested in competing, that they wouldn't truly want an explanation for why he didn't consider the sport. Not an honest one anyway. TIRA is still powered on, so he knows the AI will bring this up later.

Once practice is over and everyone has slowly filtered out of the stadium, Colin closes his program with only three new measures of progress.

The empty glass dome is quiet now. Josiah and Davin have emerged on the platforms by the lift. Colin runs through the rows below to get to the exit. Blue glass lifts are spaced around the outer halls of the stadium; most are empty at this hour. He waves his hand over the sensor at the closest door, the thin bracelet on his wrist flashing. Once the lift starts moving, he pulls off the access bracelet and shoves it back into his coat. He can't wear anything new on his arms for long, or he'll mess with it until the constant feeling of it touching him becomes unbearable.

At the top floor, light floods in from the curved glass panels that span the upper half of the stadium. Colin squints and searches for the opening to the station. The train makes a stop directly in the outer lobby. When spectators swarm the space, it's a hectic wait. Right now, only a few athletes dot the vast lobby. Colin locates his stepbrothers in record time. The analog clock above the train's sleek doors counts down the seconds until departure. The Royal Station has several golden clocks mounted on the walls as well, made in Victorian styles but digitally synced up to their system.

Colin arrives with almost a minute to spare. The boys have chosen their seats and are reclining with arms crossed and heads resting on bunched-up towels. Their dark hair is still damp and tousled. They'll probably fall asleep on the way home. They usually do. Colin doesn't mind. He adjusts his headphones until they sit perfectly over his ears, then keeps composing. Lance has already chosen his seat in the corner of the empty compartment. He has his earpiece in and is in a meeting with several figures whom his eyes keep jumping between. They're only visible to other members on the call, so he always appears to be reacting to empty seats. Josiah and Davin used to think it was funny, but they quickly grew accustomed to it.

Lance manages the money that goes into the glittering face of Kaelum: the royals and their glamour that sweeps the classes. From what Colin has overheard from his stepfather, the royals have only been set up by the government to entertain the citizens. He isn't sure why. The underhanded web of games that make up Kaelum's high society isn't something he cares to understand.

Colin focuses on finishing as much of his song as possible before they reach home. He won't have much time to compose when they get back. Colorful lights from the city beyond the train's windows flash across the floor of the train and over his hands as he plays back his short melody. The train slows as it passes through the tunnels downtown, the lights changing again as walls brighten to counterbalance the lack of sunlight. Colin still closes his eyes for a moment, determining not to get a headache from the rapid movement. Then he finds himself gazing out the window as the view transitions to towering buildings and digital advertisements in cursive Française. Lance must notice, because the moment he ends his call, he snaps at Colin, "Don't look out the windows. You're going to be complaining about headaches later."

A natural sunset glow breaks into the space as the train slows to a stop at the station inside the apartment lobby. Plants drape the walls and three-story windows. They're fed by a system of narrow waterfalls and fountains that race to long pools. After exiting the maglev, Colin focuses on the walkway ahead, determined not to be lured by all the sensory noise in the lobby. He does glance inside the pools as they pass, curious about what's been added. Since the Renaissance started, people have been eager to revitalize the tradition of "wishing wells." Since there's no longer any such currency, they toss shiny knickknacks and toys, a collection that gets swept out of the water by the chutes and sent to be recycled. Colin spies a goldfish figurine at the edge but resists the urge to scoop it up. It belongs to the never-ending, watery life cycle now.

He walks past the wall of waterfalls to the private lift. Their apartment is on the top floor, which is reserved for the nicest penthouse suites. It takes a neat ten seconds for their floor number to light up with a white glow and the door to hiss open. Once inside the apartment, his brothers disappear into their rooms, the LED display on their doors indicating that they've locked them. It's the same story every time they come back from practice.

The solar-powered lighting in the room is gradually adjusting to off-set the fading, natural glow coming through the glass walls. Changing brightness in sync, the lamps on the table and counters around the apartment give the illusion of flickering flames. Colin drags his feet across the wood floor to the kitchen counter and carefully puts down his tablet.

Lance follows, his earpiece still in. Its blue glow flashes once, and he looks over at Colin. "I have another meeting, and the boys need to rest. Make yourself useful and start the cleaning program."

His stepfather retreats in the direction of his own room with his holo tablet, soon to be a virtual boardroom. With his free hand, Lance grabs the more expensive visual aid from the kitchen table: a black-and-white newspaper with headlines about the royals splashed across its thin pages. Colin has never dared to pick one up. Lance doesn't allow him to touch his things, but he wonders what actually goes on in the gilded world of the royals.

First priority: return to composing. Colin quickly opens a touchscreen menu on the kitchen wall, scrolling a list of automated cleaning services their apartment can perform. He taps through each filter and adjusts the settings based on what random items his brothers have left about the space. Josiah leaves waistcoats, jackets, and boots strewn throughout the entire apartment. Davin is forgetful with smaller items. He left one of his cologne bottles on the corner of a table, the colorful glass mimicking a vintage chess piece.

Colin settles his headphones snugly over his ears, adjusting them a few times so it feels right. Then he plays a piece from one of his favorite ancient composers, Vivaldi. The cleaning system begins to vacuum, sanitize, and polish what it can. Sleek, robotic blades wipe down counters before disappearing underneath them to be disinfected. Colin sorts through items himself, placing clothes in different laundry compartments and gear in stacks. The lanterns above him shine brighter as the windows at his back grow dark. Kaelum becomes a constellation of glowing lights across the skyline, and the panels of the dome around the city gradually adjust to mimic a night sky.

When the apartment is spotless again, he hides the holo menus on the walls and turns the rooms to night mode. The lights fade until they leave a gentle flicker in the hall and above the kitchen. Colin retreats to his bedroom at last. It's a simple space, intended to be a walk-in closet. With a little modification and some soundproof walls for his music, it became his sanctuary.

He sits on his bed and opens his tablet. "TIRA?"

"Is it time to work on the song? You are exactly one percent finished with the composition."

Colin lies back and spins the note bead on his bracelet with his thumb. "I'm tired. Can you just pull up the numbers from my music shop? I want to see if I've sold anything this week."

TIRA's tone sounds slightly dubious. *"Opening sales page."*

He can see the glow of the tablet change out of the corner of his eye as she scrolls his admin screen. Lance was *highly* dubious when Colin first asked seven years ago if he could sell his songs and make them available for people to listen to, but after a few weeks, customers started trickling in. There's a steady demand for new music that sounds classical, so the handful of sales keep Colin's spirits high. His virtual academic program will ultimately determine if he will be assigned a career as a musician when he graduates in a few short weeks. If he doesn't get the place-ment...he's not sure what will happen to him. Probably a long factory shift somewhere he won't have time to compose anymore.

He tightens his fingers against the beads on his wrist at the thought of that possibility.

"One purchase," TIRA reports. He rolls over and studies the screen. *"The song* Pipe Organ Waterfall *was purchased by user 'Elayne.'"*

"I know that name." Colin browses his memory for something he learned in Art History.

TIRA relays the information first, displaying a small holo window to the side of the tablet with the photos. *"Elayne of Ascolat is a character from ancient Arthurian legend. She was a popular subject for painters."*

Colin looks over the paintings, scrolling with one finger through the holo display glowing over the edge of the bed. The memory is growing clearer. "I can never escape schoolwork with you around," he tells TIRA.

"You cannot."

When the city first assigned Colin a "Tiered Intelligence for Required Academics" tablet, he hated it. He could hardly grasp anything the tablet attempted to teach him. Then his mom opened up TIRA's infinite library of music one day, and Colin was fascinated for life. Every clever game, trick, and test TIRA tried to throw at him had seemed like another language, but music was the first language that clicked for him.

His language wasn't spoken. It was felt.

Every day, Colin struggled his way through required academics on the tablet until the moment he could close the education tab and discover more music.

"Pipe Organ Waterfall." He repeats the name of the song *Elayne* bought. "Let's play it." He slides off the bed as TIRA turns on his room's soundproofing. Opening his violin case, he pulls the instrument from its home. He tightens the bow and then runs the rosin across its hairs. Tunes briefly. He walks the ten paces across his small room as he plays. He can't play while standing still. He has to *move*, to flow with the music.

His violin is his prized possession. Loathe as he is to admit it, he wouldn't have it if it weren't for Lance coming into his mother's life back when he was seven. The instrument was still her gift to him, but he knew where the money had come from now. Not even a century ago, violins weren't made at all. Orchestral sounds were purely electronic. But after the Renaissance, violins like his were handmade again. Spruce tops and ebony fingerboards. It produces a sound like no other.

As soon as the bow touches the strings, he's immersed. Quick, descending notes make the piece sound like a waterfall. When he finishes the song, and the last note floats into the air, he plays two of his others: *A Song for December* and *Candlelit Rain Nocturne*. The nocturne is slower and more somber. When he finishes the final down bow, the silence feels good. He checks the time, then reluctantly puts the violin away. He should sleep.

TIRA disables the soundproofing. The lights click off after he's prepared for bed, and a soft glow from a holo notification illuminates right as he lies down. He squints and reads the announcement: *Rain scheduled for 3am-4am.* He sighs. They never seem to schedule the rain for when he's awake. If they planned a rain shower for the hour he's falling asleep, then he could listen to it and dream up a new song.

A door slams in the distance. Colin's heart races, dragging him from the precipice of sleep. The apartment has automatic doors, which makes them infinitely more difficult to slam. Lance's meeting must not have gone well.

He mouths a quick prayer under his breath as he falls asleep again. "God, please help him to sleep well tonight and to not be angry tomorrow. Tell my mother I love her and miss her."

CHAPTER THREE

THE KATRIN SHOW

The omnipresent black lenses haunt Katrin's mind as she approaches the catwalk and her assigned row in the audience. The velvet-lined aisle is empty, and seats are beginning to fill up in anticipation of the show. Katrin isn't excited. Her whole life already feels like a show. She just hopes that eyes will be glued on the display of fashion and not on her. She keeps her multicolored hair brushed behind her back and fixes her eyes on the ground as she walks so people won't stare at the blue-and-gold design on her irises until she passes.

A periwinkle glove reaches for hers and squeezes tightly as she walks to her chair. Adelaide appears at her left side, her designated friend's crinoline announcing her presence as her thick skirts brush against Katrin's. Adelaide is an icon of genetic design, her platinum hair and silver-blue eyes in perfect color harmony. Down to her lips and nail beds, the blue undertone is synchronous.

Though it's rare, Katrin has known the girl to be icier than her eyes.

Katrin's other assigned friend, Phoebe, is already standing by her seat. Phoebe has a calmer demeanor than Adelaide but a sharper tongue. She keeps everyone in the palace on their toes. Tonight, she's chosen a white dress with a ruby-studded bodice to contrast her black curls. Somehow, her genetics were modified to make her hair shine fiery red in the light and her black irises to have a thin, golden circle that makes them especially piercing.

A line of guests arrayed in sunset colors curtsey and bow to acknowledge Katrin's presence as she passes the row. She's accustomed to the response but can't wait for everyone's eyes and the lenses in the room to pan to the catwalk.

"Roland is here. Should he sit with us?" Adelaide lays a gloved hand on Katrin's shoulder.

Pausing, Katrin eyes her, debating on what her friend actually wants. Her words always contain hidden meaning. "Of course," Katrin eventually gives in. With all her changing moods, there's no way to figure out who Adelaide is sweet on. Besides, out of all the young people who flock around her like colorful birds at the palace, Katrin can tolerate Roland the best. Not because she particularly likes him, but because he never involves himself in any of the drama. He almost seems bored of it. She can relate.

Adelaide and Phoebe noticeably arrange themselves to seat the tall young man beside Katrin, then take their spots with a rustle of fabric as he claims the offered chair. Katrin's suspicious eyes cut to Adelaide, but her friend smiles demurely. Katrin turns to Roland next. He has his long arms balanced across his knees and is slumped forward a bit, clearly weary of the show already. His cream double-breasted waistcoat and collar contrast his dark skin and absurdly blue eyes. It's clear his family fashioned his genetic palette for him to stand out, yet all he tries to do is remain unseen. A walking irony.

"Was there a seating chart?" Roland asks when he catches Katrin looking at him.

She shakes her head slightly, used to minimizing her movements and expressions because of lurking video cameras. "No, but I could kick you out if that would make you feel better."

He follows her lead, barely moving his lips. "Yes. Please. Have mercy."

"What would you do instead?" she asks curiously.

"Watch horse races on the holo probably." He crosses his arms, studying the room. Over half of the nobility gathered around the catwalk is still staring at them. "You?"

"Painting probably." Her studio sits neglected too often. Her schedule is always filled to the brim with places to appear and parties to attend. Some days, by the time she gets around to setting up her supplies and applying a burnt sienna wash of paint onto a new canvas, she is too tired to keep going.

An announcement from hidden speakers silences the audience's chatter. "*Welcome, ladies and gentlemen, to the Josephine Mirror Shakespearian Collection. At this time, please turn off any holo glow to help us preserve optimum lighting conditions. Enjoy the show.*"

The lights shift on the catwalk as the first models emerge. Katrin can tell it's an 1850s-inspired collection since the meters of fabric are heavy and layered instead of shaped by a cage. The crowd admires dress after dress as they sweep across the velvet. Then couples emerge in matching designs, the men's waistcoats and the women's skirts made out of the same material.

Katrin resists the urge to fidget in her chair. She stares at each piece to memorize the way the light and shadows strike the folds so she can paint them later. If there is a later.

"If only someone would trip, then this would all be worth it," Roland whispers behind his hand.

Katrin is grateful there's music playing, or he might have been overheard. She faces forward, catching herself before she turns to him. She *almost* wants someone to fall. But the models are human, not android, and she is accustomed to the feeling of humiliation. Her news headlines practically write themselves. So she wills them to stay upright instead.

As the show comes to a close, an elaborate evening dress emerges. The crowd sighs with pleasure. The model stops near Katrin and spins. She wears a lacy white dress with matching parasol, her bodice and even her skirt studded with hundreds of pearls. Then the largest pearl at her neckline comes loose and hits the marble edge of the catwalk with a *ping*. The woman tries to grab for it with her free hand, but it slips through her silk glove. It rolls next to Katrin, and she reaches down without thinking. Roland moves to grab it at the same time.

The exact moment their hands touch the pearl, Katrin realizes she's fallen right into a trap. Roland doesn't seem to catch on, passing the pearl to the model and sitting back. But one look at Phoebe and her slanted smile tells Katrin everything she needs to know. The rest she can see in her peripherals. The guests surrounding them are locked in to where she can almost see the hungry, yellow eyeshine of the pack. Even the model in the pearl dress turns to Katrin and curtsies gracefully after taking the proffered pearl back. Katrin schools her expression, but the suffocating hand of defeat is heavier than the layers of fabric holding her down. After all these years, she's still too gullible for this game. The model dropped the pearl on purpose.

After the show, Katrin runs into her art studio, kicking off her heeled shoes at the door and continuing in her white stockings. The window of the room has been left open for her, and tiered golden spires are turning orange in the distance from the sunset. The rest of Kaelum is a blanket of lights under the palace. She gathers the caramel ringlets of her hair aggressively into a bun at her neck. She can hear the *click clack* of expensive shoes behind her, and she's on the verge of exploding.

Adelaide comes into the studio tower first, silver hair still perfectly in place. Phoebe follows, leaning against the doorframe.

Katrin wordlessly holds out a hand for the golden opera glasses Adelaide is holding. Her friend's mouth is opening to speak, but she passes over the glasses and presses her lips together. Katrin's eyes quickly focus on the screens inside the glasses. The fan holos and entertainment hosts are already circulating the news that Katrin knew they would.

Who is the Princess's New Love Interest?

Princess Katrin Attends Winter Show.

Are Princess Katrin and Roland Lark Together?

Katrin lowers the glasses, blinking the afterimage away. "Why do you two keep doing this? And of all the ways you could make me look like I had a crush on someone I obviously don't, why would you pick *that*? Our hands touching? That's the most cliché way to get a headline."

Adelaide attempts innocence, but Katrin's seen her wide-eyed, parted lips look before. *The face of guilt.* "Everyone thought the pearl would be a nice detail. That dress will definitely be selling like mad."

"Addie," Phoebe warns from the doorway.

"Everyone?" Katrin simultaneously wants to know and doesn't. "Is there a meeting I don't know about where the entire parliament, every government agency, my publicist, and you two plan my upcoming fan-fictions?"

She spins around before she can get an answer and starts organizing her oil paints, pulling the colors she'll need for later.

Phoebe approaches her canvas. "It doesn't matter if it's true or not. They'll be content to speculate, then distracted by something else later. There's no harm done," she says. Lacking all of Adelaide's bubbly enthusiasm, Phoebe can often feel like a patiently circling bird of prey.

It doesn't comfort Katrin at all. She knows why these girls are her friends. They were scripted to be. They've been "the princess's closest friends" since they were born. They have what every other girl wants: access to her inner circle and the fantastical world she inhabits. They will both inherit important roles in the empire, while Katrin spends her time at photoshoots and parties.

The only person she feels she has a real relationship with is her father, Kaelum's figurehead king, because he's the only one who understands her life.

"Maybe you could do your own live show," Phoebe suggests. "You should paint. You should show everyone your process and then the finished product. Show off the real you."

Adelaide clasps her hands together with a small gasp. "I love it! You're such a talented artist. People would die to have one of your paintings."

Katrin fights another pang of frustration. They always seem to expose her insecurities by accident. "I'm—not sure if they're any good." When she glances back at her friends, they're both staring with mouths agape.

"They are. They're amazing," Adelaide says firmly. "Everybody loves your paintings."

Katrin sits on her stool, hooking her stockinged feet around the legs.

"Of course everyone loves them. They just love them because I made them." She takes off her purple gloves and grips them in one hand.

The girls stare at her, expressions unwavering.

They don't get it. Why did she think they would?

Whenever she paints, it's always with the thought niggling in the back of her head that people who pay her compliments do so out of obligation. Because she's royal. "Let's just find Macy and start planning my birthday party," Katrin finally pivots. Adelaide and Phoebe would rather be occupied with desserts, dancing, and decorations. The spectacle must go on.

The truth is, Katrin knows that if she's going to discover whether she has any talent for painting or not, she'll have to find a way herself. She once saw a video of a class at the Studio Arts Center near the palace, rows of students with easels being trained as artists. She's tossed around the idea of sneaking into a class incognito a handful of times, but she doubts her ability to get past palace security.

"Princess." An assistant pokes her head into the studio. "The king has arrived. He'll be at the tower in thirty minutes."

Chapter Four

Candy Opera

Colin is ready to permanently move into his room and turn on soundproofing for the next decade. His headphones block out most of the noise, but the unfolding chaos is still distracting. Davin was practicing his breathing exercises in the living area by the glass walls, and just as he was about to break his breath-holding record Josiah walked by and slapped him on the back. Now Davin takes a gasping breath, which immediately fuels a round of exasperated shouting at his twin. The mood is crashing in spectacular fashion. Colin rubs the back of his neck and squints at his screen. *Why are they so loud?* The twins are eighteen now, and yet their bickering hasn't changed since they were eight.

Colin is sitting on the couch with TIRA and *attempting* to finish his school assignments for the day. His eyes are having trouble focusing now. The screen makes a single chiming tone, his assignment window closing with a flash. *"Panel Technology Module complete,"* TIRA announces.

"All assignments submitted. Twelve assignments scheduled for tomorrow. Aptitude results updated."

Colin slides the headphones off his ears, mentally exhausted. Focusing on a single tedious task at a time makes him jittery. He needs to move, listen to music, or play something. He's already been spinning his bracelet and tapping his feet frenetically for over an hour. *Aptitude results updated.* That sentence never fails to send a brief tremor of nervousness through his mind. TIRA is required to keep updating his aptitude results, and he's been nervous about what it might say for years. The government stores digital results based on every moment of schoolwork completed by students year by year. When students graduate, their career result is generated based on a plethora of data tracking where they excel. It's accurate every time, which has taken away the mystery of career options ever since Kaelum instituted the system.

Which means if Colin can't get a slot in the limited musician category, he has no clue where the system will assign him. Music is the only area where he seems to excel.

Lance appears from his study and removes his earpiece. He's wearing a dress coat and black shoes, so Colin assumes he's going out for the evening. As his stepfather stares absently at the glass panels, Colin takes the opportunity to spy on his multicolor eyes. He's always wanted to ask how expensive those eyes are but has been reluctant to bring it up. They have a silver center, a darker ring of brown, and a third ring of black to dial up the contrast. The eyes probably cost him as much as Colin's mom used to make in a year.

"I have a dinner reservation at Plunge Pool Restaurant tonight," Lance announces, turning. Colin quickly looks down at TIRA. His stepbrothers' heads snap up at the mention of dinner. "It'll be late, so bring holo contacts."

The boys spring into action. Josiah runs through the kitchen, grabbing his coat.

Colin wonders what he should wear. He likes the feel of his older clothes, so he rarely asks for new ones. Lance never offers. Plunge Pool is one of the finest restaurants in the city, so it naturally demands elevated attire. The building is a circular structure bordered by a massive waterfall. The water filters beneath the walls into an underground pool, where muffling devices in the floor suppress the deafening sound of the falls into soothing, background noise. The inside is loud enough with all the tables and guests.

Colin begins picking up his workspace so he can get ready. Lance glances in his direction. "You should stay here."

Josiah and Davin pause in the hallway. Colin swallows the initial questioning tone that nearly escapes his mouth and says, "I would like to come."

After a second of silence, Josiah lets out a short laugh. "What if you freeze when the waiter comes around, and I have to order you something from the children's menu again?"

Davin rolls his eyes, his coat folded in his arms.

"You didn't have to do that. I just needed a few more seconds to figure out what I was going to say." Colin twists the music note bead between his fingers, flustered.

Lance waves an arm in Josiah's direction. Colin thinks it means that he wants Josiah to stop talking. "I know you like the waterfall," he tells Colin. "But there are some important people from the government coming tonight, and I won't have any time for you."

"I don't need looking after. I'm not a child." Frustration tightens in his chest. He used to struggle with restaurants, with the noise level of all the voices and conversations going on at once. If someone asked him a question, he used to have a hard time responding. But he believes he can handle the noise now, enough to blend into the background anyway.

Lance's expression shifts into something Colin can't interpret. "But you and I both know your brain is like one sometimes."

Colin looks at Davin, hoping he might stand up for him. Davin is the only reason he's had a few experiences in life outside the apartment. His brother simply crosses his arms over his coat and shifts his eyes to the wall. "If you stay here, you can play music however loud you want. That's what you like, right?"

Colin wants to shout at one of them. Or all of them. But that would probably get him locked in his small room, so he manages to retreat back to the couch facing the window and place his tablet down on the table. He hears footsteps, low voices talking, the door sliding shut behind them, then the apartment's security system clicking back on.

Colin sits in silence, anger gradually morphing into resignation. Then he looks down at the tablet. "TIRA, why was I created this way?"

"You were born, not created, according to government records. December 4th, 2420."

"Mom said we were both born *and* created."

"This is not an AI question," TIRA admits.

He knows. He just doesn't have anyone else to talk to. When he was younger, the government told his mom that he had to do schoolwork remotely, but they laid out two possibilities for his future. Either he would manage to complete the normal schoolwork on his tablet and be able to access the jobs that other students were given, or he would be unable to understand it and would be given a job normally assigned to androids.

Nothing in Colin's life has ever been *normal*. His mother was considered a rare natural beauty, even though she'd never been given genetic enhancements. She'd struggled to make a living as an actress, but she'd managed to catch Lance's eye a mere month before they were evicted from their tiny downtown apartment. Her death hadn't been normal either, a lift accident that had been splashed across news feeds for months. Colin knows he should be grateful that Lance's money saved him from a terrible fate, but he wishes far too often that Lance would treat him like his sons and not just his responsibility.

He sits up straighter on the couch. "TIRA, let's compose an opera."

"A large undertaking," TIRA notes. *"What will the opera be about?"*

"Candy," he says, the first thought that pops into his head. He's hungry. He'll have to order something through the Shelf soon. A panel in the kitchen can slide away to reveal a box-shaped slot that receives all kinds of deliveries. He'll probably order some pasta and play with new melodies on the violin while he has the apartment to himself.

"Operas are typically about—"

"Mine will be unusual," Colin interrupts. These songs are primarily for his own entertainment, so he doesn't feel the need to try to appeal to a larger audience. Even when he tries to match trending sounds and styles, his sales remain consistently low. He'll write whatever he wants. "How long do you estimate we have until they get back?"

"Based on the average length of these dinners and the time it takes to travel downtown and back, it should be three hours and four minutes."

"Brilliant. Set a timer and order a...Number 7 from the Shelf menu. We'll see how much of an opera I can write in three hours."

"Three hours and four minutes."

Colin runs to his room to grab his violin, laughing a little at TIRA's insistence. "You can't possibly know that."

"I can."

Katrin gives a command to her studio's speakers, and her new favorite song bursts from the walls. *Pipe Organ Waterfall* transports her to a fantastical alternate reality faster than any VR room can. She picks up her brush again and applies a light cream color on her pipe organ in the painting. With a few touches of white at the center, the gold starts to look real. She hums along to the music as she works. She has every second of the song memorized. Each time she listens, she falls in love with it a little more. She curls her toes around her painting stool, trying to ignore her long petticoats brushing the easel. If she thinks about them too much, she'll crash back down to reality from the safe casing of her musical world.

The song's volume turns down, causing Katrin to peek over her shoulder. *Every time.*

The door slides open. "The king can see you now." The girl is a new intern, so Katrin assumes her assistant is off duty today. The girl quickly ducks away and into the hall. The palace has strict rules about interacting with royalty, namely that they can't display "fan" behavior like anyone outside the palace would.

Katrin stands to clean up. She pulls off her apron and closes the holo screen sitting dormant by her canvas. She hates to be interrupted in her precious minutes to paint, but her father being available is a rarer occasion. When she's finally ready, she brushes down her skirts one final time and steps to the doorway. A letter sits on a small, hovering pad at the threshold, a faint glow under an envelope of parchment. She reluctantly picks up the letter and holds it up to examine the wax seal.

A red shield symbol. *Percival.* Katrin's mind swirls instantly with options to fend off his flirtation. Percy has been highly tenacious. Unlike other boys that she grew up with, Percy seems both genuinely infatuated with her and eager to enhance his social standing. A dangerous combination.

She tucks the letter into one of her dress's larger pockets and hurries to the study. The hall is lit with concealed lights programmed to flicker like candles. Gold filigree lines every doorway. The holo pads by each entrance are hidden with matching gold cases designed to resemble cabinets.

Katrin flies through the study door, giving the security system less than a second to complete the scan. Her father is sitting at the couch past the desk. His shoes are already kicked off under the coffee table, a habit they share. He's still wearing a blue, formal waistcoat from the ceremony earlier that afternoon. Even tired, his face doesn't show it. His genetics are so advanced that his appearance falls into the realm of ageless perfection. But Katrin knows when he's had a long day. There are other clues, like the way he stares into middle distance near the window. The way he sits back with his right hand propping up his head.

Katrin bunches up her long skirt and plops down on the couch next to him, leaning against his shoulder.

"Been busy listening to your mystery composer?" he asks by way of greeting.

"Maybe," she admits. "I'll find out who it is one of these days. What if it's a girl my age? We could be best friends."

"Or, what if it's some old geezer on the Council?" he teases with a chuckle.

She doesn't reply. She'd rather be content with her imagination of Composer Anonymous if that were the case. "How's the Kaelumian Council today?"

"I wouldn't know."

She hopes he's teasing. He tilts his head to look at her, his cyan eyes finding her hands. Tiny streaks of paint have dried on her thumb and palm.

"How's painting today?" he asks.

"I'm not sure. I mean, I'm not sure it's any good. I've been told it's beautiful for three days now, and I know if I put the image on my Column everyone will be clamoring to buy it."

"But?"

"But I want to know if it's *objectively* worth anything."

"Well…" He tilts his head back against the couch and stares up at the ceiling. "Part of the value of a thing *is* who makes it."

"You're not helping," she complains. She tosses her thick curls over the back of the couch to let her neck breathe for a moment.

"I'm sure the great artists of the ancient world painted primarily because they enjoyed doing it. Then maybe secondly or thirdly because other people enjoyed looking at it." He waits until she looks back at him to add, "I think you should keep at it."

She just shrugs and twists her key necklace between her fingers, but she knows he's right. Painting is her escape from cameras and palace intrigue. She might even prefer that no one sees some of her canvases hidden in a corner of the studio.

"You should also post them on the Palace Column. Just in case it makes someone's day."

Something about the way he says it makes Katrin's eyes dart back to his face. As much as he gets annoyed at the government games he has to play while the decision-makers try to keep him out of anything real, he keeps subtly pushing her to engage in her own role.

A floating blue outline appears next to the couch. Her dad reluctantly taps the center of the window, and it expands into a snippet of text. "Apparently, I'm supposed to leave. You stay here and wait for Macy. She's on her way up."

Katrin frowns at his back as he picks up his shoes. "Tell them you want to stay. Macy can tick a few boxes without me."

She can tell he's far from dissuaded, but he pauses to ask, "Do you have any special birthday requests?"

She levels her gaze at the door, already preparing a complaint for her publicist about her ill timing. "To remain undisturbed for a whole day?"

He smiles ruefully before trying again. "Something I can wrap up and put in a box?"

"Well, it doesn't exactly fit in a box but...I'd love some snow."

"Sure it does," he says cheerily, swiping away another message in the air. "A single snowball."

She huffs in false irritation.

He kisses the top of her head and walks to the back doors. "I'm sure we can work it out with the city. See you at supper."

Katrin watches him disappear, then crosses her arms. Her publicist and head of security always comes bearing lists of nonsense Katrin has to do for her adoring public. She plays with the skeleton key around her neck and wonders if Macy's request has something to do with the necklace.   Months ago, as a finishing touch to one of her outfits, her stylist added a silver key. Macy and her army of seamstresses and stylists decided that the key was going to become a fashion staple—and it did. They created a store called "Katrin's Keys" and created a new key for her to wear each week. Once Katrin wore the key, the original and all copies were fair game to the city's elites. Katrin used to wonder how the designer came up with all the key designs but was disappointed when she found out that the designs came from archives of Victorian era photographs. None of them were new, just recycled.

Today's key is a frost blue color with white filigree and a long blade. It likely prompted her to request snow for her birthday. Knowing her father, he might actually pull it off.

A voice trickles down the hallway, and Katrin stands to brush down her dress. She hasn't wrinkled it much. As she makes her way to the door, she hesitates and tries to listen closer to the young woman's voice she hears on the other side. It's unfamiliar, and it sounds like someone excitedly narrating a virtual tour.

"I *cannot* believe I'm in the palace right now," the voice whispers intensely, growing closer. "There are so many hallways I thought I'd get lost or run into someone before I found her. But I just know I'm getting close. The lucky necklace works!"

Katrin's face scrunches in bewilderment. There is no way a citizen made it into the palace from outside. A thousand people and AI barriers would have stopped her.

Katrin opens the study door and peers into the hall, coming face to face with a girl in blue ruffles and bows. Her large amethyst necklace glows as a camera in the gemstone captures the scene in front of her.

After a quick gasp, the girl's navy-painted lips form a starstruck oval. She rushes across the threshold as Katrin backs away in surprise.

"It's you! Skies, everyone, I found her! Look!" A squeal escapes her, and her heels click against the study floor as she dances closer.

Katrin gapes back at the stranger in her study. She holds up a hand, mind racing. "How did the security—"

"I'm Janette. And of course, I know who you are. You are so much more beautiful in person! I might faint. And you're wearing the blue key! I just saw a picture of it this morning. I have to ask, since I'm finally meeting you, do you have a crush on Roland or Percy?"

Katrin steps back again, eyes darting between the ecstatic girl in blue and the doorframe that scans every arrival. Then her brain catches up. *Of course.* Her people planned this. They let this girl in and probably guided her down the path to Katrin on purpose so they could have this unexpected reaction on camera. Typical Macy. She probably didn't tell her because she wanted Katrin's genuine surprise to keep her fans chattering all night.

This girl is the reason they made her dad leave.

Katrin's smile slips back into place, and she straightens. "Apparently my security staff is closing in as we speak, but I have this entire palace memorized. I know some secret passages, a couple hidden doors. I can help you sneak back out. That is, if you're up for an adventure?"

Chapter Five

Secret Passages

Katrin slips her arm around the trespasser's shoulder, sliding past the camera's view and out of the frame. She knows how to sound conspiratorial. Her disingenuous friends taught her that ages ago. Janette nods breathlessly as Katrin speaks, words clearly failing her the moment Katrin touches her. Then she shuffles along obediently—voluminous blue skirts rustling—to the bookshelf at the back of the study.

Katrin removes a leatherbound book from the middle shelf and places it on the desk. Instantly, the entire bookshelf clicks into place and slides neatly into a slot behind the wall. The opening reveals a narrow hallway with pinpricks of light lining the path. Janette gasps at the sight and gives a slight twist from side to side to let her camera necklace capture the entire scene.

Katrin knows it won't matter, even though the video is likely live on the girl's Newsstand. Nothing is really live. All footage is swept into the government's river of data and is edited before being sent down the current to viewers. Katrin knows that her publicist is probably spinning an exciting tale with the pieces of this footage that she likes and discreetly hiding or cutting out anything she doesn't. The two major platforms for personal holo news, Mirror and Chronicle, have strict agreements with the Kaelumian government. Katrin can reveal any secrets she wants.

Janette follows her into the passage, her long dress briefly blocking the lights at the opening. Then, as her state-of-the-art eyes adjust to the darker space, she presses closer. "This is so incredible. I love the rows of lights! I didn't know that the palace had—"

"Shh. We'll have to stay quiet," Katrin cautions unnecessarily. She just wants Janette to stop talking, which works for a few seconds.

Janette lowers her voice to a penetrating whisper as she walks. "There are so many twists and turns. How long is the tunnel? Do we have to go through another secret passage? What about the stairs? How will we get back to the fountain level?"

Katrin considers turning so Janette can see her exasperated expression, but she walks in a straight line and stares at the blank walls determinedly. She just wanted a few minutes with her father before his staff shooed him off again, but she gets this girl instead. Snooping around the palace. Taking videos. Is her value as a princess so insignificant that she can only entertain people by walking through walls now? She takes a breath to mentally prepare the timbre of her voice, then answers, "We'll get to the end of this passage soon. Just follow me, and I'll show you where to go. You'll love this next part."

Another wall slides open soundlessly. Katrin steps into a small atrium with blue velvet curtains adorning the windows. She pushes a large section of curtain into one of the windows, revealing paneling behind it.

"What's this? I don't see a door." Janette supplies unhelpful commentary as she turns a slow circle in the empty room. Then she points her necklace camera back at Katrin.

Katrin presses her palm against the wall, which glows faintly around her fingers. After it scans her hand, there is a *ding* as a thin crack between panels opens to reveal a lift. Janette gasps and shuffles into the small box, which is lined with mirrors.

Katrin steps in after her and forces a smile. "Fountain level, please," she says, and the lift's hidden speaker verifies her voice and parrots the request. For a split second, the only sound is the sleek box's descent.

Janette stands as close to Katrin as their wide skirts allow. "This is the best day I've ever had. When I was younger, I always dreamed of meeting you and being able to have an adventure in the palace. Is the palace really the largest building ever made? Are there underground levels? Do you really have enhancements that make it so you don't have to sleep at night?"

Katrin has never heard that last theory. She does, in fact, sleep. Before she was born, she was given hundreds of enhancements, but most of them would not be exciting to the general populace. Like most of the upper class, she will never fall ill. Her vision is flawless and can translate any text without contacts. But she was administered nothing so unusual as sleeplessness. She could get so much more painting done with that ability.

"It is the largest building ever made." Katrin confirms the only item on the list she can—or is allowed to. If she shows this stranger the secret passages and also some underground levels in one day, Macy will really lose her mind. On impulse, she pulls the sapphire ring from her finger and hands it with a flourish to Janette. "How about something to remember me by? I'd give you the key, but this one is due in the shop tonight."

Janette looks like she's about to pass out from shock for a second. Katrin mentally plans how she will catch the girl and drag her out of the lift if she faints. Then the moment passes, and Janette looks up. "Thank you so much, princess! I will treasure it forever."

The lift doors slide open. At the arched doorway to the open-air fountains, a small security team waits for the girls. Macy stands off to the side, her cropped hair stick-straight to match her posture. She holds a holo tab open. Her right hand is lifted next to the image hovering in the air, and she stares at the girls, expressionless. Macy is petite and ambiguously young. She speaks only when necessary and has never divulged to Katrin a whisper about her personal life.

Katrin sees Macy as a humorless android. Always a joyous experience, running into Macy. Katrin considers retreating to her room and leaving Janette with security. But it's far too late. Her companion is stopped and questioned. The two men at the door point to invisible metal detectors and quickly remove Janette's long necklace. They take the ring from her hand before she has a beat to realize what's happening. She's ushered through the archway, then given rapid instructions on confidentiality that she'll forget a minute later.

Once Janette is gone, mind likely spinning from the pace of her departure, Macy approaches Katrin. "It's not that easy," she deadpans, holding out her hand like an exasperated parent. Katrin hesitates, jaw tightening, then lifts her right hand, allowing the ring to be pushed back onto her finger. She had to try. The ring houses microscopic sensors that interface with the palace rooms, tracking her location, heart rate, when she enters or leaves certain rooms, and mountains of other data. Her routines are so meticulously catalogued that any deviation from her intended location instantly sends up an alert to the entire palace.

It would have been nice to pass that off to Janette and give security someone new to chase for a while, but that was a far-fetched wish.

Macy steps closer, just enough to make Katrin uncomfortable. "You knew what you were supposed to do with her. Show her around, places we can *film*."

Katrin meets her gaze, defiant. "You spring someone on me, I make the rules."

"You kept my team hard at work staying ahead of that live Newsstand. They hid the footage of the passages. You put them all through quite a bit of stress if you care to know."

"I was supposed to be with my father if *you* care to know."

Macy smiles thinly, then scrolls a floating holo list with one finger. "The plans are coming along well for your birthday. Every young woman in Kaelum will want to be you before the end of the night."

Katrin feels the underlying message: *You should be grateful.* She should stop fighting and be grateful.

"Do you have any last-minute requests for me to send off?" Macy asks the same question her father did, though she likely already knows the answer.

"Please no surprises." Katrin hates begging, but she's desperate. "If anything is going to happen, just tell me. I can play it up, but please just tell me ahead of time. Let me help."

Macy looks amused now, though she doesn't take her eyes off her list. "Let us worry about programming. You should go back to your rooms. There is a stylist waiting for you. We don't have much time before the dinner tonight."

Katrin groans. She'd forgotten about dinner and wishes she could erase it from her memory now. She wants to ask if she'll see her father again before they have to sit across the table, unable to directly speak to each other, but she already knows the answer. No, she will not speak to him anytime soon. No, she will not be told what will happen at her own birthday. No, she will not ever be freed.

But that is the job, and she *should* be grateful.

She's not.

After two more days of schoolwork that bleed together, Colin wakes up feeling strange. He tries to remember the last time he felt like this, but it was likely when he was a toddler. His head feels heavy. His whole body is achy, both too hot and too cold. Confused, he takes his coat and pulls it on over his clothes. Then he sits on his bed, unmotivated to get up and traverse the few steps to his door. *Is he dying?* A distant memory of his mother nudges his brain. She felt like this once when she'd been working several nights in a row. Colin tried to take care of her. She'd explained, exasperated, that she hadn't been able to afford a genetic upgrade for this kind of inconvenience.

Colin can't remember what the inconvenience is, exactly. His mind feels fuzzy. He eventually persuades his body to stand and walk to the living area. The windows are filtering warm swaths of light into the room, and his brothers are busily packing bags for Labyrinth.

He doesn't bother them and shuffles to the kitchen to pick up pieces of fruit they left behind on the countertop instead. When Lance finally walks through the room, having just finished a call, Colin reluctantly describes his symptoms.

Josiah pokes his head up from his bag, where a digital packing list hovers at his side. "If they didn't give him Immune 1 before he was born, it's possible for him to have a cold," he suggests to his father. Then his silver-black eyes flick back to Colin. "You should come by the lab. The department I'm taking over after graduation would love to study you."

Colin doesn't have the capacity in his fuzzy brain for banter. "No, thank you."

Lance sighs and pulls his gold pocketwatch from his waistcoat pocket, the new accessory doing a brilliant imitation of an antique. "We need to leave in ten. There's probably something I can order for this on the Shelf." He glances at Colin. "How come everything that goes on with you is something I have to research?" Then he pulls up a holo tab by his face to do just that.

Colin swallows, pain scratching at the back of his throat. He looks around for his water glass. He hopes there's something simple he can eat that will fix this heavy feeling in his head. He doesn't even know what a "cold" is, but now he's afflicted with yet another rare phenomenon. After picking up a few more strawberries from Davin's abandoned plate in the kitchen, he meanders toward the windows where his brothers are.

"A complete waste of time," Lance mutters under his breath, flicking up a holo menu with one hand in irritation. As Colin sits down slowly on the edge of the couch, he adds, louder now, "Why didn't they take just *five minutes* when you were born to—"

Colin tries to explain. "Because it costs—"

"I know how much it costs!" Lance interrupts from across the room.

Why am I getting yelled at? I'm the one who's sick. In a few minutes, though, he's grabbed his tablet and headphones, shoved them in his satchel, and is standing by the lift to leave. Lance hands him a label-less white bag with an affixed straw that arrived in the Shelf. Colin examines the bag and squishes it curiously. He can't tell what's inside.

Davin and Josiah file into the lift after their father, uncharacteristically quiet. Colin stands near the back, sipping the unidentified liquid that tastes vaguely like vanilla syrup. The lift compartment seems extra cold. Still, he leans against the glass wall for support. If his mother were here, she'd probably tell him to pray about it. So, he silently asks for answers. *Mom said you weren't surprised that I was born this way, God. So, what's the purpose? Why is everything harder?* He realizes he's parroting Lance and stops. He doesn't want to believe what Lance says about him.

The lift comes to a gentle stop. A woman in a formal dress waits in the lobby when the doors open; she's a curator from a neighboring penthouse suite. Her dress is covered in a swirl pattern of crystals shaped like water droplets, a handful of them glowing a warm gold. Colin looks at the dress and wonders how she keeps from touching the smooth crystals constantly.

The woman glances at him and frowns. "Your face is really red. Are you alright?"

Colin moves the straw down, trying to come up with something to say.   As always, his brother thinks faster. "He's fine," Josiah grins broadly. "His face always does that when we talk about his crush in front of him."

Before anyone else can react, Lance herds them toward the maglev.

Colin keeps his mind on the train this time, sipping the last of his medicinal drink, then dropping the empty container in his satchel. He steps onto the train as soon as the doors slide open and sits before his dizziness gets any worse. Davin ends up on the seat next to him, so he rattles off to Colin about how they will get to attend the princess's birthday party at the palace when their team wins the upcoming championship. "We'll be the first Silver Streaks *ever* to win it."

Colin notices that Davin talks about the races as though they've already won the final today, but he doesn't point it out. He wonders what a party at the palace would be like. He can't imagine the royals settling for digital sounds filling their ballrooms when they could have a real orchestra instead. Colin would love to see a live concert, just once. Lance claims he doesn't have the time to take Colin to concerts, and the boys don't care about music. He'd have to go alone. But that's impossible.

Colin pulls out his tablet and moves his finger up to the top of his composition. Thinking for a moment, he names the piece *Cotton Candy Dance*. He is careful not to disturb the other passengers by humming aloud, even though most of them will have ears modified to isolate sounds and listen to their own music. Colin used to wish he had that particular enhancement, but he's grown accustomed to the comforting weight of his headphones over the years.

The doors open as their compartment comes to a stop at Labyrinth Station. Colin fights through a brief wave of dizziness when he stands. Once he steps onto the platform, people press in from all sides. He takes a deep breath and tries to ignore both the sounds of the crowd and the dull pain in his head. Inside the stadium, there are already giant holo images being projected through the audience, streams of swirling water that pass over heads and imitate spray when hands reach up to touch them. Boxes soaring above the stadium levels near the racing spiral hold the most powerful families of Kaelum. Josiah can name them all, point out their celebrity children, and probably explain what they did mere hours before on their Columns.

Colin stands at an arched doorway with Lance to access one of the lower boxes. This ring of seating is fashioned to look like ancient opera houses. The entrance scans his eyes as he passes, opening a narrow hall for them to walk through. Lance's box has blue stained-glass walls and a comfortable seating area near an open railing. Colin has always loved the diamond designs in the rails. He used to sit on the floor of the box and trace the insides of the diamond shapes with his finger. Of course, Lance thought it looked strange when he did it, so he'd make him sit back down on the couches. Lance was always hyper-aware of how he was perceived by the people sitting in the stadium around them who could be observing their box.

Digital fireworks pop over a section beneath them, causing a few unaware spectators to gasp in surprise. Delighted laughter follows. Colin sits at the opposite side of the box as Lance to give his stepfather some space and observes the colorful lights dancing around. He tugs his coat tighter around his waist, still inexplicably cold, then makes a mental note to compose a song about the fireworks soon. The races won't start for a while, so Colin turns his attention back to *Cotton Candy Dance*. He lifts his headphones to block out the noise of the crowds below.

A terrified scream cuts through the hum of the stadium.

Every eye looks up to the ceiling panels. A blur—a girl?—plummets from the sky.

Chapter Six

Princess Falls From the Sky

One hour and seven minutes earlier...

Katrin taps her wall, transforming the surface into a smooth mirror. "I don't look studious enough to be an engineer."

Adelaide stands behind the mirror, studying the disguise she has helpfully provided. She taps her rose-painted fingernails on her mouth. "No, I think engineers are supposed to look like nerds and researchers are supposed to look studious."

Katrin tilts her head, adjusting her hair for the fifth time. She washed her hair that morning with a dye that transformed it to a warm brown that would last a single day. A pair of apple green contacts cover her distinctive irises. Her hair is tied into a low ponytail. She eyes the white apron over her dress without much confidence. "Thanks for helping, even though this isn't for content," she tells Adelaide, since she knows she sounded ungrateful. She *is* grateful. She doubts that Phoebe would be as eager to go behind Macy's back to help Katrin disguise herself.

There is still a chance that Adelaide has laid an elaborate trap. Katrin doesn't discount the possibility. But she's closer than she's ever been to her goal.

"Where are you trying to go?" Adelaide finally asks. Katrin points her to the holo still playing footage by her bed. Adelaide takes a moment to pair her own eyes to the display to get the best view. To the left of the princess's wing of the palace, maglev tunnels lead through Kaelum's Genetics research labs. Notably, the train stops at the Crystal Palace Studio Arts Center: Katrin's final destination. The footage Adelaide watches is from a studio art class that takes place in one of its many, roomy art studios.

Katrin thinks the experience looks magical. Other art students working together. A professional artist on hand to explain how to make the painting come alive. More importantly: confirmation that she *is* meant to be an artist.

The images dance across Adelaide's icy blue eyes. Then she swipes the holo away. "It's just a class. Why don't you sign up?" She looks confused.

Katrin taps her wall again, removing the mirror setting. "I don't want to go as myself," she patiently explains. "Hence the disguise."

"Why don't you want them to know you're the princess?" Adelaide still doesn't seem to get the point.

Katrin knows that Adelaide wishes she was born to be the princess, and Katrin would gladly exchange places. She doubts Macy tracks Adelaide's movements so thoroughly.

She will today.

"Here." Katrin slips off her sapphire ring and quickly puts it on Adelaide's finger. Hopefully, their resting heart rates are similar. "It's simple. I don't want them to recognize me because I want them to be honest."

Adelaide admires the ring. "You don't think people are ever honest with you?"

Katrin ties the back of her apron in a neat bow and sits down on the edge of her bed. "Keep moving but try to stay in my studio so you won't be bothered as long as possible." She gives last-minute instructions to avoid gracing the obvious question with an obvious answer.

"Well, even if you don't believe me, I think you're a great artist," Adelaide tries again.

"Thank you." A perfunctory response. Katrin doesn't believe it, and now the thought of finally having the answer to her question in that classroom today ties her stomach in knots. She wishes she could believe her father. She wants to believe him the most. But she knows as well as he does that he's biased.

Adelaide stops her as she stands to leave. "Wait! Key."

Katrin grabs the chain and stuffs the skeleton key necklace into the apron. She's so used to the weight around her neck that she forgot about the accessory entirely. Luckily, the key of the week has just changed. This one is small with gold and gray metals swirled together to create a spiral stem. It disappears easily into her pocket.

"Have fun!" Adelaide calls to Katrin's back as she rushes out. "I hope the train ride isn't too long."

"Thanks," Katrin answers, a touch worried about Adelaide's word-ing. She shuts the door to her room and quickly runs to the study. The passages will have to get her to the train, which will take her to the other wing of the palace. She'll be cutting it close on time. In order not to leave trackable data, she refused to look at a map of the palace on her own holo displays. She found a painted map in one of the sitting rooms yesterday and attempted to memorize every detail.

The palace is bigger than most people imagine, housing government buildings, research facilities, and even data banks. Where ancient palaces contained hundreds of useless bedrooms and wasted space, Kaelum's palace is a display of spires, waterfalls, and bridges on the outside, but a web of active offices and labs within. Katrin and her father take up a tiny portion of the space in the highest wing of the structure. Her living quarters, viewed from outside, look like a tiny silver spire.

Katrin walks past hundreds of low-level government workers on her route to the tunnels. She doesn't make eye contact, trusting that she'll remain invisible, but her eyes still bounce between office plaques made to look like carved wooden signs. This is far more confusing than the map, and she murmurs the information she knows as she walks. *Two left turns. Third stop after I board the train. Art building straight ahead. Classroom is on the fourth floor.*

It's hard not to be distracted by the fact that heads don't turn to gape as she passes. She's not used to blending in, but it's oddly comforting. Her heart still races as she hurries past each person, half expecting someone to spin around and shout, "*It's her!*"

She walks into the maglev without anyone so much as giving her engineer costume or fake eyes a second glance. A group of five men and women in white outfits identical to hers board the train, so Katrin carefully walks to the opposite side of her compartment to avoid being seen. Engineers, of all people, would know she doesn't belong in their department. She sits in the last seat and looks out the window. A high tone chimes to her left, a woman's holo display synching to the maglev so she'll be informed of the stops as she watches Newsstand feeds. Katrin narrowly avoids looking at the woman's video. There's a good chance she'll be watching her own devoted fans cover every aspect of her life and latest gossip.

Katrin doesn't want to see it. *Not today.*

At the second stop, a passenger leans down and taps her shoulder. "Who are you cheering for today? Do you have a friend in Labyrinth?"

The girl is only a few years younger and has tight, golden curls and a perfect dusting of matching freckles. She's clearly upper class, but Katrin's attention is snagged by her outfit. She has a silver dress matched with a long silver cape and broach. She must be going to a race for Labyrinth.

Katrin opens her mouth to reply that she'll be stopping at the Crystal Palace, but a short chime on the girl's holo display around her wrist causes them both to glance down.

"Next stop, Labyrinth Station," the blond reads the announcement.

Katrin flounders. "Wait, has the schedule changed?" She tries to picture the painting from the palace, but now she can't recall specifics. She spins to the window. The maglev has emerged from the tunnels and is streaking toward the city center, past glass apartments reflecting a purple sunset. *Oh no.* Her fingers grip the window's frame as she takes a steadying breath.

The girl next to her grins, noticing her confusion. "Well, for the next hour, the maglevs are redirected for the finals. Then they'll be back to their normal route." She taps the holo hovering above her wrist, and the glow disappears.

The stadium? Everyone on this train seems to know this information she hasn't the faintest idea about. How will she get back in time for class? The obvious answer is that she won't. She'll have to try again another day, which is frustrating. She already has Adelaide occupied in her rooms, and the trick might not work a second time. Adelaide's last comment makes sense now. She *knew* Katrin would end up on this detour.

"Will this train go back to the palace after it stops at the stadium?" Katrin asks the blond, who's already preoccupied with a message on her wrist display.

"Not for a while. The one on the south entrance of the stadium should be. They're synced at thirty-minute intervals."

Katrin thanks her, then moves toward the closest door along with the remaining passengers. Past the glass windows, the stadium looms above her. She's only ever been to championship Labyrinth races, and only to make an appearance. She won't officially attend until tomorrow, for her birthday. She won't even get to stay for all of it. For now, she just has to hurry across the stadium to catch the next train.

A private compartment of the maglev opens just before the passenger doors she waits at. Katrin peeks through the door to see a husband and wife strolling down the platform ahead of the crowd. They're wearing lavish clothes in vivid reds and purples. Katrin can see sparkling gems placed in the woman's thick hair. It takes her a moment to recognize them. *The Lidens.* Marigold Liden is the Cultural Minister of Kaelum and can be found at practically every function of significance in the city. Katrin isn't worried about the Lidens recognizing her. She's far more concerned about their son seeing her. She angles her head away from the window as they pass.

The doors hiss open. Katrin practically bolts onto the platform and tries to blend into the closest group walking to their upper ring seats. She's not used to this kind of activity. She can feel her cheeks turning red and her fake-brown hair sticking to her neck as her breath shortens. Her brain screams at her to remain ladylike and adjust her posture, but she shoves aside her own habits.

She bumps someone's shoulder, trying to read the signs around the upper ring catwalks. "So sorry, just trying to catch up with my family." She grins up at a tall boy in a royal purple coat.

Percy. *Brilliant*, she bemoans, quickly looking away.

The ever-undeterred Percy stays on her heels, hands in his pockets, but at an advantage with his longer strides. "I recognize your voice. But, I must say, I don't know anyone from Genetics."

She ignores him, still turning her head and pretending to look at signs. She cuts a sharp left to an unmarked hallway lined with blue windows. She can still hear his footfalls behind her. Then, with one quick move, he slides in front of her, getting a good look at her face. "Even with that plain hair and those green eyes, you can't hide your enchanting face, princess."

Katrin looks up at Percy, her face likely more exhausted than enchanting at the moment. He's immaculate, as always. He was created with an Indo-Guyanese template in mind for him and his family, possibly before all those countries were dissolved or absorbed into the Kaelumian empire. His eyes, a smooth amber green that reminds her of maple leaves, are mesmerizing against his dark skin.

"It's a long story." She throws out the most useless excuse she can conjure. She edges past him, her long skirt brushing the glass wall.

"I'm sure." He studies her hair, seemingly trying to determine how she disguised it.

Katrin turns her back on him, lengthening her strides.

"Did you get my letter?" He catches up in two seconds.

She'd forgotten it in the pocket of whichever dress she'd been wearing when she'd received it. "I did get it, yes. I...haven't managed to read it yet."

"Well, since you're here, maybe I can tell you the contents myself?"

He sounds so earnest. Katrin turns another corner. Percy follows, clearly unaware of where she's leading them. *That makes two of us.* She walks through a hall of dimly lit water tanks rumbling with a low mechanical purr. The next door leads to another unmarked passage. White walls. Katrin has lost all sense of direction. A worker in a plain silver coat stops to let them pass. Katrin thinks he's stopping for her at first, then realizes again that she's in disguise and he's stopping for Percy. His father owns this stadium, along with half of the city.

Percy keeps talking, speech accelerating in time with her pace. "I'll try to recall most of it from memory, although I'll probably do it an injustice. I'm more eloquent in writing. I've been talking with my parents about you, about how ever since we were kids, I've felt like we belonged together. Even our family crests are complementary. I think you are the most perfect girl I've ever seen. Every time I see you, I think to myself: *she looks absolutely stunning.* Like it's effortless, somehow. And every time I'm being dragged to another art opening, I just think: Katrin's art will fill these walls one day. I simply can't stop thinking about you."

Katrin searches desperately for an end to the maze of hallways. Is she close to the south side of the stadium? She wishes she was bold enough to leave Percy behind. She wishes she would feel *something* with all his flattery. But she doesn't. It's all meaningless; his parents want them together, and he's playing a part.

She would *look* perfect at his side. Her art would *look* stunning in his mother's galleries. Even her crest, which has nothing to do with her as a person, would *look* nice interlocked with his. What a strange detail to fixate on. But that's Percy. She doesn't hate him for it. She would just prefer he give up trying to win her over.

At the end of a long hall, she finds a door that's already cracked open. Thin black letters above her head read: *Dome.* There is a biometric holo floating near the wall, but she hurries through, and it doesn't seem to set off any alarms. "Percy, that's very kind. I'm happy you think my art deserves to be in a gallery, that you think I look beautiful. We *would* look perfect together, I agree. I just—I don't want that. I wish I could explain. I *would* explain if I could." She walks quickly down a metal catwalk.

"Then what *do* you want? Also, why are we on the ceiling? Did you mean to watch Labyrinth from here?" He laughs once before falling silent.

Katrin finally looks down at her feet as the surface beneath her changes. The railing has ended, and she's stepped onto an echoey glass surface. She stands on decorative glass panels, in spiral shapes. Ahead of her, there's nothing but the top of a domed ceiling. Water reflections ripple across the dome. *Where am I?*

She spins around. Percy holds onto the railing at the door's entrance, looking at her expectantly, still waiting for her answer.

"I don't know," she says, voice wavering. Her head throbs. She just wants to find the maglev. "I'm sorry. I don't think it's meant to be, Percy."

He starts to open his mouth, looking miraculously undeterred. Then she takes a step back, and a loud crack echoes through the dome. Katrin eyes snap down to her feet. Stained glass panels form a decorative spiral. Beneath the semi-transparent glass, she can see the stadium. The labyrinth's twists. The open water shimmering at the top pool. Thousands of spectators and colorful projections. Light and color blur under the glass and come together into a white crack at her foot. The crack spans two meters of blue panel.

I'm at the very top of the stadium. There's colorless, weatherproof glass above her so that the domed ceiling is not open to the elements, but the decorative pattern beneath her is what the spectators see. Clearly, nobody is supposed to walk on this glass. *Hence the catwalk I thoughtlessly stepped down from while running from Percy.*

"What should I do?" Katrin whispers, frozen.

Percy's wide, frantic eyes dart between his position and the crack in the glass. He stretches out a hand. "You should probably—"

The panel shatters. Percy shouts something unintelligible. Katrin falls back, apron whipping around her. Her belly lurches at the initial drop. Images of the gaping crowd flash before her eyes among the raining shards of glass. She instinctively windmills her limbs to avoid flipping upside down. Panic floods her body as she continues to freefall. Just as suddenly, she smacks something hard and is encased in bubbles. The water is cold, shocking. She flails her arms in the blue pool, already desperate to breathe. Her feet touch the glass base, and she manages to push off the bottom to reach the surface.

Katrin breaks the surface with a gasp, greeted by muted blue light. Voices shout to her left. She blinks rapidly, the water gathering on her lashes. Her green contacts burn but remain in place. *I'm not dead,* her brain spits out, her terror fading. Young men in purple uniforms run through a narrow tunnel with a rubber walkway. One of them reaches out a hand, and Katrin grabs hold for dear life. She struggles to catch her breath as she takes in her surroundings. This is the end of Labyrinth, the place where a sensor marks a swimmer's time and they exit the water. Katrin is pulled into the tunnel. Worried voices echo around her, muffled by the water's sloshing.

"Are you alright?" a boy asks, his eyes round.

Katrin nods dumbly. He doesn't recognize her. Her back and arms sting from where she hit the water, but she slowly moves her limbs and takes stock of her body. Nothing feels broken. She knows she was given every genetic advantage to avoid injury, but this feels like a stretch. "I'm alright."

Another boy appears on her right, shaking his head in disbelief now that the concern begins to pass. "You're not part of the opening show, are you?" he asks laughingly.

Katrin tries to smile. "I wasn't planning on it." She wrings out her wet hair. Only a little of the dye has come out.

"We have an acrobatics team, if you're interested," another swimmer chimes in.

A coach ducks into the tunnel and shoos the rest of the boys away, motioning for her to follow him into the brighter room behind him. He takes her hand and guides her down the rubber walkway.

At the last second, she turns back to the team. "Thank you," she says.

As she finds herself fussed over by one person then another, a towel draped over her shoulders, she begins to think clearly. This stunt will be the biggest story in Kaelum. Even trying to escape the drama in the palace, it follows her here in spades. Why couldn't she have just looked where she was going? What will Percy do? Will he be able to keep this quiet, or will he tell everyone that the falling girl was actually the princess? Would Macy love it, or would she hate it?

She sits on a bench, her skirt dripping steadily onto the clean floor. Her panting echoes once everyone's voices fall away. The locker room smells like chemicals. Her hair smells like chemicals. As her mind begins to take inventory of the space around her, her breathing gradually slows to a manageable rate. One thing she knows for sure: the people will have something to talk about for weeks now. Even her birthday will pale in comparison to her falling from the sky.

Chapter Seven

Championship Run

"Bubblegum Aria?" Colin questions TIRA.

TIRA responds as he fears she will. *"I am not able to provide an opinion on a song name. I can provide a list of historical trends."*

"No, thank you." Colin sits next to the apartment window overlooking the gardens at street level and rests his forehead against the glass. It is silent in the apartment, which is usual for mid-afternoon. What is unusual is that Lance does not plan to come back at all. As the purse strings of the royals, he is working nonstop to ensure the princess's birthday is perfect. The palace seems to be spending a few empires worth of money. Completely alone in an empty apartment, Colin intends to fill the space with music. If he expects to be a musician when he graduates in a few short weeks, he'll have to earn it.

"Play back the A section again," Colin tells his AI, closing his eyes and preparing to return to his headspace for composing. He can come up with the exact name of the aria later. The solo piece will be near the middle of his Candy Opera, and it is already shaping up to be his favorite so far.

The song bursts from the speakers, cheerful pizzicato notes bouncing across the walls. Colin listens with intention, making mental notes on the B section he wants to add to the song today. The recording is his own violin. He performed it in his room a few hours ago. He can always tell the difference between a real violin and a digital one. There is a difference in the *air*, the space between the notes. In the slight imperfections that digital sounds delete entirely. This kind of sound has more life in it. He's sure others will notice too, so he records them himself.

The violin finishes its final downbow in the aria, and silence reclaims the apartment.

"It is now 2pm," TIRA announces.

His heart rate jumps up at the mere mention of time. "Already?" He leaps to his feet, flying back to his room to put up his violin and change clothes. He grabs his scratchy coat, which is unfortunate but necessary. Everything has to go perfectly today. His brothers and their team stayed over at a friend's high-rise on the other side of the city after they won the final. The news of their win was overshadowed only by the gossip surrounding the girl who fell into the upper pool from the dome.

Strangest thing Colin had ever seen.

The boys will arrive at the championship today on their own. Lance will come when he's finished with preparations for the palace, which means that Colin will have to go to the stadium by himself.

Resolving to give himself enough time to get comfortably to his seat, he gathers his things to leave. He can't remember the last time he traveled anywhere alone. "TIRA, turn on the security system once I leave. Activate *Empty House* protocol." He gives instructions aloud as he shoulders his bag. His coat is already irritating the back of his neck when he moves his arms, but he tries to ignore it. He glances into Josiah's empty bedroom on the way out the front hall and pauses.

There is a silver scarf hanging over his brother's chair. Josiah has been protecting this article of clothing with his life, waiting to wear it to the palace if they win the championship. He must have forgotten he wouldn't be able to come back home for it after they spent the night on the other side of the city.

Leave and forget about it. He doesn't need it. They already think I'm their personal cleaning service. Colin only sighs and steps into the doorway cautiously, waiting to see if Josiah's security will try to keep him out. No alarms begin blaring, so he grabs the scarf and folds it carefully. His brother has rarely been anything but a menace to him, but Colin adds it to his bag anyway, then leaves the apartment before he can notice anything else amiss.

"Lock doors," he says to TIRA as he leaves, hands still occupied. He hears a click behind him. Alone in the lift now, he breathes slowly and tries to prepare himself to navigate traffic on his own and get to his destination. Despite his best efforts, he hears Lance's voice in his head. *Keep moving. Get on the train. Don't make a scene.*

He begins humming out of habit the moment the doors slide open. He hums the beginning of *Bubblegum Aria* as he slips into the swarm of activity at the ground floor. Not a single person in the crush makes eye contact with him, so he walks a straight line to the station outside the lobby and stands on the platform like a statue. The maglev is nowhere in sight. Colin can't figure out why he feels so calm at first, but then it strikes him that the waterfalls aren't running today. The hanging pools and gardens sit tranquilly around the apartments. The roar of the water constantly layered behind the other sounds of the city is gone. The air is still and uncomfortably frigid.

Of course, in its place is the sound of girls nearby in fur coats and gloves talking nonstop about the princess's birthday party.

"They're doing behind-the-scenes footage of the cake being made!" One girl squeals. "It's only available in a few Newsstands, but I have a code I can share with four friends, and you can be one of them. Oh! The playlist is going to be curated and released later tonight."

The other girl chimes in the moment she can. "I heard the princess will have a special key for her birthday. I've talked my dad into bidding for it!"

Colin is so focused on their conversation the moment they mention a playlist that he doesn't notice the maglev gliding into the station at first. When he does, it's because the doors chime as they open for the passengers. He quickly stands to the side, then rushes through the open doors to find a seat. He sits near the back, but all the empty space fills up in seconds.

The third girl of the group he'd overheard settles into the chair next to him, long skirts rustling. Her eyes are a mosaic of color, and her coiffed ringlets, perfectly arranged lace, and broach make her look more like a holo projection than a real girl. She spares him a single glance in return, likely noticing his lack of genetic enhancements, then looks away.

Colin digs his headphones out of his bag and puts them on. He plays Rachmaninoff until the maglev arrives at the stadium. The crowd is sparse since Colin is early. He cranes his head to look out the window, then leaves the music playing as he dashes from the train to the walkway.

He barely remembers the way to his brothers' locker rooms, but after some second-guessing, he pokes his head into a curved room with a silver logo emblazoned on the wall. Josiah's locker is labeled and also locked, but there is an empty shelf just above his head, so he takes the scarf and places it inside. Once he's satisfied that it's visible enough, he turns to go.

Beep. He jumps when the music in his headphones stops abruptly. Has he ever received a call on this holo tablet before? After his brain catches up, he sits on the silver bench between the lockers and pulls out his tablet. The image materializes in the air just above his eye line. There's a blue glow to the projection and a seeming lack of depth due to his non-enhanced eyes, but it's functional.

Lance is standing in a hallway in the image, his coat and scarf on like he's preparing to leave. Colin doesn't recognize the marble floor or unmarked doors behind him, but there's a flashing red light that keeps washing out the holo. His stepfather looks absolutely furious, something about his eyes and the set of his jaw. Behind him, Colin catches a glimpse of Josiah walking across the background with his lab coat slung over one arm.

"I need you to listen, okay, because I'm not repeating any of this," Lance says loudly. Even though he is trying to raise his voice, Colin can barely hear him. The holo connection must be trying to scrub out some other background noise.

What is going on? Colin just nods, hoping Lance can see him. "Of course."

"I went across from the palace to one of the research facilities. The boys met me here from the north side so we could go to the stadium together. The building went into lockdown a minute ago, and we can't get to the trains. I'm going to make some calls and get us an open door in the lobby."

"Why is there a lockdown? What happened?" Colin fidgets with his bracelet. He's never heard of a government building needing to lock its doors. Lance doesn't seem afraid, just angry. If he *is* afraid, it's certainly not showing through the blurry projection.

"I don't know, Colin. It doesn't matter. I just need you to remember to tell Coach Manlow that we will be there, but we may be cutting it close."

"I can tell him."

"Are you *sure*?" Lance glares pointedly.

Colin tries not to be annoyed. After all, his stepfather is stressed and currently trapped in a building with lights and alarms. Colin would hate that. "I'll tell him," he repeats with more assurance.

The holo vanishes. He drops the tablet back into his bag and tosses it over his shoulder again. He can do this. He just has to find his way to the coach's office, which is probably where Coach Manlow will be until the team warms up.

Wandering through the main concourse and back to the upper ring, Colin watches the first of the spectators arrive and chat by their seats. Parents mostly, dressed to impress for this special occasion. He quickly tears his eyes from the crowd and presses on. As the minutes tick by and the hallways become increasingly unfamiliar, Colin worries that he's drifted off course. He finds some offices, but they have sensors at the doors that won't let him through. Switching strategies, he runs back to the locker rooms. The team will have to come through eventually. He checks the time and speeds up.

Back in the locker room, a few of the boys glance up at him curiously. They're still in school clothes, bags tossed under the benches.

"What's wrong?" a boy asks, forehead wrinkling; he clearly doesn't recognize him. Unless Colin has briefly crossed paths with them on the maglev, none of the team members know who he is. He looks nothing like his stepbrothers.

"I'm just looking for Coach Manlow," he says after a second. He considers telling the team about the delay, then wonders if that would be a good idea. He tosses his options around in his head until he realizes that another boy behind him is talking.

"He'll be here in a few minutes. But only team and family members are supposed to be back here."

Colin spins around. "Yes. Josiah and Davin are my brothers—"

"Really?" He's met with instant skepticism from the boy in front of him. Colin can understand the confusion. Sibling sets are usually meticulously planned and genetically coordinated by their parents.

"Yes," Colin replies, trying to come up with something more convincing. His mind is blank. He's saved, however, by the commanding presence of the coach jogging through the door behind him and clapping his hands.

"Let's go!" he calls to the team scattered across the room. "We've got warmups. Get everything off the ground and in the lockers. I want to see everyone geared up and waiting at the tunnel in seven minutes. Let's start this like a champion team!" He pauses and looks down at Colin, half a meter shorter than him. "What's this?" He dials back his volume a click.

The boy beside him shrugs. The rest of the locker room has launched into a flurry of activity, the lounging team following their coach's orders. Colin steps closer, trying to arrange the words in his head before they come out wrong. "My brothers are in a government building downtown. I'm not sure what's going on, but I was told that there's a lockdown.

They can't get out any of the doors, but they're working on it."

"And your brothers are...?" Coach Manlow's thick eyebrows scrunch together.

Colin's face heats. Part of him wonders how the coach has never seen him loitering around the stadium during practice, though. He's not exactly been hiding. He must have an utterly forgettable face.

"Davin and Josiah Meador," he answers after a second.

The coach looks understandably upset. "Government building lockdown? What kind of political drama nonsense...?" His mutters fade away with him as he stomps across the room to an open doorway and taps a holo screen on his wrist. Colin hopes Manlow plans to get more information so he won't come back to him for updates. He can still hear the man spitting out as a call connects, "This would happen to me the one day that nothing can go wrong..."

There is no flash of blue light from the door, so Lance clearly can't or won't answer right now. The other boys keep filing around Colin to begin warming up.

Should he leave now? He wants to get to his seat before the last-minute arrivals crowd into the stadium. Colin leans closer to the entrance of the tunnel and watches the first boy dive into the clear water. The swimmer's silver wetsuit in the distance disappears as he swims around a curve in the glass.

The moment Colin decides to get scarce, Coach Manlow emerges from the adjacent room and points at a boy sitting behind Colin. "Will! Get in there. We'll need an alternate if they're late."

Colin moves out of Will's path to the tunnel. The boy appears to be one of the shorter of the team and has an analogous color scheme of copper hair, eyes, and skin tone. Colin determines he has a friendly face and isn't sure why. The boy's brow furrows as he hesitates at the walkway. "What if they don't make it at all? I'm the only alternate."

Manlow swivels around without hesitation. "Can you swim, kid?"

It takes Colin nearly three seconds to realize that the question is directed to him. "Yes. Wait—no. Swim Labyrinth? No."

"But you can swim." It seems like a statement and not a question.

Will is still standing at the door in his wetsuit, peeking out the tunnel to check his place in line. He studies Colin for a moment. "Your brothers are on the team. You know how the races work, right? There are seven swimmers, but only the top five scores are judged." He shrugs. "Technically, both of us could swim the worst times and it won't hurt the team's chances."

Colin knows this at a cognitive level, but he also knows why all seven swimmers complete Labyrinth. The glass design changes every time, and anyone can bomb a course. Also, competing in front of thousands of people? Not happening.

Will runs off before Colin can say anything in response, diving in without hesitation to complete the practice course. Colin waits for the splash, then tries to think of a respectful way to decline the coach's offer.

Before he can speak, Manlow motions him toward one of the lockers. "Your brothers are likely on the next train, so they'll be here on time. I just need you to put on the uniform and wait, because worst case, we have to forfeit if we don't have a seventh."

Another swimmer at the back of the tunnel speaks up. "Can *my* brother get here fast enough?"

"No. And he's out of the age range as of last month." With this thought, the coach spins back on Colin. "Are you seventeen? Eighteen?"

"...Yes." Colin spins his music note bead, round and round the bracelet. He doesn't even want to imagine what Josiah and Davin will say when they walk in to find him wearing one of their suits as a possible substitute. They won't stop talking about it for weeks. He can already hear the packed stadium cheering as the announcers open the night. The sound causes his stomach to drop. "But I won't have to swim since—"

"Even if they get here late, they can still compete. Josiah is our last swimmer and our best."

Colin nods. He thinks he understands. The coach will already be able to calculate which scores to drop at the end of the competition if he doesn't have to worry about the last one. He lets go of his bracelet as the thought occurs to him that the coach doesn't know Colin is Kaelum's one anomaly. Manlow doesn't know what he is capable of. He just assumes he *is* capable. It strangely emboldens him. Colin finds himself wanting to suit up and wait simply because of the vote of confidence.

As soon as Colin gives the slightest nod, Coach Manlow waves Will back over, who's passing back through the rubber walkway. Will's face shines with water from the warm-up run, and he's breathing hard, but he immediately jerks his head toward the back of the room. "Come on. I'll find a suit for you while we wait."

Colin follows Will and listens to his instructions. The other boy doesn't seem to be anxious about the possibility of having to sub in for a championship race. Maybe he is nervous, but Colin can't tell. Or maybe he just knows his score will likely be dropped anyway. Colin tugs at the long sleeves of the wetsuit he's borrowing when he's finally managed to put it on. It's rubbery and was a more challenging process than he'd expected, but now he tucks his bracelet under the tight sleeve, letting it snap back over the beads.

Will looks on, sitting on the middle bench with a towel around his neck and pointing at his arm. "Dude, if you go in there with that on, you'll get the whole team disqualified."

Colin instantly pulls the sleeve back, but Will just lets out a short laugh. "I'm kidding." He gives him a look that makes Colin wonder if that was one of those things he should have picked up on right away. He's too jumpy right now to try to determine if people are teasing him or not.

"What should I do now?" he asks. The suit is tight, but instead of making him uncomfortable, the weight of it strangely puts him at ease. He looks less out of place now that he matches everyone else.

"You should watch the races—see as much as you can. I can try to give you as many pointers as possible, but it probably won't be necessary."

Colin notices that the wording has changed to *probably,* and he doesn't like it. *Probably* is a big jump from *worst case.*

He takes a set of narrow stairs down to the starting pool of the labyrinth. The roar of the crowd and the voices and music over the speakers is dialed up to thunderous at the opening. Colin resists the urge to cover his ears. The other boys talk and move around him, completely ignoring him for a few minutes. Then one of them dives off the end of the platform to deafening cheers, and Colin realizes that the race has begun. He feels a sudden, cold shock. He turns but doesn't see Josiah or Davin miraculously appear behind him. He prays a quick prayer that they'll do just that.

"Watch." Will's hand lands on Colin's shoulder again, and it takes everything in him to concentrate. There is so much noise and movement. The team around him is shouting and responding to the swimmer's every fraction of progress through the glass maze. The boy in the distance is cutting through a straightaway with a breaststroke. Then he kicks at the outer wall of the glass to divert into a curved tunnel. Colin can try to remember what the movements look like, but the one thing he knows he can't do is hold his breath for as long as they do.

"I can't hold my breath that long," he turns to say to Will, raising his voice as cheers break out in the stadium. He hopes Will can't hear the slight tremble in his tone.

"Just surface," Will finally responds calmly. "You'll be deducted each time you surface in the main sections, but you'll be fine. As long as you know how to swim, you'll make it. Those branch-off tunnels are short. You'll go back to the open water each time, and you just surface in both pools as much as you need to."

A digital scoreboard above the labyrinth displays three sets of numbers in elegant calligraphy. In a few minutes, another boy disappears in a blur of silver, streaking through the water. A swimmer in red from the other team appears in the labyrinth next.

"How do I know if a tunnel will be a dead end?" Colin asks next.

Will grins, shrugging with one shoulder. But his smile quickly disappears. "That's just Labyrinth. You never know. You just have to get through each dead end fast and find the right path to the top. Everyone will get it wrong at some point. If..."

He trails off, and even Colin notices that he's distracted by the scoreboard. "What?" Colin tilts his head back to see the numbers.

The remaining three boys huddled around the entrance murmur in frustration. The stadium has erupted again. This time, Colin does put his hands over his ears until they calm back down. The score that's been updated is bright red, so he assumes that the other team, Tsunami, had a great run. Maybe one of the swimmers even managed to get lucky and guess every passage correctly. That would put the Silver Streaks behind.

A red, digital glow passes over the spectators like a wave, sparking a chant that goes on for several minutes.

"Now would be a great time to have Josiah," someone mutters on Colin's left.

The other two swimmers look frustrated, but one of them grabs Will's arm and pulls him over to the platform. "Don't surface three times like you did in practice or Manlow won't let you come back at all."

Colin stays in the back, as far from the opening as possible. The shouting and tension are unnerving. He can feel his heart racing as the next swimmer vanishes into the water. He counts the seconds. The labyrinth has changed entirely. New tunnels. New openings. After six minutes of searching and swimming through glass passages, the boy finally emerges in the spiral's pool, then ducks under again. Colin watches him, feeling *himself* hold his breath after a few seconds and intentionally exhaling. He should not be doing this. Will is calmly executing breathing exercises before he dives in, the smarter move. Both remaining swimmers regard the back of the walkway with stony frowns.

No twins.

Panic sets in as the next swimmer jumps off the platform. Will finally meets Colin's gaze. "Make sure your toes are behind that red line. Then jump in when you hear the long whistle." He doesn't offer additional encouragement or advice. He simply looks away, expressionless, and gets ready for his race. In seconds, he's vanished, leaving an empty, churning pool of water behind.

There is no way my brothers are still stuck in that building. There is no way I'm jumping in that glass canister with every enhanced eye in this stadium watching. It's not happening.

Colin's body feels like someone else's as his feet station themselves on the rubber platform. He's completely alone now. They waited until the last possible moment, but the moments are spent. The last Tsunami swimmer's score flashes above the labyrinth, and Colin can hear the hydroelectric maze of glass above his head reshape itself.

His eyes drop to the water. In his ears, the crowd has worked into a frenzy of cheers again. Hardly any attention was paid to the last Tsunami swimmer. Maybe his score was intended to be dropped from the start.

For someone whose score is technically supposed to be dropped out of the top five, Colin is getting far too much noise from the audience. It scares him, because it might mean that the Silver Streaks are moments away from losing the championship. And he has to finish anyway.

His brain swirls with apprehension. *Lance is going to be so furious—at whoever is in charge of that building's lockdown protocols, at the coach. Probably at me, for some reason. Josiah and Davin will hate me even more. Even though they know it isn't my fault.*

Colin's eyes drop to the agitated water. The noise around him has reached a fever pitch. His brain riots and wants to shut down, but one thought saves him.

Underwater, there is no sound.

It is quiet.

The whistle erupts from the speakers, short chirps followed by the longer one. Colin takes a sudden, deep breath, and plunges in.

This is his only way out now: *up*. Up into the glass.

Chapter Eight

Candlelit Rain

Underwater, the sound mercifully shuts off. All he can hear is his arms moving the water around him. The current isn't strong but gives him enough power to continue. His eyes are stinging, which he assumes is a lack of a simple enhancement that he didn't know he needed until this moment. He can see a little. The glass is barely visible. He can see streaks of moving color—the crowd—past the reflective surfaces. A tunnel branches off to his left, so he turns into the darker passage and tries to adjust his stroke. After a few seconds, he thrusts his hand in front of him and hits a wall with a muffled *thump*.

He spins around and kicks hard against the wall with both feet. Emerging back in the spiral, Colin notices more light seeping into the space. He swims forward for a few heartbeats, then has to kick to the surface. He can hear his gasping breath echo in the empty chamber. Water sloshes around him. He wants to go home. His thoughts are a jumbled mess. From watching the practices every week, he knows for a fact that he's swimming far too slowly.

There's still only one way out. He dives, resuming his quick strokes. Another passage to the right opens up, a smooth curve that twists out of sight. He angles awkwardly into the tunnel and finds himself at the next level. Glowing, purple designs reflect through the open spiral, part of some light show that's distracting to his barely functioning eyes. At some rational level, he knows he has no chance of beating a single swimmer's score. Still, he tries to conserve breath and hurry this time.

The first tunnel is another dead end. He gets lost in the reflections for a second, spinning around until he finds a smaller tunnel underneath the first. He swims down, then follows the twisting glass into a larger chamber. He's still not back to the spiral where he can reach the air, so he tries to navigate. The tightness in his lungs has started already. He tries to ignore it. *Stay focused. Get out of here.*

To the fearful rhythm of his pulse, Colin swims into a new opening. His body fights him, trying to force him to inhale. It takes only a few seconds to follow the tunnel toward the dancing lights.

Thud. His hand swipes down glass. He's only found another wall. Confused, he looks behind him. His body is fighting him, trying to force him to breathe against his will. Suddenly, lightheaded, he wonders briefly if the safety divers really do have hidden trapdoors everywhere. Surely they save swimmers all the time.

Please don't let me die in here. He trusts his prayers in his last moment of consciousness more than the divers. He releases his last breath out of necessity and becomes more buoyant, rising to the ceiling of the tunnel. His hand, reaching above his head, feels cold.

Cold? *Air.* Desperately, he lifts his head. His muddled brain takes a few beats to catch up as he chokes in air. There's an air pocket. He's heard of air pockets hidden in Labyrinth. In each course, there's only one, and it's barely visible under the water. He breathes for a long time, knowing that air pockets don't even count as a deduction. It doesn't matter much to him either way. He'd rather *not* be unconscious.

"I'm never trying out for this sport," he whispers aloud in the small space, his voice echoing faintly. Diving again, he kicks against the tunnel and retraces his path. His eyes start to burn again, but he's single-minded. *Find a way out.* A second passage that he missed earlier sits temptingly in the ceiling. He lowers himself to the base of the glass, then pushes off, gliding upward. It branches in both directions at the top. The left turn clearly takes him to the open spiral, where he'd be able to breathe, but the right turn is a straightaway that looks suspiciously like it cuts all the way to the finish. Something in the back of his mind tugs at him to turn right, so he swims fast in case he chose wrong.

The straightaway leads to an open pool, the very top of the spiral. A red, painted wall catches his blurry eyes, so he reaches for it. When his head emerges from the water, he's assaulted with the roar of the stadium again. He blinks a few times, trying to regain his bearings. There are bright lights, numbers flashing above his head, so he must have triggered the final scores. Luckily, Will had told him before that when he sees a red wall, he should touch it. The noise is too much for him to process, but the physical sensation of a hand reaching around his arm brings him crashing back to reality.

A flood of silver packs around the rubber walkway, boys crowding the exit and trying to yell over the spectators. The arm pulls him out of the water, and Colin barely stays upright when he finds his feet. Cold water drips down his face, and he swipes rivulets out of his eyes.

"One air pocket, and we're going to the palace!" a boy shouts to his left, pumping his fist.

A blurry, copper figure takes shape to his left. "If we dropped your score, we were going to lose by a point. We weren't going to tell you," Will grins widely.

Colin isn't sure what happened. "I—but I was slow."

A swimmer to his right waves enthusiastically out the opening to the stadium, then turns around. "You were at the beginning, but you solved the second half fast. And we haven't had a one-breath run since the finals!"

Colin opens his mouth, but Coach Manlow barrels onto the wet rubber mat and starts shouting louder than the rest. "The Silver Streaks! First time champions!"

A raucous series of cheers and whoops circles around, echoing from the water. The boys form into a tight huddle, smashing Colin along with them. He's not used to this kind of wild frenzy of excitement and isn't sure how to join in or what he'd look like if he tried. Still, he allows himself to get lost in the middle of the chaos, and his eyes bounce between all the new and sudden visual information to process. *Are Davin and Josiah here yet?* The thought enters his head, and he spins around to look for their dark hair. *They're not here,* he realizes after a moment.

It doesn't occur to him until he's back in his street clothes and sitting in a maglev between two energetic Silver Streaks that the night has only begun. Exhaustion drapes Colin's entire body like a weighted blanket, and as the other team members talk and laugh ceaselessly, he sits like stone. The city passes in a distant blur outside the windows, but his eyes remain unfocused. They're still slightly irritated from him opening them underwater. He blinks at a faster rate than normal. The young men around him suddenly rise from their seats in chorus and press their faces to the window. Colin follows their gaze.

The train eases to a stop under towering spires. Snow begins to fall.

They've arrived at the palace.

Colin stands in a hallway, contemplating his disastrous outfit. The long marble hallway is bookended by security stationed at arched doorways. Coach Manlow is standing at the front of the line and is waved through the freestanding arch. It glows a faint blue and admits him into the palace. The team shuffles forward to be let into the birthday party.

"I didn't know I was coming, so I didn't bring anything," Colin whispers to the closest teammate waiting in line.

The boy, hands in coat pockets, looks him over. Colin is wearing the most basic of school outfits, long-sleeved shirt and trousers with a tweed waistcoat and long overcoat. His shirt isn't quite long enough for his arms. He resolves then and there never to take off the coat. His shoes are scuffed on the sides and about three styles behind the current trend. He looks Victorian enough, but the boys around him have clearly prepared for the nicest event of their lives. They are wearing matching suits, bright colors, coordinated hats, and even watch chains. Colin looks like he wandered in off the street out of curiosity.

The last hour barely feels real. After the award ceremony, the coach finally heard back from Josiah and Davin. The building lockdown was over. Even their dad with all his government influence couldn't get them out in time. They were going to meet the team here at the palace. Colin hopes they can still enjoy themselves. He can't imagine how disappointed they must be to have missed their own championship. This was supposed to be their night, not his.

He shouldn't be here. His throat is still scratchy when he swallows, either the last standing symptom of his cold or from all the swimming. He's already mentally exhausted from nearly drowning and from the resulting chaos surrounding the team. The boys practically forced him to attend their award ceremony, but he hung back as much as possible to stay out of the camera lenses and eyes of the crowd.

"Name?" a voice asks loudly to his right.

Colin lifts his eyes, emerging from the backlog of his mind. The security officer at the doorway stares at him. It might not have been the first time the man has asked, so he replies, "Sorry. Colin Burke."

Surprisingly, he's instantly waved forward. A satisfying blue glow announces his admission through the doorway. Once he passes a row of white columns, Colin finds himself at the garden level of a massive ballroom. For a few seconds, the sight is so overwhelming that he can only spin around in place to take it all in. To his left, three-story windows overlook a candlelit garden in a glass dome of tropical flowers and waterfalls. He squints at it all, trying to determine if the sight is just a holo projection, but it looks and sounds perfectly real.

The ballroom sprawls before him, ending in two matching staircases that lead to a live orchestra, tables set with crystal, and a third staircase. The final staircase is lined with velvet and emerges at a third level, which Colin can't see from his position. When he tilts his head back, he's thrilled to spot huge chandeliers above his head, all arrayed with real flickering candles. Wax drips from the tiers. He's always had an obsession with chandeliers, though not quite as passionate as his love for music.

In the sea of colors and display of wealth, Colin slips unnoticed through the ballroom. The rest of the Silver Streaks fan out and disappear to find friends or seek out entertainment. Colin walks into the garden first, admiring the still-falling snow past the glass walls. It hasn't snowed in over a year, so he's surprised it's scheduled now. He shoves his hands in his pockets and stares at all the waterfalls. This party's environment is noisy, and he's not sure what to do, but he can definitely get some inspiration for new songs while he's here.

A halo of light near the center of the garden draws his attention, so he walks over to find the source. A low wall of white stone about a meter tall wraps behind the back of an alcove. An easel is placed in the grass. It's surrounded by candles lining the wall. Colin studies the canvas resting on the easel. The painting is of raindrops falling, hitting the ground and forming puddles on a murky gray background. It's fairly unremarkable except that the flickering light all around the painting from the candles creates clever little shadows and spots of light on the rain. It reminds Colin of one of his songs. *Candlelit Rain Nocturne*. One of his favorites.

The rest of the garden is a collection of flowers and various man-made waterfalls and streams. After a couple, arms linked, passes by the rock path, Colin leans forward on the decorative barrier and holds out a hand to the closest waterfall. The mist coats his fingers and drips to the ground. The water is warm. He wipes his hand off on his sleeve and seeks out his next destination: the orchestra. He might just stand and watch them perform for the rest of the night—or until Lance finds him here and sends him home.

It would be easy for his stepfather to find him near the musicians, but

Colin doesn't care.

Crossing back into the open ballroom, he slips through the crowd to reach the staircase. He hums to himself, singularly focused on the path to the orchestra. All around him, guests are enjoying refreshments served by androids, holo scavenger games, and even a silent auction in rows of glass boxes. He presses on.

Just past the stairs, he hears the music change. The strings swell in a recognizable tune. It's the Kaelumian anthem. Colin hears the distinct pattern of the flutes and looks up with the rest of the guests at the third story staircase. The song is a variation of the anthem, one written specifically for the princess. An eventual silence falls upon the crowd, the eyes of the palace turning to her entrance.

"Presenting Katrin Elayne Vaugner, Princess of Kaelum," a disembodied voice fills the air. Whispers trickle through the ballroom the moment she appears.

Colin's seen holo images of the princess, like any young person in the city has, but she looks more impossibly perfect in reality. She has a flawlessly set smile painted onto her lips and the most regal posture in her cascading dress. It's pale blue with a train that keeps going and going, layers of fabric studded with tiny gems. The sparkles are all in her hair too, which is no particular color. Colin can't decide if her long curls are caramel colored, bronze, or even gold. He decides it must be all three, made to look seamless. Her eyes are pinned straight ahead on the garden windows, unblinking. They look like a kind of blue marble that has rivulets of pure gold carved in. This young woman was clearly enhanced with great care by the best geneticists to stand out in any crowd.

The music continues as applause eventually dies down. Another young woman in a blindingly red dress with long platinum hair approaches the princess first. She flashes her a comfortable smile and takes her hand. She chatters easily as she guides the birthday girl to her close circle of friends and admirers. Colin notices the princess cast a single look over her shoulder, her vivid eyes locking on the windows once more. Then she turns gracefully back to the man in front of her who's offered her a plate of refreshments.

Now that the excitement has passed, Colin resumes his path to the small orchestra near the balcony of the second floor. A section of velvet chairs and low tables forms a lounge near the strings. Most of the people upstairs are relocating from their corners to be able to see the princess. They chat about finding better lookouts to see her dress and note her interactions. Colin can't imagine hundreds or even thousands of people studying his every move. He would be bound to embarrass himself every day if that were the case.

He sits unnoticed on a chair in the shadows, watching the violinists play. He's enraptured hearing the full, rich sound of live music. Currently, they are performing Vivaldi. It's not The Four Seasons, which he would have assumed they'd play for the easy recognition, but the Concerto in D. A human waiter, the only one he's spotted so far, passes Colin's seat to offer a couple on the other side of the lounge crystal glasses of water. Then the waiter turns and hurries down the stairs. Colin's mouth quirks in the direction of a smile for a fraction of a second. *I'm the reigning champion of invisibility.*

Chapter Nine

Birthday Cake Castle

They have not listened to a word of my requests. Katrin stands in the ballroom, at a party in her honor that likely cost more than any attendee's lifetime salary and feels selfish for being disappointed at all. The party is magnificent. The dress she is wearing is heavy but stunning. She loves the way the light hits all the gems. Her birthday cake is a replica of the palace, towering two meters above its table. She has gardens and musicians, entertainment and the best food engineered in the city.

Still, none of it feels like it's for her. She doesn't know most of the people her publicist invited. Tiaras she's worn at prior birthday parties are being displayed and sold in boxes. She can hear the orchestra in the background playing Vivaldi instead of her favorite composer. They must have taken her notes on what she wanted for the party and thrown them away. The only thing that catches her eye that looks right is the snow. She glimpses it from the back of the ballroom, falling gracefully outside the windows.

The king can still call in a favor around here. Katrin smiles faintly. Then she obediently follows Phoebe over to the cake so she can be captured blowing out her candles for all the Columns in the city. The candles are positioned like flags on the towers, so she has to walk to each corner of the cake to blow them out. Phoebe points subtly to her neck as she passes the first candle. Katrin follows her eye line and adjusts the key necklace so it can be seen on camera. As with all her movements, she takes care to make every moment seem perfect and planned. This may be her birthday, but she knows good and well that she's just a prop.

Phoebe stands near her parents until Katrin blows out her candles. The Drakes are wearing official black-and-gold outfits, customarily intimidating even at a birthday party. They glance around the room in slow, subtle movements, faces unreadable. Phoebe says something to her mother, then rejoins Katrin. Her friend's dress is long and sleek, matching her waist-length hair. Her lips are deep red and her expressions few and deliberate.

"Enjoy yourself," Katrin says on impulse. She doesn't want her bird of prey circling her all night. Not tonight. "I'm going to make my rounds, and you don't want to get stuck by my side for this. Escape and eat fruit while you can."

She knows that Phoebe's weakness is exotic fruit and that her patience for Council members wears thin faster than she'll admit.

Phoebe smiles knowingly. "You'll just escape and listen to boring classical music from a distant perch, won't you?" When Katrin doesn't reply, she gives up. "Don't let me stop you." She melts into the crowd with ease, vanishing in a moment.

When Katrin's completed a few more necessary tasks, including greeting people from the government she doesn't know and taking a golden box from the stacks of presents, she wanders up the stairs. The gold present is tucked tightly in her hands. It's a tradition, her gift from the king. She refuses to open it in front of these people and their roving cameras. She knows it'll be the only gift she'll be given with any thought put into it, the only gift from a person who truly knows her, so she keeps it for later. She has to open it alone. In her room. Preferably in her nightgown with her hair a royal disaster. That would be perfect.

She can feel holos and eyes following her on the staircase and turns, anticipating her father's presence nearby before she even sees him. He greets her softly before touching her arm, clearly trying not to surprise her on such a stressful night. "Happy Birthday. Have you gotten to experience your present yet?"

She carefully turns, gathering the thick fabric of her dress so she can hug the king with one arm. His hand settles on top of her glove. "The snow is beautiful. I haven't been outside yet, but I will, I promise." She moves her lips minimally, from habit.

He's wearing a black suit tonight, with blue details that subtly match her outfit. She pulls back, looking up to inspect his telltale eyes. He still looks indecipherably tired, but his smile is genuine. He is truly happy to see her. She wishes she could talk to him about something real, something other than small, unserious comments that everyone expects at a birthday party with all the eyes and lenses fashioned upon her and her father. "Love you," she says instead. She smiles a fraction.

He kisses her forehead, trying to avoid both her complicated hairstyle and intricate makeup. "That's supposed to be my line."

"Well, pick something else." She tries to turn her head to where cameras can't see her words. She wants this exchange to be theirs and theirs alone.

"It was just yesterday you were eight years old, and you wanted slippers shaped like cheese for your birthday."

"Did I really ask for that?"

"You did."

Katrin giggles, mood improving instantly.

"And now my little girl is an amazing, talented, kind, beautiful woman and I couldn't be prouder." He lowers his voice. "I'm sorry the orchestra didn't seem to get my note, but it's your birthday, so tell them what you want. I'll try to lead some of this crowd downstairs for you."

She nods, hugging him again. He knows exactly what she wants: some space, and her favorite music. After he leaves, taking some of the guests with him, she hurries over to the musicians at the top of the stairs and interrupts the conductor. "I'm so sorry. Would it be too much trouble to request a song?" she asks quietly. She'll probably be overheard anyway.

"Of course not, Princess," the conductor blinks in surprise, but quickly smiles at her enthusiasm. "This is your birthday after all. What would you like to hear?"

Luckily, the movement they are playing ends in less than a minute, so Katrin watches the conductor type the song title into his holo display, fingers deftly moving across the air. Once he locates her song, he taps once more, and the displays of all the musicians sync to the new piece simultaneously.

Satisfied that she'll have her favorite song played now, Katrin steps back to watch. The lounge beside her is fairly deserted for now, but she knows that will change once more guests find her and rearrange themselves to be nearby. There's only one young man sitting in the corner of the lounge, paying rapt attention to the musicians. Katrin decides that he's the only one with any taste. She studies him discreetly. She's used to every person in her circle having perfect genetics that make them look like holo projections. He has the most normal face she's ever seen, plain brown hair and pale gray eyes against pale skin. He even blinks every few seconds, which is a universal indicator of natural eyes. He's so utterly ordinary that she's actually intrigued as a result. *How did he get in here? Is this another trap set by Macy somehow?* She glances around but doesn't see anything unusual. Stray guests near the stairs have congregated around the balcony to watch her, pretending to listen to the music.

Katrin makes the decision to walk over to the stranger, knowing she'll probably scare him half to death, but even more intrigued now that the first downbeat of her requested song is playing. He blinks quicker, expression changing. He seems to recognize the song after only two notes but looks confused. She's too curious to reverse course now.

"You picked the best seat in the house," she says with a smile, sitting in the closest chair as elegantly as her jeweled dress will let her. She sets the gold present on the floor atop her skirts.

He jolts at the sound of her voice, as if coming out of a trance. He must have been *deeply* engrossed in the music if he didn't even notice her approach.

"I see you recognize the song. I just discovered this one recently, but it's my new favorite," she adds as the music drops into the sweeping melody.

He blinks again, surprise on his face as his eyes bounce between her face, her eyes, her jeweled hair, and back to her eyes again. It happens with every ordinary person she's ever met. It's like they have trouble processing that she's real. She's used to the reaction. There's even a conspiracy theory floating around the Columns that she's just an advanced holo and that is why no one outside of the palace is allowed to touch her. If they did, she'd be nothing but a shaft of colorful light. Phoebe likes to mock that side of the fanbase.

"Your Highness." He tips his head slightly, clearly unsure of the protocol for speaking to her. She'd prefer never to hear the title again, but it comes with the job.

"What's your name?" Maybe his surname will clear everything up. There are a few mysterious families among the Kaelumian governing class.

"Colin."

"Just Colin?"

He looks embarrassed now, which was not her intention. "Colin Burke."

That doesn't help at all. She mentally thumbs through her database of names but can't come up with a single Burke. Something in the back of her memory suggests that she saw the name on a Newsstand instead, but she gives up the search for now.

Colin, meanwhile, seems to come to his own conclusion. She can see it in the way his eyes drift in thought. He looks back at her. "Your middle name is Elayne. Did you just—purchase this song last week?"

Now it's her turn to be surprised, even concerned. Nobody but palace security can track purchases on her private holos. "How could you possibly know something like that?"

"I'm sorry," he's quick to apologize, his speech coming quicker but more stilted now. She chalks it up to his shock. "I should have explained. It caught me off guard that you listen to my music. I had no idea you were a fan. I mean—" He gestures to the orchestra. "This one. This song. I wrote it."

She leans forward, crossing her long gloves over her skirt. An amused smile sneaks onto her face. "*You're* Composer Anonymous?"

He hesitates. "Yes," he says, blinking.

She laughs, a bright laugh that the guests that have gathered around the balcony can probably overhear, but then she lowers her voice so they can't decipher her next words. As always, she barely moves her lips so they can't read them. "I'm sure you are," she teases.

Eyes still wide, he nods a fraction. "Thank you."

She realizes after a second that he didn't pick up on her sarcasm. She sits back, trying to determine how to read Colin. *Something's off.* Everything that comes out of his mouth sounds too genuine. At first, she thought he was playing the game with her, teasing and pretending. It's a game as common as breathing to her, as common as the posturing of her myriad admirers and fans.

"How did you know I found this song last week?" she asks, changing tactics.

"I have an admin dashboard that shows me who's listening to the songs and where they're from. Although, the username Elayne just had an asterisk that said: *Court 50.*"

The music in the background seems to fade away as her thoughts crowd in. That *is* her location code. She lives on the fiftieth level of the palace. No one knows that, though. How could a complete stranger know that, unless...

"You really are Composer Anonymous," she whispers, turning her head further from the sight of guests and letting her long curls fall in front of the left side of her face.

His gray eyes flit between the orchestra and her face, brow furrowed. "I—yes, Your Highness. That's what I was saying."

He looks absolutely lost, but suddenly Katrin doesn't care if she understands. She forgets that Colin is a complete stranger. She forgets how completely out of place he looks with his outfit and demeanor. Composer Anonymous has been a mystery to her for so long, and now he's *here*. Right in front of her. Of course he'd be sitting here, listening to music.

She brushes more curls over her shoulder, blocking the less-than-composed expression that comes over her face. "I am the *biggest* fan. I love all of your songs. I listen to them when I'm painting!"

A flicker of understanding and recognition finally touches his face. "The painting in the garden. *Candlelit Rain Nocturne*?"

"Yes!" She struggles to keep her voice down. The song is ending, so she pulls up her wrist display and types a few quick words into a box. In a few moments, the conductor at the balcony receives the name of a new song and searches it, sending it again to the rest of the musicians. Katrin waits, a breathless smile on her face. Colin's reaction is perfect, a sudden smile the instant the song begins. She likes how his blinking speeds up a click when his excitement grows. No one she knows does that.

"*A Song for December*," he says in disbelief. "You really know them all?"

"Of course! This one isn't quite *Pipe Organ Waterfall* for me, but it's a completely different kind of feeling. I have to listen to this one when it's dark and moody outside."

"Yes, exactly," he agrees instantaneously. He still looks like he's seen a ghost, a distant frozen expression of shock on his features.

"I've always wanted to ask: Why do you compose anonymously?"

He angles his head a bit, one hand absently spinning a bead on a thin bracelet around his wrist. It's barely visible past the sleeve of his coat, which he oddly didn't drop off at the coat check. *It's not like anyone would steal that coat.* Katrin berates herself instantly. That wasn't a nice thought. She's been far too rich for far too long. She probably couldn't even understand someone like Colin.

"My stepfather thought it was best. I'm not exactly a public figure. I didn't think much of it when I first started. I didn't think anyone would ever listen to my music."

Katrin wants to laugh at that idea, but she stops herself. His music is incredible, as good as any of the classical composers she's ever listened to. But maybe even the classical composers doubted themselves when they first started. Now they're in books and Newsstand archives.

"Are you working on anything new?" Katrin asks. She'd constantly been checking her holo by her bed, in her studio, even at dinners when no one seems to be looking. She always wants to see if a new song has dropped.

"I'm actually working on an opera. I'm getting close. I've been staying up at night sometimes, soundproofing on, just writing. Playing it back."

"Skies!" She squeals, feeling like that giddy girl Janette who snuck into the palace all of the sudden. She doesn't care. She's happy *she* gets to be a fan for once.

Colin's eyes actually dart upward at her exclamation, which makes her want to laugh. Then he seems to gather that it's an expression and recovers. "It's, um, about candy."

"Wow. Skies, that's so creative! I can't wait. I really can't believe I'm meeting you. My father is practically going to faint when he hears about this. I talk about you *all* the time when I'm with him."

"He won't actually faint..." Colin's brow hikes, concern in his eyes.

"Oh, no. He'll just be surprised." Colin's dryly delivered humor is amusing. *A Song for December's* last notes bring her back to reality, and she realizes that she needs to keep making her rounds before people get suspicious. If Colin intends to keep writing anonymously, she should not call any more attention to him or spill his secret. He probably doesn't want her to tell. She quickly and stealthily removes the chain around her neck with one hand and lets the key fall into her palm in one motion. She places her glove next to his sleeve and whispers, "Take this. Please, come tomorrow for lunch and give this to the man at the door of the north garden and he'll let you in."

Colin turns his hand and takes the necklace, chain wrapped into a ball of gold. "I can't—don't you need this?"

She smiles brightly. "This key doesn't go into the shop until tomorrow night, so you have a whole twenty hours to bring it back."

Quickly, he blurts out, "My stepfather might lock me up forever if I did that." Then he presses his lips together firmly, seemingly regretting the sudden comment.

Katrin laughs. "Why would he do that?" Then she stands, blocking the view of the guests for one last moment. Colin quickly rises to his feet, observing protocol he's probably read about. She realizes once they're both standing that he's a head taller than her. Whoever programmed her height must have wanted her to appear delicate and dainty, because she's shorter than *everyone*. "Please, come if you can. I'll keep your identity a secret either way. I know a little about wanting to avoid attention."

Colin glances over her shoulder, noticing the many eyes fixated on them from the balcony. His face pales, his hand tightening around the hidden key. "I should go."

Katrin wonders at the unusual look that's entered his eyes. She feels guilty. He must *really* not like attention. Before she can say anything, he hurries around her, hands disappearing into his pockets. Heads turn curiously as he rapidly takes the stairs back to the first floor and weaves his way into the crowd.

I'm sorry, she thinks to herself. This mysterious composer clearly doesn't want to be seen, and she arrived in all of her glory to inadvertently make him the center of attention. She resolves to find several more guests to talk to so that no one will think anything of their brief interaction. At least, for the few moments they talked about music, she sensed his excitement for the subject. He also seemed surprised by the sight of her, but not absolutely smitten the way most young men were when they approached her. She knows without even asking: his true love is music. And how could it not be? His songs are some of the most moving, breathtaking experiences.

She selfishly hopes he comes back. Not because she needs the key, but because she has a thousand more questions. Does he actually play his own music? When is he going to release the opera? Did his family choose his appearance for a reason? She still wants to know how he got here, and who else knows who he is.

This whole thing might still be a trap. Her paranoia checks in to her mental conversation. Katrin doesn't love mysteries; she prefers answers—truth. Probably because her life provides little of either.

But this time, she doesn't care if the interaction was planned. She just met Composer Anonymous. And he's nothing like she expected.

Chapter Ten

Something New

Colin doesn't stay for food. He barely looks over his shoulder, his eyes locked on the only door he remembers to get to the maglev. He still can't believe he told the princess who he is. Maybe it was because she caught him off guard. Maybe it was because he never would have guessed that one of his few listeners was royalty. She knew his songs. The orchestra was *playing* his songs. She even *painted* one of his songs in the garden. He is torn between elation and terror. The moment she finds out who he *really* is—

She won't, he decides. He won't show up at the palace tomorrow. Maybe he can find a way to return the key safely back to her, but he has to stay away. He drops the necklace in his pocket for now, not sure who he could possibly hand it to who wouldn't keep it for themselves.

The trip back to the apartment blurs together in Colin's mind. He's exhausted from Labyrinth and from the constant fanfare after. His stomach rumbles, but he's determined to get home. He played the invisibility game well enough when he was in the lounge at the ballroom that even the servers passed right by him with their trays.

Both hands pressed against his temples, he keeps his head down on the maglev as the vivid colors of the city night streak past frenetically. The lights hurt his eyes, especially this late. By some miracle, he gets off at the correct stop. He's never seen the outside of the apartment in the dark. The snow also obscures the view. At the station, he stands on the platform, which is coated with a dusting of white, and looks up. Flurries catch the warm light of the lanterns outside the lobby doors. He pauses a moment, mesmerized by the sight.

Once he's upstairs, the door scans him and unlocks the empty apartment. Lights slowly illuminate the hallway. The windows remain frosted black, still on night mode. He disengages it so he can watch the snow fall, then drops onto the couch. His coat is still buttoned. He doesn't move to take it off. Instead, he pulls out his tablet and sets it on the glass table by the window.

"TIRA," he says.

"I am here."

"I met the princess tonight." He's not sure why he needs to tell her, but he's talked to her for most of his life. It's almost like she deserves to know, even if she's just a program.

"It is statistically unlikely to meet or interact with Princess Katrin."

"Well, I did. She also listens to my music. She said that *Pipe Organ Waterfall* is her favorite song." He pauses, and when he speaks again it's slower, with increased disbelief. "I wrote her favorite song..."

"Was the princess nice?"

He thinks about this for the first time, brows scrunching together.

"Actually—she is. She is nice. I never thought someone like that would be very nice to me. But...it's probably because she likes my music."

"Yes, this is a considerable likelihood, seeing as you are nondescript and very plain."

Turning the key in his pocket between his fingers, he lays his head back on the couch and stares at the falling snow. "Although this analysis is true, TIRA, I would rather have *not* received it."

"You proposed reasoning for the princess's actions which I felt compelled to—"

"Yes, TIRA. Thank you. I understand the logic."

His brain often functions like TIRA's, straightforward and direct. But he is still human, so he doesn't *like* to think about being unusually inferior.

He doesn't realize he's fallen asleep on the couch until the apartment door opens, deactivating the security system with a chime. He jolts awake, neck sore from his angle on the cushion. It's still dark. The snowfall has stopped. He squints and shifts from his position to look back. With a stiff left hand, he slowly unbuttons his coat.

His family has arrived, a sad company hanging up coats and scarves in complete silence. Josiah throws his bag on the floor, kicking it up against the wall and out of the hallway. Davin walks to the kitchen with a stony expression and pours himself a glass of juice.

Colin knows what he should do, so he quietly approaches them and holds out medals he pulled out from his right pocket. They are gold plated, with a silver logo that was emblazoned on both sides mere minutes before the ceremony.

"Here," he says quietly. Everyone's eyes shift in his direction. "These are yours. I promised your team I would get these to you tonight."

Josiah grabs them both, then steps away, heading for his room. Suddenly, he spins around and tosses the medals back at Colin. A walking manual on slow reaction timing, Colin barely ducks away in time. The metal clangs against the wood floors. Lance looks up, halfway through the door to his room with his hands full. The boys glance at him for an instant, but he doesn't interfere. He just shakes his head slightly and shuts his door behind him.

"What's wrong?" Colin looks back at his stepbrother, his brows dipping.

"What's *wrong*?" Josiah bursts out, flinging his waistcoat in the hallway next to his bag. "You are *completely* incapable of understanding anything." His black eyes are wide with intensity. "What's wrong is that we've been working for this for three years, and yet when we finally made it to the championship, we didn't even get to go. What's wrong is that you've never even tried it, and yet you got lucky. Now you hold a *Labyrinth record* that I've been trying to set my whole life, on accident. And you. Don't. Deserve it!"

Colin nods. "Yes. This is all correct." He hesitates, reviewing the logic of the statement in reverse order. "Except...I am capable of understanding some—"

"Did they give you one too?"

After a moment, he realizes what Josiah is asking. He takes out the third medal and holds it at arm's length. "You can have it," he says quietly, trying everything he can think of to calm his brother down.

They stare at each other, tense. Colin studies Josiah for pre-attack indicators that he might throw the third one too. Davin ends the stare down by walking by and picking up the two medals on the floor and swiping the third from Josiah's hands. "There's no point," he mutters at his twin.

"I'm sorry about the record," Colin apologizes. Surely it will help, even though he's not sure what he could have done differently. "Maybe I can talk to someone?"

"That's not how this works!" Josiah throws his hands up.

The door to Lance's room slides open, and he stomps out, waistcoat half unbuttoned. Colin knows exasperation when he sees it. His stepfather waves a hand in a sweeping motion at the twins' rooms. "Even I don't have good enough soundproofing for all this shouting." He steps around them, shooing them toward bedrooms. "Everyone, go to bed. Get out of here. It's late." Then he points at Colin, who hasn't moved yet. "You. Go."

Colin gets inside the threshold of his door, then turns, remembering something. "Wait. I haven't eaten yet."

"You had all evening to figure that out." Lance picks up the tablet from the glass table. "TIRA, close door A4."

"Override accepted. Closing door A4."

Colin stands in the dark after the door shuts, then finally pulls his coat off and hangs it up. His lights sense his movements and form a faint glow around his path to his closet and back to his bed. Then he pulls the key necklace out of the front pocket of the overcoat and sits by the window, holding it up. The key is thick and blue, matching the princess's dress. It has gold edges and small diamonds lining the stem. He runs a finger across the stones and wonders if he's ever held something so valuable in his life. This necklace probably costs more than the entire apartment.

He looks around the room for a place to hide it. If either of his brothers see it, they will know exactly what it is. If he tries to wear it, he'll never fall asleep. It'll be hard enough to fall asleep hungry. Eventually, he drops it into his lamp. Even when turned on, the lamp's blue dome is completely opaque, and he can easily grab the necklace's chain from underneath the shelf it rests on.

When he finishes dragging his feet and finally prepares for bed, eventually lying on top of the covers to stare at the ceiling, he changes his mind about the princess. Anything would be better than staying here, stuck with three people who don't want him around. Surely he can find a way to visit the palace again. He doesn't know what the princess wants, but at least he'll be doing something different. Something new. He didn't know if he had the courage before, but this life is not what he wants. And today, he has done something new and different, even if it was an accident. Even if it was a miracle, more like. His mother would call it a miracle that he made it through that underwater maze.

Miracle or not, he made it. He jumped in. He swam through it. He finished it. All because someone let him try. Because he let himself try.

Tomorrow, I will try again, he resolves. *Tomorrow, I will do something new.*

Attempt 2. Katrin grips the armrest of the seat and leans forward to check the window again. The maglev is flying through a tunnel, so her view consists of steel beams and flashing lights. She sits back and tries to relax. Her hair is a new color, a warm ginger. She has to distance herself from the older disguise. Even now, she can faintly hear the voice on the Column in the neighboring seat, a holo display teasing her with the view

of her falling.

"Katrina, Carmen, Catherine, Arwen, Corinne. We've compiled lists of the possible names we could have heard shouted from the stadium's ceiling. But many still speculate that we heard 'Katrin' for several reasons. Although the girl from the images doesn't look like Katrin, we've been unable to find any available footage of the second person who was on the ceiling at the time of the incident. Also, no one has put forth a legitimate claim about the mystery girl. Those who say that she was Katrin have many more questions: What was the princess doing there? What led to her dramatic fall into the labyrinth?"

It still surprises her how little the public knows. She thought that everything would be discovered in a matter of minutes. Yet somehow, her staff has prevented more information from being released. Percy's parents also own the stadium and all of its cameras, so that probably helped.

The maglev stops. Wrist displays next to her flash with the announcement, then resume their programming. Katrin jumps to her feet and moves to the doors. She tips her head back once she's standing on the platform and admires the crystal designs lining the Studio Arts Center's exterior walls. The stones form three-dimensional patterns like gem facets.

Fourth floor, she recites in her head, then gathers her skirts to rush up the stairs. Inside the building, a tall android in plain silver guards the front desk. Its eyes scan several screens forming a semi-circle around the counter. She quickly walks past the atrium to the lifts. Massive canvases decorate the walls on all sides. The class starts in ten minutes, but she wishes she could stop to admire them all. There's a canvas with a blue splash of paint that turns into the hair of a woman, ending in a striking profile of her face. The painting between the polished lifts depicts the sunlit dome of Kaelum, reflections of the skyline in the panels.

Standing underneath these paintings, Katrin feels small. She wants to laugh at her own audacity, thinking she can do this. But she stubbornly stands at the back of the next open lift and waits, heart pounding.

Adelaide is wandering her rooms back at the palace, but Katrin doesn't trust her. Adelaide knows what class she's trying to attend. She could have warned the professor ahead of time. Every interaction Katrin has at this class might be prepared. The other students might even pretend not to recognize her.

For a moment, she's trapped in indecision. Then she passes the fourth floor. The fifth. *If I go to a different class, a random one, then I'll be sure,* she decides. Two other women stand in front of her wearing aprons similar to hers, so she follows them out the doors once they open. They lead her to a bright studio with a row of easels set up next to standard holos. The painting displayed on all of them is the same. The two women select their stations silently, joining other students busily arranging their supplies.

Katrin glances around the room and finds the professor. A blue apron is tied around his waist, one that looks like it's been put through several hundred hours of projects and several thousand layers of paint. His studious face features deep-set, probing eyes. He clearly has decent genetics but is starting to show some signs of age in the tips of his hair and small wrinkles around his eyes.

Naturally, he spots Katrin looking lost right away. He consults a tablet in his hand with a puzzled expression. "Good morning. Did you sign up for the last class? I don't seem to have you on my—"

"Yes," She answers quickly. "Maybe my connection to the database was interrupted, but I'm sorry I couldn't make it the other day. An issue with the trains and that Labyrinth final."

The professor frowns, clearly upset at the mention of the sport. "Athletes!" he spits out the word, suddenly walking at a fast clip to the back of the room. Katrin hesitates, then falls into step behind him. She tries to hide a shaky sigh as her ruse appears to work. "They think they should be the center of attention. But art, now that's where the heart of a society truly lies!"

His voice is low and gravely, and Katrin almost strains to hear a few words. She just nods along since he doesn't seem to be angry at her for missing the first class. *At least he's not blaming me.* He stops at her blank canvas and looks over the supplies laid out. "How much experience do you already have with oils? We should have put that question in our sign-up form in the database, but we forgot this session."

She nods again, looking away from his intense gaze. He doesn't seem to be doing it on purpose, but she's already nervous enough. She keeps trying to pick up on signs that he may know her, but she doesn't see anything definite yet. "I do have experience. I should be able to follow along alright today."

"Brilliant," he says, leaving his tablet on a cluttered desk at the back of the room and shoving both hands into his worn apron pockets. He wanders away without another word, greeting other students as they arrive and get settled at stations. Katrin turns her attention to her own preparations for the master copy. The whole class will be painting a portrait of Adonis from ancient mythology. She doesn't remember much about the painting or even the original character from myth. Something about a mortal that becomes a god. Katrin's worries multiply. Faces are not her favorite subject. She prefers landscapes and flowers. She has no choice this time, so she uses two fingers to zoom in on the projection by her easel and study the values of the face, light and shadow.

When the class begins and the other students lift their brushes, she takes a deep breath and makes her first trembling brushstrokes. After fifteen minutes, her hand becomes steady. She steps closer to the canvas as she applies the first layer. The professor strides past her section and taps her shoulder. "Back up a little. Get a good look at the overall composition and don't get trapped in the details too quickly."

She nods eagerly and takes a step back. He continues down the line, giving more instructions and making general observations about the original work and its significance. Katrin hardly listens, intent on her progress. She loses all sense of time as the task sucks her in. Even without music by Composer Anonymous—*Colin*, she remembers—painting still enraptures her completely. She layers the darker values onto the face, the deep-set eyes like the professor's and dark grays near the hairline. Eventually, she moves on to more transitional shades. Then highlights, spots of white meticulously placed.

She is so immersed that she hardly notices when everyone halts. Students put down brushes, arrange the paints they used. She hears light *clicks* from brushes being dropped into water glasses. The professor is speaking louder now, calling the attention of the room. Katrin politely stops her work and sidesteps to watch him around her easel. He picks up a canvas from the opposite end of the room and uses it to praise the lighting, anatomy, and coloring. She isn't even familiar with some of the words he's using. Then he walks towards Katrin's end of the room. Her heart races, and she finds herself hoping he doesn't make any comments at all about her efforts. Now that she's looked around at her neighbors, she can see a difference between her painting and theirs. Actually—lots of differences.

The class ends without the professor roaming anywhere near her copy. She stands in front of her easel, staring at it dumbly as other people around her clean and pack. Suddenly, she feels distant from her own work. She never dreamed it would feel like this. *That's not true,* she reminds herself. She did worry about this, day after day, and told herself it wasn't true.

I have no talent at all.

She lets the thought settle in her mind for a few moments. It's a thought that pricks at her, like she's swallowed something irritating and it has to travel slowly down her throat. She *wanted* to be good. But now she's met with reality.

The professor's heavy steps announce his presence. Katrin snaps back to herself, standing in the bright studio, far behind the crowd. "I'm sorry," she rushes to apologize. "I'll be going. I just got distracted."

The professor smiles at her. She imagines the expression to be a touch patronizing. Her distress is too obvious. "Don't worry," he says in his low voice, looking over her canvas. "Skills develop greatly with time. Your work may not be where you want it to be now, but it can improve. Not everyone has an eye for it right away, and certainly few are naturally gifted. It's a process."

She doesn't know what to make of this speech, but she latches onto parts of it in her discouraged state. *I don't have an eye for it. I'm not gifted.*

"Thank you," she says, even though it sounds like an odd response in her own ears. She's not sure he helped her. She's not sure what can help. What she does know is that he doesn't recognize her. He told her the truth.

Chapter Eleven

Performed Live

The ride back to the palace feels long. Katrin stares blankly out the window. Art students chatter around her. Her brain transforms it into a vague hum. Doubt and disappointment circle her thoughts. *I was right. I'm not as good as they say.*

She takes her ring back from Adelaide when she gets to the tower and stands in her art studio staring at the paintings leaned up against the walls. Now that she knows the truth, they all look less inviting, less creative, less skillful. She retreats to her room and does her best to remove all traces of her disguise, hiding the contacts in case she ever needs them again but disposing of the temporary dye. She closes her vanity drawer with a hard *thunk*.

Her friend doesn't ask questions for once, retreating to her lunch party. Adelaide has decided to star in a perplexing love triangle, barely offering her two love interests glimpses of her attention. This lunch will be traveling the gossip circles in hours, and Katrin wants no part of it. Instead, she has lunch delivered to the gardens on the fifth floor. It's more of a modest patio balcony than the sprawling waterfall gardens outside the ballroom. A girl brings small trays of bread, jam, cheeses, fruit, then a tiered cake stand with white petit fours arranged in a pattern. Katrin picks at the dishes halfheartedly, gazing at the man-made clouds dotting the sky.

A notification beeps on her wrist. Birds are chirping in the fruit trees bookending the patio, drowning out the ringing, but she catches it in time to open the call.

"Your Highness." It's Jarred, one of the new security members downstairs that Katrin finds *least* suspicious. She gave him instructions about her key last night, so she sits up in her chair and enlarges the holo display to see his message. "I was handed a key, just like you said. It might be a forgery though because this boy looks like he's from Underwater Level—"

"It's a disguise." Katrin says the first thing that pops into her mind. For all she knows, it might very well be a disguise. Colin's appearance is still a mystery to her. She doubts he's from Underwater though. The city calls the network of cheap apartments, factories, and water reservoirs that contribute to Kaelum's weather system the Underwater Level because of the humid air. Over time, it's turned into a euphemism for the lowest class citizens. Katrin despises the term. "Let him up," she tells Jarred, not bothering to mention her location since he can check it from her ring.

Within a few minutes, Colin appears at the glass doors. He's being escorted by a different security member, and his head is on a constant swivel, glancing from the ornate doors to the fruit trees to the sky. Katrin nods her thanks and watches the security woman return to the hall. Colin looks the same as he did the night before: simple clothing, well-worn but originally from a designer Katrin recognizes. She decides to attribute it to the historically eccentric nature of composers. He looks like he's about to bow, so she quickly asks, "Would you like to take a seat? I'm having brunch if you'd like anything. I got a late start because of last night."

He glances at the chair across from her, then sits, eyes bouncing between all the trays on the table. His presence is so disarming that Katrin finds herself relaxing the moment the door shuts behind her. She tries to settle on one of the thousands of questions she's accumulated to ask him. "How did you like the party?" It's a simple, polite one to get started.

"I liked the chandeliers in the ballroom. I liked the waterfalls, and the music, of course. I liked that it snowed. That was a surprise."

"You liked that?" Katrin grins, leaning back in her chair. "I put in a special request."

Colin blinks once. He tilts his head at her. "You made it snow?"

She laughs lightly. "Sort of. I just requested snow. I assume the weather officials made it happen."

"I would like to write another song about snow," he states matter-of-factly.

"Please do." Reminded of something, Katrin taps a quick message on her wrist display. After it's sent, she pulls a tray of fruit in her direction and takes a few pineapple chunks. She pushes it in front of Colin. He looks down, then selects three strawberries.

"Thank you for coming," she says after a second.

"Thank you for inviting me." Colin suddenly moves his hand, dropping it into his coat pocket and pulling out the key necklace. He carefully sets it down on the table, as though it's made of glass. "I would have come sooner, but my stepfather had to remember that I existed this morning."

She grins, then picks up the key, struggling for a moment to reclasp it around her neck. "So, I heard that I missed all the excitement at Labyrinth after I left. I wish I'd stayed. I heard you subbed in at the last minute and swam the best run of the night."

"It was a miracle I made it through. I'm not a strong swimmer," he admits.

"A miracle?" She pours herself a glass of raspberry lemonade, laughing inwardly. She only hears that word from one person she knows. "My dad would like you. He represents all of our progress in modern genetic engineering, yet he believes in God, in miracles. Drives some of the government officials mad." She isn't sure why she's telling Colin this, except that she has no one to talk to about these things with.

Colin just smiles. "My mom believed in miracles. She said that we all have worth, not because we can accomplish certain things, but because we were created." After picking up one of his strawberries, he adds, "What about you? What do you believe?"

"I'm still thinking about it." She looks out at the city past the balcony. She knows she should redirect the conversation to something safe, but she's starting to accept that she met Colin purely by chance. Maybe Macy didn't set this up. Maybe she's talking to a *person* for once, a person who has no script. "There are certain things I wish I could accomplish, though. Anything special, really. I wish I could write songs or invent things. Or paint. I wish there was something that I could be good at, so I wouldn't just be..." She nearly says, "*a prop*," but she knows she shouldn't say something like that out loud.

Colin frowns, immediately fixated on something she said. "Wait, I thought you said you painted the canvas in the garden at the party."

"I did. But I'm not a very good artist. Be honest, what did you think of the candlelit rain painting?" She knows it's not fair to ask him to be honest. She's a princess; he's her guest. He can't say anything rude, and he's bound to know it. "I won't be upset," she adds, though she knows it's not enough.

He still takes several seconds to gather his thoughts. Then his gray eyes stick to the tablecloth. "The rendering wasn't particularly realistic, nor adherent to a specific Victorian style. Although, it'd probably be best categorized as impressionistic. The lighting was its strongest feature, added to the creativity of setting the painting with the physical lighting setup of the candles. To me, the overall effect was intriguing."

Katrin gazes at him with wide eyes. Then she pulls herself together and takes a drink of her lemonade. His analysis feels honest, yet it doesn't disappoint her at all. Standing in the Crystal Palace classroom and comparing her study to the other paintings, the truth hurt. But she prefers it over the litany of lies she lives with. "Thank you. It does seem like you're telling the truth."

Colin appears even more hesitant with his next statement but speaks up after a second. "I am. You asked me to be honest, so—I was."

"It's not you," she smiles sadly. "It's just, people tend to lie to make me feel better about everything."

"I'm not very good at lying."

Her grin widens. "I believe you."

"Do you not like your paintings?" He circles back to her question.

"I thought I might have a gift. Turns out, everyone's been saying I'm the greatest artist they've ever seen to make me feel better."

"Do you like it, though?"

"Now you *sound* like my dad. Except he also thinks I should put my painting progress up on my Newsstand."

"Videos?" he asks. When she nods, he seems to think for a moment. He's abandoned the food. "Well, are the paintings for them or for you? If no one ever saw them again, would you keep painting them?"

She hasn't been asked this question before, so she takes her time. "I've never thought about not having an audience. I feel like I'm always watched by someone all the time. But if no one ever saw another one of my paintings again, I guess...I'd still do it." She looks up. "Yeah, I'd keep doing it." He just waits, letting her process the answers to her own questions without further comment. She finally decides to lob one back. "Why did you start putting your songs out there?"

His eyes dart away, a sudden shade of embarrassment coloring his cheeks. "I said I wasn't good at lying, so the truth is that I did it because I wanted validation."

She tries to make light of it, since she can tell that he didn't want to admit it. "I mean, everyone wants validation in some way. It's just that most people don't talk about it. I wanted validation for my paintings. And, when I didn't get what I wanted after I went to a class, it felt like my whole identity had been stripped away." Saying it out loud makes it sound silly and shallow. But the frustration is real—and she *isn't* good at anything.

Her wrist display chimes with a notification. She swipes it away with one finger in midair as the glass doors open. Colin looks up at the newcomer. It's the same girl who brought their food, dressed in a simple aproned uniform. She holds out a silver case to Colin wordlessly.

"I figured you couldn't bring a violin here, but would you mind playing one of ours? I had Dahlia bring up the nicest one she could find." Katrin knows only a handful of people will be able to see footage of them on the patio, but she's prepared to tell security that Colin's an *expert* on song covers, as any good musician could be if they tried.

Colin eyes the case, head tilted curiously, then sets it down on a chair to open the lid. For a moment, he admires the craftsmanship of the violin inside, taking it from the velvet inlay and examining it with reverence. Eventually, he seems to notice that he hasn't replied to her question. His eyes dart back up to her, then down at the bow in the case. "Yes. Yes—of course. Wow, this is a nice violin. Do you know who made it?" He sits, turning something on the bow that Katrin didn't even know could turn. Then he searches the case and finds a compartment she didn't even know was there.

"I have no idea. I don't know much about music," she reluctantly admits, stacking her plate with some cheese. There are few foods, natural or engineered, better than cheese.

"What would you like to hear?" Colin raises the violin to his chin and plays a few notes. Katrin realizes after a second that he's tuning. He seems more confident holding a violin, like it's a familiar routine for him.

"Anything. I love it all. Everything. What about... Did you mention something about songs for an opera the other night, or was that my imagination?"

"I did." He brightens even more, lifting the bow to the strings. "I just finished working on this one. It's called *Bubblegum Aria*."

"Skies! I get to hear an unreleased song?" Katrin automatically falls silent as he begins playing, determined to catch every note. She's instantly mesmerized by the sound. There should be no way a violin can mimic a bubble expanding, then suddenly popping, but it does. A single laugh escapes her when she recognizes the sound, but she watches silently for the rest of the song. She eats cheese with one hand, fingers searching blindly on her plate since she refuses to move her eyes from the violin. She claps when the song finishes, and Colin smiles sheepishly at the response.

"I've never had such an enthusiastic audience before," he says.

She knows he's not joking, since he's chosen to remain anonymous. Surely his family supports his composing process, though. "I love it!" After a second, she adds, "And I'm being completely honest. It's amazing. How did you even learn to do that?"

He places the violin across his legs. "Well, it was challenging to start. I liked music, but the violin itself was difficult to get used to at first. The feel of the strings... It was hard, but eventually it became a habit. And the songs? I don't know. They just start playing in my head, and I try to get it recorded as fast as possible."

"I understand none of that." She laughs again, amazed that songs can just *appear* in his head. "But it's incredible."

She listens to him play a few more songs, some of her favorites and even a few she knows she's never heard before. She remembers every detail of how *Pipe Organ Waterfall* and *Canopy Crown* sound, but his performance of each of them is different. He adds extra nuances into the songs, and she realizes that what she's hearing is completely unique to this moment. The song will never be played the exact same way again.

When Colin halfheartedly announces that he should go home before his family gets back, Katrin has a container of food put together for him to take since he hardly had time to touch any of it. He adds in more strawberries than anything, likely a favorite food equal to her obsession with cheese.

"I don't know how to say this," she says quietly before security arrives to escort him out. "I really enjoyed talking to you and listening to your songs, but don't feel like you have to come back just because I'm the princess. You don't have to if you don't want to. It's completely up to you. I won't tell anyone who you are regardless, I promise."

Just as she begins to feel herself rambling trying to get her point across, he nods. "No, it's okay. I liked it. My house is really quiet. And I liked talking to you too. And I believe you."

She smiles, nodding back conspiratorially. He trusts her not to tell anyone his secret. It feels good, feeling like she can trust someone too. She's never had a friend that she's *chosen* before, one that's not been intentionally placed in her orbit. She's still nervous that Macy and her security team won't leave Colin alone, but she tries not to dwell on it. She knows what she'll tell Macy.

Right now, she's experiencing an exciting feeling: she's inspired to paint again.

Chapter Twelve

Holo Music

Colin pulls up his tablet's display the moment he gets back to the apartment. He opens the box of fruit on the kitchen island and eats strawberries while he tries to search for images of Katrin's other paintings. Surely some images are available. He wants to determine for himself what he thinks of her artwork.

"*Search query not within academic parameters*," TIRA reports.

Colin drops his head down to his arm on the counter in frustration. He keeps forgetting that the school tablet, the only one he has so far, doesn't allow him to access databases beyond strict categories. Fortunately for his sanity, classical music falls under an accepted search.

"Okay, new search. Open my store's sales report for this week."

The results pop up in a separate holo above the counter, organized for easy perusal. He only made five sales, but one of them was the princess's alias. He taps the name again: *Elayne.* The limited data from the sale flashes onto the display. She'd heard all of his other songs, but this was the only sale by this name that he's seen. The palace must have been covering their tracks until this sale. Maybe she bought the song on a different device, which confused a security firewall long enough for Colin's admin account to register the information? He doesn't have a clue how it all works.

The apartment door shuts, pulling Colin out of his analysis. He quickly closes his displays, leaving the tablet on the countertop. Then he takes a bite of his strawberry.

"Where have you been?" Lance asks, almost sounding concerned. He appears in the kitchen in his long coat, newspaper stuffed in the pocket. He taps the wall and quickly orders a few items to be delivered to the Shelf. Colin realizes that he hasn't taken his overcoat and scarf off yet. That was his mistake. Colin makes eye contact for a second too long. Lance adds, "You've never been able to lie, so don't even think about trying it."

Colin starts to think of a way out of explaining everything, but he knows *something* on his face will give him away, so he begins, "I...left. I left the apartment to get on the train—"

"If you want to ride around on the maglevs just to look at waterfalls, *wait* for one of us. I don't have time to go find you if you get lost somewhere or miss a stop." Lance immediately launches into his speech, which oddly saves Colin from continuing. "If you get distracted even for a moment by the noise or whatever it is that bothers you, you could end up in another *district*, and someone would have to come get you. I'm not leaving in the middle of a meeting to do that." His voice slows down. "Do you understand what I'm saying?"

Colin nods quickly. "Yes."

Lance finally looks down, noticing the strawberries. Then he rounds the corner, examining the rest of the apartment. He gestures widely to the space. "If you're so bored, why don't you do something about this mess instead of wandering around. I'm busy enough without having to monitor all this." He reaches out and takes the strawberry that's halfway to Colin's mouth and drops it back in the box. Then Lance retreats to his room, a waiting call beeping on his wrist. His voice changes to a brighter tone as the doors automatically shut behind him. "What can I do for you, Lark?"

Colin reluctantly abandons his food, not knowing how long the call might last. He might be able to finish cleaning and retreat to his room before Lance's meeting is over. He doesn't particularly want to stick around for any more speeches. His fingers fly across the wall display, programming the various tasks. Then he runs into the living area and gathers Josiah's waistcoat and collectible books he'd been counting on the floor. He looks hard for the random trinkets Davin usually forgets around the apartment but can't find any, so he takes his palace fruit and goes to his room. The door slides shut behind him.

Opening his violin case, he takes a slip of worn paper out of the compartment to stand it up on the velvet lining. This is the only writing he has from his mom. Just twelve words, something she'd slipped into the violin case when it was given to him. He sits on the floor and eats his strawberries in silence, reading the words on loop.

God is our refuge and strength, a very present help in trouble.

Colin switches on the room's soundproofing so he can talk aloud. "I need very specific help. I don't even know if this is possible, but I would like to see the princess again. I don't know how I can do that. Can you please help me? She is nice to me, and I haven't met someone who's been nice to me in so long. I just want to see her again. Please."

"You cannot see him again."

"Sorry, what?" Katrin hates being cornered by Macy when she's trying to enjoy her sitting room in peace but hates even more that this is her opening statement. Macy usually reserves her most cordial sentiments for the beginning of a conversation, so if the interaction is *starting* in this fashion, Katrin doesn't want to envision the ending. She fluffs a pillow on the couch and sits in an ocean of scarlet skirts in the middle. If she's going to be miserable, she might as well be miserable sitting down.

Macy continues as though Katrin has made no reply, enlarging and flipping a holo display so Katrin can see. "We've done more research on the young man you encountered at the party and invited here." *Of course she has.* Katrin's jaw tightens. "He was flagged as a rare genetic anomaly at birth. Neurodivergent, virtually impossible according to our research. Our Genetics branch offered to take him off his mother's hands as an infant, assuring her that we'd undertake sufficient research to ensure that such an anomaly would not occur again if she chose to have another child. She refused and kept the child."

Katrin swallows, not sure how she can even believe a word of this. Something in the back of her mind from her conversation with Colin earlier is now flashing to the forefront. His mother said: *We all have worth.* Of course she would keep him. Still, her mind swirls. What was the genetics branch planning to do with him if his mother had turned him over? These people don't know him. They haven't watched Colin play a violin with their own eyes, the incredible passion he infuses into his music. They don't know that his songs—*his*—can pull a person into a heavenly world of dreams. They don't know everything. Even if he couldn't do those things, he doesn't deserve—

Before she can interject, Macy continues, "This, of course, is a classified file that we've been able to access. There used to be more public information about an autistic boy in existence, but his current guardian is our treasurer, now CEO of the Kaelumian World Bank." Macy lifts an eyebrow and flashes Katrin a warning look. "So, he has some—sway, let's say, in his insistence that his ward remain entirely unknown to the public for his own safety and the safety of his family."

"I...had no idea," Katrin manages, overwhelmed.

"The Meadors have taken great pains to ensure that this boy is provided for and is not unnecessarily made into a public spectacle." Macy offers a sympathetic smile, one of her better attempts. "I'm just saying that we both know that public spectacle can tend to be both your occupation as well as your occupational hazard, and for once, this is a family that we can't drag onto the set."

"I didn't know," Katrin repeats, still trying to make sense of it all. She learned at some point about neurodivergent traits that existed in the 2200s, but it has been a few years since the class. Did the class explain anything about genius composers? She doubts it. Also, the Labyrinth championship must have seriously been an accident if they were truly avoiding attention. Yet, again, Colin managed that in spectacular fashion, so...

"I understand you didn't know," Macy says soothingly. She closes the display in the air with a tap of a finger. "That's why we did our own digging. Now, don't worry about it. Everything's handled." She walks out briskly, leaving Katrin with the peace and quiet she wanted.

Well, maybe not peace. Guilt swirls in Katrin's chest. She recalls Colin's anxiousness when she spoke to him at the party, how quickly he ran off. She didn't know that he was composing anonymously for *this* reason. When she asked him about it, he said, "*My stepfather thought it was best.*" She highly doubts he lied. That was probably true. But one thing still doesn't add up to her. If he and his entire family are so keen on keeping him a secret, then why did he come back? His family has means. Clearly. Why didn't he just send the key back? Why did he come?

She can only come up with one conclusion: he's lonely.

Resolving to keep investigating on her own time, Katrin stands to her scarlet heels and proceeds to the firing line—what she calls her next meeting. The rest of the attendees call it the Kaelumian High Council. A pretentious name, in her opinion. She walks through the halls, quick scans flashing in the corners of her vision at doorways. When she comes to the room, an arched entrance gives way to a high, domed ceiling and a long table. A golden runner cuts through the middle, separating the collection of lounging young people. Phoebe sits in her customary end seat, eyes rapidly skimming thin air, signifying that she's reading a book on some invisible holo her eyes are paired to. Percy sits to her left, elbows across the table as he leans forward in heated conversation with the troublemaker across from him. Roland, as always, lounges carelessly in his chair. He already has his riding boots on, so Katrin knows exactly where he's headed as soon as he can get away. He's starting an argument in the interim, which is to be expected. Adelaide has brought desserts from her lunch. She's stylishly dressed but spilling bits of chocolate on her skirts distractedly. She clearly has an ear tuned to the boys' conversation.

Katrin sits down at the foot of the table unannounced. Adelaide's attention flicks across the table so she can share a quick eye roll in silent commentary.

"You can't call it that! There already *is* a Kaelumian High Council," Percy exclaims, clearly on his last nerve already.

"Fine," Roland says breezily. "Then we can call this the Kaelumian High-ish Council."

"Now you're just mocking me. Or perhaps you're mocking all of us; I can't tell."

"I like to keep it that way."

"How about this: The Future Kaelumian Council Stakeholder Round Table."

"I don't even think Phoebe's book has that many characters," Roland deadpans.

Phoebe's fiery eyes break their pattern, glancing over at the mention of her name. There's a sizable enough pause in their pointless argument that everyone turns and notices Katrin. Adelaide swallows a bite of raspberry chocolate, lowering her napkin delicately to the table. "Should we address the elephant in the room?" she says in a sugary sweet tone.

Katrin glowers. "There are no cameras in this room. If you're referring to me, I will dump those chocolates into your lemonade."

Adelaide laughs brightly. "No, silly. Not you *exactly*. Just...this maybe?" She pulls up the video in the center of the table, where none of their eyes can escape from it, a distant shot of Katrin falling from the stained-glass ceiling at Labyrinth.

"Could we not?" Percy complains, and Katrin wonders if he's still upset about being rebuffed.

Katrin shifts her attention back to Adelaide. "Addie, future Department of Commerce, did you put me on that train on purpose?"

"Of course." Adelaide sighs, eyes still fixed on Percy. "The principal character over there ruining everything was most definitely not my fault, though. I told him you were coming on the next train." She glances at Katrin, whose face is betraying some of her exasperation. "Surely you didn't think Percy just *happened* to run into you at that exact moment, did you?"

Katrin groans quietly. Her life is such a tangled mess of strings from people trying to pull her one direction or the other that she can no longer discern between coincidence and premeditation. "I suppose that was a bit convenient," she says, defeated. She hesitates to ask if they all planned her second trip to the Crystal Palace, if she was successful in disrupting their plan by spontaneously finding a new class to crash. The palace is too large for Security to watch cameras, so the doorways only scan for levels of access. When Katrin passed through, Level 1 access wouldn't have attracted much attention. Still, somehow, her companions seem to know everything.

Percy finally speaks again. "Katrin, I promise I had no idea where you were going. I was just following you when you ended up on the dome. If you had gotten hurt, I would never forgive myself."

"Thank you," she replies mechanically. He's already trying to get back in her good graces. "I'm grateful to hear it wasn't part of the plan to have me plummet to my potential death."

Roland leans forward now, elbows planted on the tabletop. "What was it like, though? Was it exhilarating, falling that far?"

Of course, Roland would ask that. "It happened really fast. My neck still hurts," she answers. "Look, can we get back to the fact that I didn't know any of this was going to happen? Is it too much to ask to be *told what's going on*?" She's losing her cool. At the end of the day, though, it doesn't matter what she wants. These people are the future Kaelumian High Council for a reason: Roland Lark the Genetics department, Percival Liden the Cultural Minister, Phoebe Drake the Justice department. Then there's Katrin—the pretty princess they play with. They can play with her emotions, with her future, with her life, and no one can stop them.

She can only beg, and she hates begging.

"We will, we promise," Adelaide soothes. "I'll plan something fun this weekend, just the two of us."

Katrin puts on her best imitation of a smile. What's crazy is that Adelaide would probably still trade places with her if she could. Addie's confessed that she hates that all of her genetic enhancements are custom to the role she'll inherit. Otherwise, she'd find a way to switch positions with Katrin in a heartbeat.

"This weekend? I thought you and Phoebe already had plans."

She shrugs, selecting another chocolate. "Maybe I want to spend more time with you."

Katrin narrows her eyes. "Or maybe Macy told you to distract me to keep my mind off that musician I invited here."

Phoebe swipes a hand across the air and closes her holo book. She turns her attention to the conversation, sharp eyes fixed across the table. "This one's easy, Katrin. He's not good for our image. He couldn't be seen with any of us in the event that his—condition or whatever it is—gets out." Her gaze cuts across to Roland. "Unless he hangs out with you. People would theorize that you were trying to cure him."

Roland gives a short laugh, clearly amused at the idea.

Katrin feels herself mentally shrinking from the wording. "It's not like he has a *disease*."

"Of course not," Phoebe agrees. "*That* the Larks could cure."

Giving up the fight, Katrin steals one of Adelaide's chocolates from her plate. "Fine, this Saturday. Can I at least pick the venue?"

"No art museums this time," Addie says. "They're unbelievably dull."

"Hey!" Percy glares. "I help curate those, you know."

Adelaide chooses to make things worse. "Oh, I know." She dabs her napkin to her lips and reaches for Katrin's hand. "I'm sure there's something else we could do, darling."

Katrin has suddenly had her fill of this meeting, and they haven't even arrived at the items on the official agenda. Roland stands from the table as though he can hear her thought, stretching lazily. "I'm going for a ride. If anybody needs me, call the lab I guess."

Percy sits upright. "Wait, you can't just leave!" he huffs.

"I'll be back to vote on the name, don't worry." He winks at Percy and turns to go, slinging his coat over one shoulder.

"Unbelievable." Percy shakes his head.

Katrin's eyes follow Roland out the door. She has an idea.

Chapter Thirteen

Star Sparkler

Katrin stands in the stable, absently wondering what this dirt is doing to her white, heeled boots. The sun is still blazing, but the temperatures lately are scheduled to be frosty, reminiscent of winter. She doesn't mind, since she often wears multiple layers regardless. The air is eerily quiet out in the green fields north of the palace. Only a handful of people are allowed to roam the soft grass owned by the Larks, and Katrin is one of those select few.

She doesn't have to wait long before Roland appears in the corner of her vision, leading his horse toward a stall. *Ivan*, if she recalls correctly, and she has a suspicion about whom Roland named his horse after.

"I knew you were going to follow me. You had that look in your eye," Roland observes, stopping near the stall she's blocking. Ivan studies her for a moment, then lowers his head to the side of her face in a silent request for attention. She obliges, softly stroking the horse's diamond marking.

"Then I think you may already know what I'm going to say," Katrin adds. She's surprised he so easily predicted her movements, but she doesn't want him to know that.

"It wouldn't have anything to do with a certain musician, would it?" He smiles smugly, though his eyes betray a hint of concern.

She might as well get right to her point. "You knew about him already. You must have," Katrin states. "Your parents know about every genetic breakthrough and anomaly in every domed city in the empire. I also happen to know that he's not the only neurodivergent individual. You told me about your family when you were five, remember?"

"Yeah, I wasn't the brightest at five."

"Roland—"

"Yes." He adjusts the reins in his hand, pulling one shoulder back when Ivan tries to nudge him off balance. His lips are a thin line. "Yes. My family found a way to isolate psychopathy. My whole family is the same. They thought that for our work, some of the things we do, it would be best for us. It would make us better suited to it." As she opens her mouth to argue that maybe there shouldn't be jobs that lend themselves best to psychopaths, he quickly adds, "Don't get me wrong. I don't despise it. I still believe I should have been given a choice. Sometimes, though, I feel like I see things for what they are and people for what they are, in ways that everyone else seems blind to. I see through the charade—everyone's charade. Even yours, right now."

Katrin adjusts her weight against the stall door uncomfortably. One thing that being psychopathic has always granted him is a direct manner of speaking. But he could still be hiding most of his real thoughts. She strokes Ivan again with one hand, then laces her fingers together. "You may be right. Here's what you probably suspect: Colin's not what they think. He has a gift. But it's his secret to tell, not mine."

Roland steps closer. "I *am* right. But you calculated correctly. I want to know. Genetics is going to be my life's work. Shutting down naturally occurring neurodiversity was a decision that was made long before me, but it's a decision that I might have control of later. I want to know what he can do."

"Why?" She can't help but ask, even though she has her theories. They led her here in the first place. But she can't be too careful when it comes to Roland.

"You know I like to study the brain. All the new, young researchers coming into Genetics want to keep moving forward and leave neuro-divergence behind for good. I have different theories. I think it may be useful, that it happens for a reason. I want to prove that I'm right."

"Well, I've been told not to bring him to the palace, but I can still make contact. If you can obtain something untraceable for me, I'd be in your debt. Also, if you prove that you can be trusted to Colin, maybe he'll tell you himself. But like I said, it's his secret to tell." She doesn't want to make promises on Colin's behalf. Colin may be even more distrusting than she is, especially with how secretive his family appears to be about him.

"Attempting to acquire contraband by offering me a mystery." He lifts a skeptical eyebrow, but then smiles wryly. "It's a good plan."

Muscles in Katrin's shoulders relax. Maybe she's made the right move. "I can get you a VR room. The equipment for it can be mailed, and the technology allows for complete privacy." Then he adds, "You say you'll be in my debt if I help you. I already know what *I* want. It's a research assignment I know you can pull off, seeing as you're a master of disguises now."

Katrin's anxiousness springs back into her chest, stronger than before. *Research? Disguises?* Katrin takes a quick breath, ready to refuse and let Roland out of the deal immediately, but her curiosity gets the better of her. "What is it?" She blames her boring schedule at the palace for this unfortunate craving for intrigue.

Roland's eyes pierce hers, like he's weighing her every expression for hesitance. "I'm going to have a friend of mine meet with you. He's from Genetics." Katrin knows Roland doesn't actually collect friends, just information, so this *friend* must be a genius to have Roland's attention. "You can take a lab tour when offered. Don't act surprised by anything you see. Then report back to me."

The *report back* grates, as if she'll be a subordinate on a work assignment. Still, the more pressing issue is the Genetics lab. She stares at him, mystified. "Where is this friend supposed to meet me?"

"He'll find you, I promise."

She doesn't like the vague answer but stops herself from complaining. She has more to think about. "Don't you already have complete access to all of Genetics?"

"Not this place," he says, more serious now.

"*That's* comforting," she mutters, emphasizing the irony. He can't be serious.

"You just take a short little tour, then come back to your palace." He cocks his head. "Think you can handle that?"

Annoyed at his condescending tone, she responds too quickly. "Fine. But if I get in any trouble, I'm blaming you. I'm not allowed to be *anywhere* in Genetics unescorted, much less somewhere top secret."

"I'm sure of it."

She remembers something else. "The alarms. The shutdown the other day at the labs. Was that you?"

"Why would you think that?" Not the response she was looking for. He's obviously unwilling to give up any of his secrets.

Katrin leans back, uncertain. Ivan nudges her hair with his nose, startling her. She'd forgotten that the horse was still over her head.

Roland gradually tugs him back. "No. Stop flirting. This girl is trouble."

Katrin gives him a look to say, "*we both know which one of us is trouble,*" then clears the path to the stall. She tries not to look nervous, but she has no idea what kind of trouble he's gotten himself into—or what he's about to get *her* into. She can't back out now, though. She has the VR room she needs at her fingertips.

Night creeps into the apartment, and it's darker than normal. There are no visible stars. No moon. The city is running tests on the dome before the upcoming light show for the new year. Colin sits on a stool in the kitchen, staring at the checkered lights of the skyscraper across from their high rise. He's been sitting here, caught up in the sights, for too long. Now his attention recalibrates, and he spins around on the stool.

Davin walks through the kitchen, lights on the floor glowing in step with his socks. He sets a plate in front of Colin wordlessly. The place is silent. Lance and Josiah are in their rooms, probably sleeping.

What is he doing awake? Colin's eyes drop to the white plate, and he pieces it together.

"I ordered it from the Shelf. No big deal," Davin whispers.

The plate has a single cupcake in its center, vanilla with a swirled chocolate frosting. White sprinkles. It's a combination that Colin would likely never pick for himself, but he appreciates the gesture. His chest tightens a little when he notices the almost-invisible gray stick in the frosting.

"It's that firework thing you used to like," Davin explains.

"Star Sparkler," Colin corrects on instinct. Then he swallows. Draws the plate closer. "Thank you."

"It's no big deal," his stepbrother repeats casually, turning to close the panel over the Shelf's delivery compartment.

It feels like a big deal to Colin. He remembers what his birthday used to be like, with his mom. They didn't have much money, but she knew how to decorate a one-room apartment like a movie set. When she remarried, and they moved into a larger home, Colin's birthday became even more elaborate. They all bought star sparklers, and three energetic eight-year-olds chased each other around the patio in dizzying trails of light.

Being eighteen somehow feels exactly the same as seventeen and yet completely different. Colin lights the sparkler on the cupcake, arms crossed over the counter, and watches it burn down with transfixed eyes. He can't take it in his hand and twirl it around. He can only sit in the dark and watch the magic unfold. Then fizzle with a crack. Die into smoke. The kitchen filtration system purifies the air a moment later.

He looks across the counter, eyes adjusting back to the darkness.

Davin is watching too. Colin knows his brother's rehearsal for his graduation was today. Lance had meetings straight through dinner. Everyone was busy. Colin hadn't expected anyone to even notice that it was his birthday.

Davin leans against the opposite counter. "Look." He lowers his voice, even though the bedrooms probably all have soundproofing enabled. "I don't think you're dumb. Not like everyone thinks. You can swim a championship race, so you must not be that incompetent. But why don't you ever stand up for yourself? That's what I can't understand."

Colin blinks, taking a second to process his unexpected statements. Either Davin's insults sound like oddly worded compliments or his compliments sound like insults. He can't tell. "What would it change?" he finally asks.

Davin shrugs, pushing off against the countertop. "I don't know," he says unhelpfully.

Neither of them says the unspoken. Colin lost his "privilege" to celebrate his own birthday from trying to stand up for himself. It doesn't work, and he knows it.

"If you don't know, then I definitely don't." Colin stands, taking the plate with the cupcake to his room. It would make him nervous to eat it out here.

"Wait," Davin calls to his back, immediately softening his voice to a whisper again. "Two boxes came in the Shelf. Dad will probably want them to be put in his office tomorrow morning." He stacks the packages at the edge of the counter. Then he stalls for a moment. "Goodnight."

"Goodnight," Colin answers, brow wrinkling. The packages, he understands. It's one of his jobs to make sure they get taken from the Shelf and put in a specific corner of Lance's office. Davin's last word he does not understand. He doesn't understand his brother's sudden curiosity about his behavior. He doesn't understand the cupcake either, but he'll gladly take that. Even if he can't reconcile it.

Colin squints to read the first package's label, some technology company's return address. He picks up the smaller box and turns it over. A cold shock travels up his spine. *Colin Burke.* He's never seen his own name on a package in his life. His first response is fear. *How?* Then he reads the vague return label and spies the word: *Court 50.* Could the princess have sent him a package? On edge now, he stacks the cupcake on top of the small box and carries them both to his room in a near run.

Once safely inside, he opens the package with shaking hands and pulls out a single item. It's a sleek black set of goggles. They are thin, cushioned with seamless leather around the eyes. Where the shape touches the temples, two metallic nodes glow a faint blue in a ring. Colin sits down on his bed and carefully fits the device onto his eyes, adjusting the fabric strap around the back. It blocks out all the light from his vision once the cushions press around his face. He makes a few more minor adjustments for comfort, then realizes that it doesn't matter. The nodes touch his temples, and his mind leaves the room instantaneously.

He gives a short gasp but can't hear it. The world has gone black. A neat line of white text appears in the center of his sight.

Please make sure you are lying down, your head and body fully supported.

He presses down with his hands, barely feeling a blanket under his palms. He tentatively settles down onto the center of the bed. The tech must be able to sense him following directions because new text appears in his vision.

Scanning.

Colin doesn't see anything strange, but he feels something warm briefly touch his skin. Then a new line of text pops up.

Confirmed: natural eyes.

He feels a twinge of embarrassment at the words, even though he knows he had no say in what kind of eyes he was born with. Then a new message:

Entering VR room.

He looks at the word in awe. He's heard of VR rooms. They're new tech, expensive, tapping into the brain's ability to dream in order to trick the mind into creating and experiencing an environment without sensing the difference between virtual and reality.

In the time it takes for Colin to form a thought, he is standing in an empty VR room. He can move, walk around—all from the safety of his bed. He tilts his head back and looks at the blank ceiling. The room looks like what Colin pictures a theater's backstage might. There are red velvet curtains in the door, lights strung across the walls. Bright, striped wallpaper. There's a wooden writing desk against the wall. Colin walks up to it and runs a hand across the surface. A thin layer of dust accumulates on his fingers.

"Incredible..." he murmurs aloud, in awe of the realism. He can *feel* it—or his mind thinks he can, at least. He lets the dust fall through the air, watching it disappear. Even the wooden floors under his feet creak faintly as he walks. Colin reaches instinctively for his music note bead and realizes he has brought it with him somehow. He is wearing his school shirt and waistcoat, mismatched gray trousers and brown shoes. It's an outfit he's put on within the last week, something his mind would have easily been led to.

He opens the top drawer of the desk, curious if he'll find anything, and pulls out a folded program. The title is printed in gold ink and embellished.

Composer Anonymous
In Concert

A bright chime alert causes him to spin around. A second occupant materializes in the room, a smiling Princess Katrin. She's wearing a simpler dress than before, lighter skirts. She's not even wearing shoes, only stockings, which strikes him as interesting. This is how she must see herself, or how she's been able to program herself to appear in VR. She comes closer to the desk, still beaming. Nothing about her glows or glitches or looks fake. It feels like he's standing in a room with her, and he marvels at the technology.

"Do you like it?" she asks, clasping her hands together. She glances at the decorative program, so Colin assumes she's referring to it.

"I've never seen anything like this before." He motions with his free hand to the rest of the space. "Did you make this room?"

"I got it ready earlier today. It's actually one of my default options." Her eyes move to the corner of the room, which causes Colin to wonder if she can see settings he doesn't have access to. He's never been inside a VR simulation before. He definitely doesn't have the advanced destinations package.

"This is a default...?" Colin lifts the program in his hand, worried.

"Oh. No, I put that there!" She grins. "I was hoping you'd find where I hid it."

"I'm surprised you sent me VR tech, but it's amazing. Thank you." He lays the folded program back down. Then he makes a small adjustment, lining the paper up with the edges of the desk. Why'd she go to all this trouble?

Her smile falters a little. "I persuaded someone to do a favor for me. I was told that it wasn't...prudent to invite you to the palace again. But I wanted to be able to explain why I had to revoke my earlier invitation."

Now Colin's face falls in response. He should have seen this coming. She's a princess. She probably has instant access to any information about any person she wants to investigate.

"My publicist had your file," she continues reluctantly. "I'm so sorry. I didn't know your privacy was that important to you and your family."

Colin nods numbly. *She knows now.* He knows she's probably disappointed. She'll do what everyone does now. She'll start to speak differently, then eventually find an excuse to leave. And he'll never see her again.

At least it was fun to visit the palace. It was fun to play the violin for her and see her rapt attention fixed on the music. She is a true music lover. He will miss her.

"But if you want," Katrin adds after a moment, "my friend assures me that this VR room is untraceable and unhackable. So, we can meet in here instead of in person. At least in VR, we can travel anywhere on the globe and go on whatever kinds of adventures we can dream up."

Colin stares for a few beats as she stands in silence, waiting for his reply. His mind spins. He doesn't understand. He doesn't understand her lively smile. "Wait, you said—you said you've seen my file."

"Yes. I didn't ask to see it; it was shown to me. But I am sorry for the invasion of privacy. My security team is wound a little too tight in my opinion."

He's surprised at the apology, a little thrown off by it. But he sputters out the rest anyway, "N-no, it's okay. I mean, you know who I am. You know *what* I am. Why do you want to meet with me?"

Katrin's brow knits tightly as she steps closer to the desk. "Why wouldn't I?"

"I've been told I am not easy to talk to."

"Besides my dad, you're the easiest person to talk to I've ever met."

Colin loses the reply he'd been forming. He stands motionless, trying to read Katrin's expression. He wants to believe her. He wants to give himself a chance, to try to connect with a person for once. It's been nearly a decade since he had his mom to talk to. What if he fails?

If you leave, you will have already failed. The thought appears out of nowhere. All he can do is try. And if he fails, he fails.

"Okay," he says quickly, aware that there has been a pause. She doesn't seem upset at the hesitation like his family usually is. His stepbrothers will raise their eyebrows, hold their palms up, exclaim, *"Well? Planet Earth to Colin!"* She just waits, eyes locked on his. "Okay," he repeats. "I accept your invitation. Where would you like to go, Your Highness?"

"Katrin, please." She beams, taking a finger and scrolling through a menu that Colin can't see. "Would you like to see a musical? Symphonic band? Ballet?"

"I love all things with music," he responds, a light feeling entering his chest.

"How about The Nutcracker?"

He has never seen The Nutcracker, only heard some songs in TIRA's library. "I would love to go, yes."

"Then let's go!"

Katrin spins around, opening a velvet curtain that inexplicably leads to an indoor ticket booth in a circular foyer. Crowds mill around them in black and white suits and dresses. Colin ducks through the curtain and follows the princess into the brighter space. She has transformed with the scene, wearing a white gown and matching white hat atop her curls. She glances back with a wide smile, and Colin looks down at his arms. He's suddenly wearing a three-piece suit with small gold buttons and a watch chain. He's never worn anything so nice. But, as the thought hits him that he should do his best to look the part, Katrin gets an impish look on her face and snatches the black top hat he didn't even know he was wearing. Then she tosses her white hat atop the ticket booth without the nearby usher even glancing at the disturbance. "What do you think?" she asks, adjusting the black hat on her head.

Colin realizes when he sweeps the crowd with a questioning look that the people surrounding them are programmed to attend the performance, but not to react to anomalies. Katrin can seemingly do what she wants. She must like this kind of freedom.

"It is absurd," he states matter-of-factly. "You should keep it. It's funny."

"Then I shall." Katrin reaches back for her white hat and perches it on top of the other, arranging the long white ribbons to fall down the sides of the top hat.

When he laughs, she twists around. She looks pleased. He wonders for a moment if she did these antics just to get him to laugh.

They are shown to seats near the middle of the theater, in the perfect position to observe everything. Colin tips his head back and turns in his chair, trying to see every facet of the large building.

As he admires the chandeliers above them, Katrin leans over. "Would you like to watch it with the audience or without?"

Colin glances around at the people sitting in their seats, a low hum of crowd noise in the room as the orchestra pit below prepares to begin the performance. "You can watch it without?"

"Of course. Look at this!" Katrin swipes something on her personal settings panel, and the room is suddenly emptied, rows of red velvet seats surrounding them void of occupants. The theater itself changes, the air around him echoing. It's just him and Katrin now.

"I like this better."

Katrin nods like she agrees. Then she sits back comfortably and removes the stacked hats, setting them on the empty seat on her left.

Colin looks at her head and reluctantly points a finger in the direction of her thick curls. "Um, is it alright if I fix it?"

"Oh, yes. Go ahead." She reaches with one hand, feeling around unsuccessfully.

Colin picks up the ringlet that was displaced by the hat and moves it to the other side of her head, dropping it in place.

The *Miniature Overture* begins, lively, lilting notes filling the room. Colin is instantly pulled into the performance. He watches the musicians play, the curtains part, and the dancers gradually fill the stage. He's always wanted to see a live performance. If this is as close as he ever gets, he'll be happy. This sounds and looks as real as anything he's ever experienced.

To his left, Katrin shifts after a few songs go by, moving a foot. He glances over, remembering that she's here. Her gaze is locked onto the performance, transfixed, so he turns back.

This is the perfect birthday present.

Chapter Fourteen

Candy Palace

Roland's VR room has access to every major domed city in the world, from Beijing to Mumbai. Katrin takes herself and Colin to every location that strikes their fancy. They build an exhaustive list of places they want to explore, and they sail across oceans and walk across mountain peaks. They visit the beach, and Katrin watches Colin pace barefoot across the sand. He bends down to pick up small shells and collect them in his hand. Neither of them has ever seen a real beach, so they have to trust that the programmer knew what a beach looks and sounds like. The waves crashing on the shore are louder than she imagined, but she doesn't turn the sound down. She wants the experience to be authentic.

Colin walks back to where she's situated herself in the shallow water and holds the shells up for her to see. "I wish we could take them back."

"Some VR destinations have items you can purchase, then they show up at your door back in Kaelum. But not shells. Not yet anyway," she tells him.

He tosses them one by one back into the waves, each shell making a satisfying *plink* in the water.

As the days have gone by, the only obstacle to their virtual adventures has been scheduling. Katrin has busy days, packed with required appointments. Colin insists that his stepfather should be gone from the apartment when he uses the technology. Apparently, his stepfather has override access to the door of his room, which gives Katrin pause the longer she thinks about it. As she spends more time with Colin, she begins to toss her preconceptions. He's a virtual library about certain subjects and is more passionate about an array of things than most people are about a single fascination. He collects sights and sounds and turns them into music, a gift she can't comprehend. None of these things were in his file. The more she gets to know him, the more she's disappointed that no one else has.

She also waits nervously for the time when Roland's price for the VR room will come due, but as the days go by, the nervousness fades to the back of her mind.

Katrin takes Colin to a candy palace after the beach so they can brainstorm the remainder of his opera. He takes in the structure slowly, pausing at each furnishing and examining it. The walls are made of colorful slabs of rock candy, and swirling layers of icing coat the tiered gables. Katrin steals a lollipop from the garden of candy flowers out front, her brain filling in the taste as she carries it into the halls. Colin finds a bridge made of licorice and gingerbread planks suspended between towers above her and calls down, leaning over the licorice rope, "I think I should do a song about gingerbread, like a mellow, cozy kind of song. What do you think?"

Katrin stares up at his face peering over the edge of the bridge. "Honestly, all of your ideas are good ideas." She searches the room for a staircase to follow him upstairs.

It takes her a few minutes. By the time she crosses under a chocolate doorway and steps onto the bridge, he's sitting with his legs hanging over the gingerbread slab and arms resting on a licorice rope. She sits down beside him and swings her feet back and forth in the air. It may be a fake palace, but it has a nice view of ice cream mountains.

She mimics his posture, crossing her arms over the red licorice, lollipop in hand. "What was your mother like?" she asks, hoping it's a topic that doesn't trouble him. She asks everyone about mothers. It's a habit she can't shake, a missing piece of her heart.

A small smile flickers across his face. "She loved everything. She loved life. She loved acting. She loved me. She could talk to anyone, make friends with anyone. I never understood how she did it."

"I'm sure you could do it."

"I cannot," he says with an assurance she isn't sure how to contradict. "Do you not have a mother?"

"No. I guess...it was planned from the beginning that I wouldn't have one. I mean, technically I have a mother. But I don't know who she is."

Colin's face crumples. "That's cruel, not to give you a mother on purpose. Everyone should have a mother."

His honesty and direct manner of speaking keep surprising her. She's never had anyone directly condemn that decision to her face before, but it validates the ache she's always felt. It's like she's always known she wanted both her mother and her father. She quickly moves on to her next question. "How did she meet your dad?"

"I was too young to ask, so I'm not sure. He died when I was three.

Some kind of accident in Hydro. Underwater Level."

Katrin frowns at the unexpected information. "People have *died* working in the hydroelectric plant? I've never heard of that happening before."

"You wouldn't hear about it," Colin replies casually. "They don't put news like that on those." He points to her wrist holo, probably referring to all the Columns that people watch every minute of the day. She's only ever glanced at the Chronicle's city-wide news page. She thought one of the only ways people died anymore was from old age.

"I'm so sorry," she murmurs, still trying to process what he said. "I had no idea." Her world is filled with dresses, dinners, and drama. She'd assumed that Colin knows less about the world than she does, since he is mostly confined to his high-rise, but now she questions what *she* knows. Her world is practically a movie set. Who's to say it isn't completely fake? "What about your stepfather?" She cycles to the next question on her ever-growing list.

Colin doesn't react, serious expression unwavering. "He'd seen her movies. He was a fan. He managed to find her and would send her gifts and notes. She reached out and started visiting him just before we lost our apartment."

"Your brothers are your age, right?"

"Yes. They are. Just a few months older." She senses his reluctance and tries to think of something else to ask, not sure why he doesn't want to talk about his family. As she opens her mouth to change the subject, he adds, "Josiah doesn't like me. Davin is more complicated. I don't really understand, but it has something to do with his friend group and how they might not be friends with him if he spends time with me."

Unfortunately, Katrin does understand this never-ending game. She's played it her entire life and can relate to his disillusionment. The constantly changing dynamics are exhausting to keep up with. "It should be a lot simpler, shouldn't it?"

"It's hard. I try to love them. My mom used to be able to bring us all together. She could make them smile. She would make up games. Now they just want to be left alone."

"Did they graduate this year?"

"Yes, just four days ago. They actually went to the academy downtown in person, unlike me. Davin is learning finance, to do whatever it is that Lance does. Josiah has been working in Genetics some already, but he says he'll be heading some kind of research department now. Sometimes he asks if he can study me in his lab. He wants to"—Colin pauses, shifting uncomfortably before finishing his thought—"prevent more people like me from being born. I think Lance pulled some strings to get him that job, even though his career assignment put him in research. He wants to coach Labyrinth someday too."

Katrin determines then and there that she doesn't like either of Colin's stepbrothers. *Does Roland know Josiah?* she wonders, a twinge of concern pinging in the back of her mind. "What about you?" she asks, adjusting her arms on the licorice rope. She's glad the VR room's creator wasn't mischievous enough to make the surface sticky.

"I—just finished my program. Hopefully, it assigns me some musical aptitude."

Katrin laughs a little at that, not surprised he's being modest about his abilities.

"How does school work for you?" He finally lobs a question back. Though she's figured out he doesn't mind talking, he doesn't readily try to make conversation, so he must be truly curious. He also makes very little eye contact. It's such a relief from the constant attention always focused on her.

"A program like yours, probably. Also tutors. They have the worst possible job, trying to cram facts into my head. I have no false modesty when I assure you that I am not academically inclined. If I had to be given an aptitude assessment like most graduates do, I wouldn't have much of a chance. I'd probably land a job at a textile factory."

He looks at her briefly, then stares across at the ice cream mountain, a small frown tugging at his mouth now. "Well, at least worth isn't determined by a government aptitude assessment."

This again. Katrin knows she was genetically enhanced in several ways before she was born, things like her eyes and her hair color and immune system. But how much control could geneticists really have over her mind, her personality or beliefs? If they had control over those things, then she'd be better suited to her role. So would her so-called friends, who also struggle to fit into their inherited positions. She thinks about Roland for a second, and how he wishes he could have chosen how his brain works. It causes another question to appear in her mind.

"Do you think you're perfect the way you are? Say you could choose for yourself to be born like everybody else? Would you make that choice?" The words are out before she can realize the impact they'll have on him, and she cringes when he doesn't respond.

It takes Colin longer to answer, as she fears. He lowers his arms from the bridge, spinning the white bead on his arm like he always does when he's thinking. When he finally answers, he doesn't look at her. "Perfect? I mean—I don't see it that way. We're not perfect, any of us. This world isn't perfect. We keep trying to get there, improve people to perfection, but I don't think we're meant to be perfect—in this life anyway. Do I think that good things can come of my being this way? Sure I do. Do I believe I'm perfect or wish everyone were like me? No. No matter how people see me or treat me, there are difficult things. There will always be difficult things." He swallows and keeps fiddling with the bead. "But whatever I'm meant to be, I trust that I will be it, perfectly and completely, in the next life. Not this one." His eyes meet hers again.

Katrin is struck by his words. He says the most surprising things, things that she's never even thought of. She *really* wants her dad to meet Colin now. He would love this unexpected, thoughtful, savant musician. She looks into his natural gray eyes, regretting ever entertaining the idea that Colin is ordinary.

She was wrong. In the best possible way.

Something beeps, the settings panel she hid reappearing in her vision at the worst time. She casts her gaze down halfheartedly to the white string of numbers where the time is flashing red. Colin hasn't noticed what she's doing, so she says, "It's telling me that the timer we set has gone off, for when you wanted to go back."

He nods reluctantly, taking one last look at all the trappings of the candy palace surrounding them. She can't wait to hear what kind of song he dreams up from this inspiration.

"Tomorrow?" he asks. "Same time?"

"Same time. Rome. Don't be late!"

"I'm never late," he states dispassionately, standing up.

"I know."

Colin cuts the timing close, but he wanted to spend every possible minute with Katrin that he could before he has to take off the VR eyewear and return it safely to his closet.

He emerges from his room with seconds to spare. He doesn't sit idle, rushing through the halls and arranging shoes instead. He picks up trash in the kitchen and scoops it into the waste incinerator. Then he picks up the dinner reservation that arrived from the Shelf while he was in the VR room and arranges the food. He lines up all the forks with the edges of the plates, taking care with the placement of each item.

The front door opens, and Colin silently watches the twins meander into the kitchen and pick up plates of food. They disperse without a word, Davin to the table by the window and Josiah to his room to finish packing. Josiah will be moving out soon, which makes Colin wonder what will happen when he gets assigned a job as a musician. *If* he gets assigned to be a musician. Will he get instructions about where to go? Where he's supposed to live and in what part of the city? Colin is nervous just thinking about it. Lance has never talked to him about it before or taught him how to live on his own. Most of what Lance talks about is how Colin *can't* do anything himself.

Colin can tell that the twins have eyes paired to their holo Columns, so he doesn't interrupt. He silently eats his own meal in the kitchen. Katrin unearthed some old memories for him about his mother, so he thinks about what dinners were like with her. She used to make the whole family sit at the table together. She would pray over the food and say things like, *"Bless all the wonderful chefs at Shelf Shop downtown."*

This tradition has long been tossed out. Now everyone eats whenever and wherever they want.

Lance walks by and picks up his plate, briefly noticing that Colin is standing in the kitchen before going back to arguing with someone over a holo call. Now that Colin has heard Katrin talk about all her rich government friends, he listens to his stepfather talk about politics for the first time. He hears names he recognizes. *Larks, the geneticists. Drakes, the lawmakers.* The two are connected somehow. Lance is questioning why a law hasn't passed yet. The law has a number, not a name, which makes it impossible for Colin to understand what's going on.

Suddenly, Lance ends the call and walks back into the kitchen. He throws his overcoat onto the island and looks directly at Colin. "Come over to the couch. I need to talk to you about something."

Colin doesn't see any signs of anger, but his heart rate still spikes. Locked in place at the counter, he manages to move his feet after a few seconds and follow Lance into the living area. His stepfather is already seated and using the holo panel on the glass table to adjust the window panel. The sun is low in the sky, hitting the couches. The light shining across their faces slowly vanishes as the window turns an opaque white.

Sitting slowly at the opposite couch, Colin hopes his expression isn't giving away his fear. He crosses his fingers together, then drops them, placing his hands over his knees. He looks at the window, sees nothing but a plain white panel, then stares at the table instead.

"I received a digital report at work today," Lance starts. "Your results from TIRA."

Colin's eyes snap back up. He's been waiting and praying over this moment for years. Fear bleeds into anticipation. He has to be able to be a musician. He *has* to be.

"Your scores were competent for the most part, better than we'd anticipated several years ago. However, you were not placed into the music performance category you were wanting."

All his hopes dashed in a single moment. Colin steeples his hands against his face as his throat tightens. If he can't be placed as a violinist, which was a very limited position to begin with, then he has no other skills. What Katrin joked about is going to happen to him—a factory job somewhere with long hours. He won't have time to compose music anymore.

His chest aches. He can't even process the loss.

The touch on his shoulder startles him. Lance has switched couches and is sitting next to him now. "Look, we don't…know, for sure, how you would do living alone," he continues, so uncharacteristically close. "We don't know if you can handle a permanent job. So, I've spent most of the day putting together the holo documents for legal guardianship." Colin looks at his face searchingly, trying to believe that this is real. "So that you can stay. You can stay here with me. You can keep playing your violin. You'll be safe, and I won't have to worry about you."

"I don't have to leave?" Colin feels hope trickling back into his mind. For an instant, he'd been trying to make peace with never being able to compose again. But now, he's being handed a lifeline.

"Not if you don't want to. I have a few more documents being sent from the office tomorrow, but it's pretty simple. I sign it and confirm I'm going to take care of you, and then you sign it."

Numb, Colin nods. Handwritten signatures haven't been used for anything but ceremonial documents for a few hundred years, so Colin knows that his real signature would just be a combination of biometric data taken from his voice and simultaneously from his hand. The device reads his heart rate and compares his voice to hundreds of hours of vocal patterns saved. He has a distant memory of doing it for school when he first got TIRA.

A flood of relief crashes into him, his eyes stinging as they fill. He can't even think of something to say, but he feels Lance's arm wrapping around his shoulders and holding him. It's a strange feeling, but he's moved by the gesture.

Going from being inside the apartment for most of his life to being expected to live on his own, completely alone, was a fear that had haunted him. Now, it's gone. Forever. Now he can release his opera and not disappoint the princess.

"Thank you," he finally manages. "Thank you."

"Colin, you don't have to thank me. I'm your father. This is my job."

Chapter Fifteen

Surpassed

Katrin dabs forest green paint onto her canvas, ears paired to the music of The Nutcracker. In class today, she's painting a landscape, a cheerful meadow of flowers blooming to the lively tune of Hungarian Dance. She has made the mistake just once of glancing to her left at the neighboring student's painting, which puts her attempt to shame. She refocuses on her work determinedly and tries not to look up.

Colin and her father would both approve of her deciding to paint because she loves it. But she also remembers what the professor told her about skill and reluctantly steps back, watching the younger girl beside her layer in transitional green shades. Katrin won't improve unless she learns. She wipes a dab of paint onto her apron, careful not to get anything on her still-crisp engineer uniform. She has gotten faster at donning her disguise since her first trip outside the palace. She keeps her ginger hair around her face, falling across her cheeks to curtain her off from curious eyes. She's prepared her makeup to slightly change the contours of her face. Her new contacts are expensive, but not particularly rare. She can only hope that it still holds up.

After the class wraps up, Katrin quickly begins to clean while the professor walks the lab and comments on paintings he likes. To her surprise, he appears by her side after she's removed the apron from her engineer costume. He picks up her small canvas from the back and holds it up for the students to admire.

"This is excellent work here—the colors and contrast, especially of the trees in the foreground."

Katrin tries to keep her eyes glued to the canvas as every head in the room swivels in her direction. *It's not that excellent,* she can't help but think. After he carefully returns the painting to her easel, she speaks up softly. "The girl here to my left has done a better job with the color matching if you wanted an example. I was mostly trying to copy her."

The professor flashes her a smile, eyes wrinkling in the corners, as she reluctantly reexamines the landscape beside her. "That's very considerate of you, Your Highness."

Wait, what? Her eyes flick back to his face. Then she slowly regards the rest of the room. The few students within earshot of their conversation are clearly listening in and know he made a mistake. Their eyes are wide. When her gaze falls on them, they turn away to busy their hands cleaning brushes. Now that she's aware, Katrin can see the rest of the room trying to sneak glances in her direction between packing their supplies. Now hushed whispers pass around the studio, and the students begin to file out one by one.

So, the High-ish Council didn't just find her here. They prepared the scene for her this time and told everyone what to say. Told them who she was. She was too distracted to notice at first.

The professor remains near her easel, so she continues, trying to keep her voice quiet. "That's not what you said last time. You didn't say my work was excellent before."

He cycles through a few micro-expressions of worry before settling on a reassuring look that she recognizes. "Well—it most definitely is exemplary. You did brilliant work today. You are making great strides in the medium."

She can tell he means nothing that he says, but she feels sorry for him. He probably feels like he has no choice but to talk to her like this now. Katrin keeps her voice low. "It's only been a few days. I can't have improved that much. I would really like to hear how I'm actually doing. That way, I can know what to work on."

The professor drops a hint of his false tone since she's clearly not buying his praise. His voice softens as well. "I think your friends want you to be encouraged, Your Highness."

"Well, maybe I need to hear the truth sometimes. Maybe I *need* to be critiqued."

He doesn't seem to have a pre-programmed response to that, but his eyes seem apologetic now, so Katrin turns to go. "Thank you for what you said last class. It changed the way I think," she says, knowing she won't come back. She's cleaned her space already, so she leaves the small study on the easel to dry and walks away under the stares of the remaining students.

She hurries out of the building, wondering every step if she is being watched. The maglevs don't have cameras, just sensors tracking holo devices, but she doesn't know if a watcher or two isn't stationed inside to keep an eye on her movements. She disappears into the restroom, then comes back out to slip on board the next train seconds before the doors hiss shut.

The maglev is full, so Katrin stands near the door and brushes her fake hair away from her face. Someone taps her shoulder, and she smothers a shriek. She's thankful she didn't react, because she twists around to find a man in an engineering uniform. The blue symbol on the sleeve matches her pocket logo. *More trouble,* she realizes. She should probably know him.

"You must be Nellie. You're a little early, but I'm glad I ran into you here. I'm Michael. I can take you up to the lobby where the lab tour will start."

She nods, pretending to understand. Then the words actually make their way into her brain. *A tour. Of the Genetics branch.*

He hands her a silver card. The moment she looks down at it, a pin-prick of white light in the center flashes. Then the edges of the card glow blue before returning to blank silver. She flips the card over curiously. There's a small logo in the corner. No text.

"This is your temporary ID until we can get the real one to you in a few days."

Katrin opens her mouth, then hesitates. This was what Roland was talking about when he gave her the VR setup the other day. He told her what kind of favor he wanted in return for his help, other than more information about Colin. Roland assured her that the man who would meet her is an associate of his, so she tries to measure her breathing and respond quickly. "Thank you, Michael. Glad I ran into you." She tucks the silver card into her uniform pocket.

The doors open at the Genetics building before he can say anything else. Katrin looks up at the sleek, modern skyscraper when they step onto the platform. It's a rare sight, a building untouched by the Victorian Renaissance. Genetics sits under the shadow of the palace, between the elegant towers to the left and the Crystal Palace Art Center's tapered glass to the right. Inside the building's doors, she's hit with cold air and tries not to shiver. Michael walks confidently to the lifts with long strides, looking perfectly in place with his crisp uniform and stellar genetics. Down to the shape of his face and placement of his features, he's a product of the most cutting-edge enhancements.

She wishes now that Roland had been more specific with his directions. He probably *wanted* her on edge and thought it'd be amusing. She's tried some reckless things in her life but hasn't yet considered breaking into the most secure facility in the city. Michael better have high clearance. She may be the princess, but she has no official access to any of these top-secret wings. If she gets caught, she's prepared to name-drop the Larks.

The lift doors open, and she steps inside with her guide. The walls are also made of glass, but they project images of blue lines swirling together to form the Genetics logo. Michael isn't chatty, which is a lifesaver, but he points beyond the glass a few times as they pass floors, loosely explaining the different areas in scientific terms Katrin can't understand.

The lift stops, and she walks out, arms crossed tightly against the chilly air. Michael notices her discomfort and apologizes as he falls alongside her. "Most of us wear the standard issue blue jackets up here. You can tell why. We'll get you one this week." A handful of techs in crisp uniforms pass them on either side, so Katrin just brushes a handful of hair over her face. He should know she'll only be here for minutes, not weeks, so he's talking for the benefit of curious ears.

Katrin stops briefly. She looks up at an arched corridor, a massive stone quote carved above the entrance.

HOW IS MAN TO BE SURPASSED?

She slowly walks under the quote, her brows drawing together in curiosity. A small cluster of similarly dressed engineers waits in the middle of the bright hall, talking in hushed tones. Katrin stands on the outskirts, clasping her hands and trying to blend in.

Michael whispers, "Good luck. Enjoy the tour. I'm off to the lab," then retraces his path to the lifts. She watches him go, mouth open with a protest forming on her lips. But he's too quick. She's on her own for this next part.

Katrin studies the other young engineers. At least she's in the right place. Everyone here must be new to the department as well if they're getting a tour. A woman appears from a doorway with a holo display hovering at her shoulder, reminding Katrin of Macy. Her waist-length chestnut hair falls in delicate curls, and her eyes match perfectly. She nods once at the group and waits for the conversations to die down.

"Hello, and welcome. I am a 12th Generation Android, and I will be your guide today. You may call me Alice if you have any questions during the tour. As you have been informed, this wing is engaged in experimental and highly classified research, so all holo devices not paired to our system will be disabled at this time."

Katrin studies Alice again in surprise. She's the most realistic android she's ever encountered, more advanced than anything she's seen commissioned to the city. At first, she hadn't even noticed that Alice wasn't human. It's strangely unsettling. Alice's eyes move between the new employees, landing on Katrin for a split second. A measure of relief trickles into her brain as she realizes that Alice's eyes don't *feel* right. If she ever looked a 12th Generation in the eye, she could tell the difference.

The android continues with the prepared speech. "As you've noticed, we have a quote written into our wing of the building, the words of an ancient philosopher, Nietzsche. *'Man is something that is to be surpassed. What have ye done to surpass man?'* It is the objective of the research and innovation here to accomplish this, to achieve the next stage of evolution. Each one of you could witness this breakthrough or could make the discovery that unlocks the final piece of this knowledge. Please, follow me as we tour the building, and be mindful of those who are working."

Katrin falls into step at the back of the group, everyone silently shuffling through a glass door that slides open for Alice. The first lab is a web of countertops and machining stations, brightly lit and filled with engineers. She can see the vague shapes of legs or torsos spread across the countertops with an array of shiny, metallic parts inside. The engineers' eyes are paired to holo screens that follow their movements, showing them the mechanisms next to lines of white text that Katrin can't read. *Interesting.* She'd expected to see something even more confusing, actually: the genetics stuff. Another hallway opens up past the lab, the tile floors forming blue spirals.

"The first lab is for specific areas of innovation strategy. Much like Research and Development, they pinpoint improvement. This next lab you will see is entirely focused on fine-tuning accurate machine learning of the face." Alice steps against the wall and allows the group to file into the next room. Then she continues, "Breakthroughs in AI development of human micro-expressions began in the 2300s but continue to this day. The human face has twenty-six muscles, and the ability of AI systems to respond in real time, utilizing all the features of the human face, is progressing quickly. The human eye, of course, is the most difficult feature to replicate. Ancient peoples used to claim that the eye was the 'window to the soul,' attempting to communicate the reality of its complexity."

Katrin stands at the back of the lab, watching rows of motionless researchers study high definition holos of faces, accompanied with rows upon rows of code. She's not surprised that they seem to have trouble perfectly replicating eyes. She's already noticed the issue. Alice referenced the eyes being a *window to the soul* somewhat flippantly, as if it were just a saying. But Katrin isn't sure. Her father would take that maxim more seriously than anyone in this building. He believes people do have souls.

Alice stands in front of the next doorway, facing the group. "Genetic improvements were only the beginning. The next phase of research spotlights the most pressing problem in human evolution: aging. Despite the advancements in the field, humans continue to age and die. Now, this department focuses on the solution. Would anyone like to share what this solution will be?"

A man near the front of the group lifts his hand, then answers, "Replacing the human."

"Exactly," Alice confirms.

Katrin feels a shiver of concern travel up her spine, more than the cold air of the lab could cause. She had been ready to come back to Roland and tell him that he was overreacting, sending her here to see boring scientists work on boring experiments. *But replacing humans?* Worry settles like a rock in her stomach.

Alice moves to the door. "Replacing the body with an android body is the simplest part of this solution. The advancements in this area are endless, and the product is nearly perfect. The breakthrough yet to be discovered is how to fully transfer the human consciousness into the body." She opens the door, and the engineers begin to fill the room. Katrin patiently waits her turn, hearing hushed whispers of surprise. She peeks around the doorframe and tries to hide the cold shock that washes over her when she sees the android standing in the room.

It's *her*.

The android is positioned in the center on a short platform like a doll on display. If she'd caught a glimpse of the android in the mirror, she wouldn't second guess the image. It *is* Katrin, the spitting image of her. Every detail is flawless. The skin, the hair color, the irises. The exact shape of her face and the pleats of the scarlet gown she wears all the time.

Alice's voice turns to muddy noise in the background of her heartbeat as she steps closer. The other engineers gather around the android to examine it. Katrin stands face-to-face with it, expressionless. She desperately tries to find a flaw, something that differentiates her from this android body. She has no spots, though, no freckles or scars or birthmarks. Everything about her is perfect, and she'd never considered it much of a disadvantage until this moment. Until she realizes that she can be replicated this easily. Her android twin has soft curls just like hers, swept over her shoulders. Her skin and lips have perfect texture. The eyes, though unblinking, have an identical design to her real ones.

She feels strangely cheap, standing here across from her replacement. Her upgrade. *Is this what Roland wanted me to see?* She wonders anxiously if Roland knows something more about this android copy than he's letting on.

"You look a little like her." A girl next to Katrin snaps her out of her staring contest with the motionless android. She reluctantly meets the gaze of the smiling, blonde engineer at her side.

"I wish." Katrin tries her best to laugh lightly, as though she felt she didn't deserve the compliment. She consciously tries not to turn around or look over her shoulder. Alice is still standing behind her, watching with her Generation 12 eyes. Katrin's just seen the lab filled with programmers cataloging every micro-expression known to humans. The AI might be able to detect a lie on her face. *Or have facial recognition.* If Alice could determine her identity, the android would know she's not authorized to be here.

Katrin backs away from her artificial twin, glancing with her peripherals at the other engineers. They walk around her, studying the machine. Her heart still races. Alice might be able to detect elevated heart rate too, unless her "tour guide" programming is not as advanced as Katrin fears.

Alice speaks up, and Katrin holds her breath. "Please, follow me to the next lab."

The group gradually peels off, leaving only a few curious men and women standing alone in the center of the room, studying the android. Katrin hesitates, then lowers her head. She swipes hair over her face and chases the disappearing tour. Questions continue to race through her mind. *Are there more replacements? Did they make my father? Adelaide or Phoebe? Will they eventually make everyone or just the genetically enhanced citizens?*

What about someone like Colin? Somehow, she doubts they would work to transfer him.

She resolves to ask her father about all this if she makes it out of here. Surely, he knows something about this work.

If he doesn't...that possibly scares her more.

Colin opens his eyes in the VR room. He's a little early, so Katrin hasn't arrived yet. He's been waiting with nervous excitement all day to see her. Their adventures together in the VR room seem to go by too fast. A quick blink, and they're over. Her schedule only allows for small slots of time, but they make the most of every minute.

He roams the waiting room, looking at all the decorations he and the princess have added to the wooden walls. Since the room is supposed to look like a backstage area, they've added trunks of costumes in the corner, a large mirror in a gold frame, and an upright piano. Colin added posters onto the wall from a Victorian database, making them yellowed and wrinkled at the edges.

Since he has to do something besides bouncing up and down on the balls of his feet while he waits for Katrin, Colin sits at the piano and begins to tinker with the instrument. After a few minutes, he mostly works out the pattern of the notes compared to the violin. He tries to play *A Song for December* by picking out the melody gradually with one hand. He gets so wrapped up in the process that when he sees Katrin's reflection in the mirror he nearly jumps off the bench in surprise.

She laughs behind him. "Don't stop. You were almost to the best part."

He stands up, facing her and trying to contain his excitement. "I'd like to tell you something first."

"Of course!" Her grin is wonderful. It makes his day when he gets to see it.

"Do you have any new notifications?" he asks.

Her smile grows. She moves a finger down to her settings and opens her holo notifications. She moves her hand up and down, scrolling for a second. Then her eyes widen.

"Wait!" she exclaims, shutting it and looking back at him. "Colin, have you released the opera?"

"I did," he answers proudly. She looks happy with the surprise, like he hoped she would.

She squeals in delight and dances around in a small circle. "Skies! I can't wait to listen to all of it as I paint! I can't believe you did all of that so quickly. You're a marvel!" Her arms wrap around him before he realizes what is happening, squeezing tightly, then turning loose a second later. "Oh, sorry." She looks up at him apologetically. "I should have asked. Do you do hugs?"

He hesitates, mind tripped up briefly on a memory. She hugs like his mom used to, a sudden, brief squeeze of joy before letting go. That was back when he was eight, he guesses. "Does—hugging a princess break a Kaelumian law? I haven't checked."

"I haven't either. Let's assume not."

"Then I like it."

"Excellent! Now, off to Rome?"

"Yes, I'm ready." Colin doesn't say everything else he is thinking. Yes, being hugged reminded him of his mom, but this is something different entirely. Whenever he is around Katrin now, he keeps wanting to be closer to her. When they walk, he wants to reach out and hold her hand. When she's gone, he closes his eyes and pictures her smiling. He's not sure what all this means, but he worries about getting too attached to someone he can't even see in reality.

Colin waits for the VR room to change. He blinks once and is standing on a long street, flats stacked along either side with narrow balconies. An occasional open-air restaurant has tables dotting the edges of the road. It's sunny and warm, and he takes a deep breath instinctively. At the same moment he thinks how nice it would be to have some ambiance, he moves his right hand and realizes that he's already holding a bow. He lifts his violin to his chin and starts down the street, playing a new melody that's been bouncing around in his head all morning. He wanders around Rome like the Pied Piper from ancient folklore, except the only follower he picks up is the princess. Rome is one of the closest domed cities of the empire to theirs, but it might as well be on the other side of the world. Travel between them is rare, but all of them get a steady flow of entertainment from the Broadcast city, Kaelum. Colin can hardly imagine videos of Katrin being watched in Seoul or London, but they must be.

He comes up to a fountain with three bowls of cascading water at the end of the road and circles around it, working out the song as he goes. It's hard to concentrate with all the new sights and sounds, so he pauses a few times. On one pause, he looks back at Katrin and notices lines creasing her forehead. Her lips are pinched. He lowers the violin. He may not be an expert at facial expressions, but she's clearly not herself. She usually rushes headfirst into their new locations, excited to explore. Now she looks off to the sides distractedly.

"What's wrong?" he asks, turning and walking back to the fountain where she trailed behind.

She tucks her hair behind her ears and squints a little in the warm light. "Sorry, I don't mean to hold up our sightseeing. I'm just trying to process some things."

He waves the bow in the direction of the stone fountain. "Here. Sit down." He reconsiders the suggestion a second later and realizes that he probably shouldn't be telling a princess to be doing anything. It's too late. Besides, she wordlessly sits down and laces her hands over her skirts, eyebrows pinched together.

"Sorry," she says again. He wishes she wouldn't apologize. "I saw something earlier," she goes on. "Something that I don't think I was meant to see."

Katrin explains in a flood of words, picking up speed as she progresses through the story. Colin does his best to follow, his brain visually picturing the things she saw. He tries to imagine what the labs looked like. He tries to imagine the building. When she describes seeing an android replica of herself, Colin can definitely picture that. Still, he frowns. "So, you know what they plan to do with it?"

"They said they're trying to put our consciousness into the android bodies."

"That's impossible."

"So far."

"I don't think even geneticists can locate a spirit."

She doesn't look very heartened. "Even if they can't transfer us, what if they try to replace us? Androids might be less trouble for the empire than humans."

"That's true," he concedes, thinking about his dad all of the sudden. If Kaelum could replace human workers with androids who didn't have to eat or be housed or be as susceptible to injury or death, they might save money. And if there's anything Lance *has* taught him, it's that money controls everything. "What are you going to do?"

"Well, I want to talk to my dad about it. I'll also have to follow up with Roland at some point."

"You said he wanted to meet me?" Colin is curious about Roland, but also cautious. His mother's wariness of scientists and doctors has rubbed off on him, and he's acutely aware of it. Roland is a scientist of sorts.

Katrin curls her hands around the stone wall and leans forward. "He does. He says he just wants to learn more about you. I'm about eighty percent sure he's telling the truth. It's hard to tell with Roland. But he did give us this VR room."

Colin grins. "It's great. It was the perfect birthday present." He lays the violin in his hands carefully on the stone surface, even though he knows he can't really hurt it. The direct sunlight turns the wood a bright cherry color.

Katrin's voice changes. "Wait. Colin, your birthday is the day after mine?"

"I guess so." He notes the surprise lacing her eyes and realizes he's never mentioned it before.

"That's so interesting. Why didn't you say anything?"

"I don't know. I don't keep up with it very well." He knows it must sound strange, seeing as her birthday party was a massive affair covering three stories of ballrooms and involving hundreds of guests.

Katrin adjusts to entirely face him as well as she can in her long skirts. "Colin, I'm...worried about you. Are you sure you're alright? You talk about your family as though they don't like you very much."

"Well, they—they don't. But my stepfather is doing his best, I think. I can't—" He pauses, struggling to put into words what he thinks about himself. It's oddly hard to say out loud. "I can't do things that other people can. I'm not normal. I can't do anything on my own."

Katrin just leans closer. "But do you *know* that? Does he let you try?"

Colin didn't realize he'd feel defensive, but he finds himself trying to find an excuse for Lance. For himself. He hesitates several times before finally steepling his hands and blurting out. "I—don't know. I know some things are harder for me, but there are things I adapt to."

"You swam that race the other day. You write operas," she supplies.

"Right," he allows, suddenly feeling like he's discussing math equations with TIRA when his process is completely wrong.

Katrin smiles a little, then it quickly disappears. "Just think about it, okay? I don't know if your stepdad is holding you back or you are, but I don't want you to think that you can't do *anything* on your own. I think you're far more capable than that. Maybe if there's something you want to try"—she shrugs slightly, her pink sleeves rustling—"you should give it a try."

He nods in assent. It is a lot to think about. He doesn't tell Katrin about the holo documents he's about to sign, but he suddenly feels a tug in his spirit to wait a little longer before doing so. He needs to discover some things first.

And Katrin clearly has her own answers to uncover. He can't imagine what it must be like to see an exact android copy of yourself. He wonders if he'd be in awe or if he'd be repulsed by it. "I will think about Roland too," he says, changing the subject as his mind wanders.

"Good," she says, pushing off the stone fountain and standing up. She brushes down her skirts and holds out a hand. "Now, let's go find the forum before we have to leave."

Colin picks up the violin, now warm from the virtual Italian sun. He springs to his feet and walks behind Katrin this time, finding his place in his song. The princess leads with elegant strides, her curls catching the harsh light and turning blindingly gold. *She is very beautiful,* he thinks. *Just as the geneticists intended.* The way she talks though, her concern and her encouragement, that was all by her choosing. Nobody forced her to be as beautiful on the inside. But she is. He meanders through both the narrow street and the melody, discovering it as he goes. Slowly but surely, the song is being pieced together. He already knows what he wants to call it.

164

Chapter Sixteen

Waltzes and Sketches

Katrin sits down at the table, her mind on anything but lunch. She sets her purple leather sketchbook beside her plate. "Good morning."

Across the table, the king smiles at the sight of the book. He's dressed in a casual jacket, so Katrin assumes he has a rare afternoon devoid of meetings. The green in his eyes is more pronounced this morning, which usually means that he's tired, but Katrin doesn't bring it up.

"Morning," he says after he arranges the trays closer to her plate. "Have you been using it?"

Katrin nods, flipping through a few pages of her sketches so he can see. The subject matter is all the landscapes and unique architecture she and Colin have seen in the past week: beaches, mountains, cities, and caves. She doesn't show him the pages where she's tried to sketch Colin's face as well. Those are covered in erased pencil lines because she finds herself woefully terrible at portraits. She can't possibly capture that unique light in his eye when he spots something he's fascinated with and gets inspiration for songs. She gave up after a few attempts.

"It was the best birthday present." *Other than meeting my favorite composer in person, of course.* "The other presents were mostly designers giving me clothing or jewelry items hoping I'll wear them and bring in customers for their brands. There was one box that had glow-in-the-dark paints in it, though. I know the person who gave it to me is still hoping I'll use them for my Column so they can brag about it to their friends."

"Are you going to use them?"

"Of course I'm going to use them," she says with a laugh. "I feel like a little kid that has to try out her new toy."

"Have you been exploring with a VR room?" he asks astutely when he recognizes the different landscapes in her sketchbook.

"Yes," she says simply, locating a cheese Danish and adding it to her plate. "I've been—somewhere else too. I wanted to talk to you about it." She closes the book and finds a safe place for it on the tablecloth away from the food.

"Sure," he says, leaning back with a curious look in his eye now.

She explains the android of herself she saw and the tour guide's explanation of their goals with the technology. Her dad's face falls as she tells the story, but he doesn't look surprised by any of her revelations. She opens her mouth to ask her question, but he quickly whispers with an intensity she doesn't expect, "Roland doesn't even have clearance to give you access to that wing of the building."

She lowers her voice as well, though if somebody really wanted to listen it wouldn't matter. "We might have also incorporated an engineer disguise."

He didn't hesitate. "You *cannot* go near that place again. It could be dangerous."

She looks down at her sketchbook. "I don't intend to. I've seen every-thing I needed to see."

They're both silent for a few moments, his eyes glued to his plate and her mind scrambling to order her anxious thoughts. *How much did he already know? Did he know about the android? What does he mean by "dangerous"? Dangerous for me? Or dangerous for him? Could that android I saw really replace me?*

"How are AI androids different from humans?" she finally asks, wor-ried that there isn't a good answer.

He still looks concerned. For a second, it seems like he won't let go of the topic to oblige her new question, but he eventually answers. "Well, like I've said, we have eternal spirits."

"Aside from that."

"As far as the brain of the system goes, androids aren't capable of mak-ing fully autonomous choices. Programmers can possibly input different commands at different points that contradict, but there will always be a hierarchy to it that the program will refer to. No matter what subroutine kicks in under what circumstances, the programmer is still ultimately the one that decides how the android acts and thinks."

"Can AI feel love? They've tried to figure that out, right?"

"They have, and no. Not really. They can simulate simple emotions and even some complex ones, but love can only really be programmed as set responses to different kinds of communication or time spent in inter-action. The AI can't really love, because even if the effect was simulated, it would be sets of commands that it would have to execute in sequence."

"How do you know so much about androids and AI?" Katrin is impressed by his answers, but worry still pierces the back of her mind.

Has he been looped into all this experimentation from the start?

"I used to be really fascinated by it."

"Used to be?"

"I studied everything I could. All these same questions you're asking. But I realized at some point that no matter how hard we try, we just can't replicate humans. I think the persistence, though, comes from our desire to make something in our own image. I eventually walked away from it because I worried that if we're flawed, and we make something like us, then what will we create?"

"Well, we are flawed, so what does that say about our Creator?"

"That, unlike androids, we are autonomous enough to make our own choices. It says more about *us* than we like to admit." He seems to study the conflicting emotions playing across her face. She knows she looks uncertain. "How does it feel to be puppeteered by people all the time?"

"Not good." A royal understatement.

"Just because we know the right way to live and behave doesn't mean we always do them. We *can* be selfish. We can be cruel. We can be prideful. But no family, society, or community will thrive like that. We know how we should be. It's a matter of deciding."

"Most of Kaelum doesn't believe in God, and it's still thriving."

He allows a small ironic smile at that insinuation. She knows as well as he does that it isn't entirely true. "All empires benefit someone." He doesn't explain further. Now Katrin is concerned that he's trying to spare her from the reality.

"Certainly not everyone," she says.

"Exactly."

They eat the rest of their lunch in silence, but as he eventually stands to leave and walks behind her to the door, Katrin twists around in her seat. "Did you know about my android replacement?"

His face clouds with concern again, but he steps next to her chair and bends to kiss the top of her head. "You're irreplaceable. I won't ever let them replace you."

He didn't answer the question, but Katrin has a sinking feeling in her stomach that he *did* know. He did know, and they probably threatened him with it. He's one of the only people in the world who would know or care if Katrin was traded in for an android. Even if they didn't try to dispose of her entirely, they could use the android for all her public appearances.

She doesn't feel irreplaceable.

Lunch is highly unusual, mostly because everyone is in the same place. Lance took some meetings from the apartment, then stayed to eat. Josiah and Davin were both lounging around in the morning, silently engaged with their own holo entertainment. It is a quiet and lazy day, and Colin decides it's perfect for what he is about to ask.

Lance has ended up at the table facing away from the windows, and the twins have gradually migrated that direction. First, Colin sits next to Josiah, which he's never done. But Josiah is moving out today and will start working full time at the Genetics branch, and Colin will probably never see him again. So he has to ask now. When Josiah flips over from his Column to a different page to start a new feed, Colin quickly interjects,

"May I ask you a question?"

Josiah sighs and disconnects his ears temporarily from the connection. "What?" he says sharply.

"You said you work in a Genetics research wing, right?"

"Yeah, it's my department. Why? Are you finally offering to let my lab study you?"

"No."

"Pity."

"I was just curious. Genetics is always trying to improve humans. Why is it so important to become immortal?"

Josiah narrows his eyes at him, and Colin isn't sure what all he suspects. He just hopes his brother will answer the question. "Well, that's the only thing we haven't done, you know? We've created life to be what we want now."

"Modified it."

"Modified it, and soon we'll create and sustain it. That's the last step to becoming, you know, like the gods we were meant to be."

"Why do we need to be gods?"

"Didn't you just say you had *one* question? I don't know. Maybe the ancients made up all these stories about gods because that's what we're intended to be, in the end."

"Or because they were running from the real God."

"Coliiiinnnn." He places his hands on the table and tilts his head back, exasperation clearly kicking in.

"I'm just saying, even the word 'intended' implies intent."

"Well, it's our intent now. That's what matters." Josiah frowns, turning away and tapping his display, starting a new feed about eye enhancements.

The pictures are fuzzy to Colin's eyes. His fingers tap the edges of his chair. Lance and Davin have also paused their own displays as they listened in on the conversation. Now they're eating with ears fully attuned to reality. He knows he's already failing at looking self-assured, but this is his chance to propose what Katrin inspired him to. "I—have a proposition to make," he opens haltingly, looking at his stepfather.

Lance puts down his glass, and his eyes shift from his screen. "Proposition?"

"Yes." Colin nearly abandons his mission at the look Lance shoots him, but he coaches himself for a few seconds before continuing. "I would like to sign the documents. I would like to stay. But before I do, there's a few things I want. Just two things, then I'll likely be satisfied to stay right here and never cause any trouble."

"Like what?"

Lance sounds annoyed as well as confused, and Colin knows that's not a good start. But he has planned what he will say, so he finishes. "I would like to see a live concert. With musicians. And I would like to see the New Year's show from the tower."

Lance's eyebrows are halfway to his hairline. Josiah and Davin even look up again from whatever they were watching to eavesdrop. Davin looks especially interested in the conversation, and Colin wonders if it has to do with his question the other night about him standing up for himself. Colin's never asked for anything like this before, certainly never this way.

"Colin, it's not like I'm trying to keep you out of the world because I can," Lance says. He casually picks up his glass and takes a sip. "It's for your protection, and it's something I take seriously."

"I know."

"And we've been over this before. I don't have an evening to waste at a concert right now—"

"I'll take him."

Everyone's attention abruptly shifts to Davin. His arms are crossed over the table, and his eyes bounce eagerly between the two.

"I thought you hated concerts." Lance's confusion only grows as he addresses the interruption.

Davin just shrugs nonchalantly.

"Fine." Lance takes his plate and walks back to the kitchen without another word.

Colin hangs back, not sure what to do. This didn't go at all like he'd thought. None of his pre-planned responses fit the scenario anymore. "Um, is that a yes to the other one?"

Lance responds from the kitchen. "I have no idea what possessed you to make demands today, but I have to warn you: the second demand is loud. It will be loud all night. And not just crowd noise."

"I think I can handle it."

"We'll try," Lance says after a moment, as close to a yes as he'd hoped for.

Elation balloons in Colin's chest. He looks at Davin. "Thanks." He's still shocked that Davin volunteered to help him.

Davin looks away, at his holo display. "There's a concert tonight, specifically some kind of concerto by that composer whose name I can't pronounce."

Colin looks at the ground, thinking. "Um, like Rachmaninoff?"

"No. Well, wait. Actually yes, that guy." Davin scrolls with a finger down a program Colin can't see from his angle to the windows.

"Sounds riveting," Josiah remarks in a tone that Colin interprets as sarcastic.

Davin doesn't look particularly excited about it, so Colin resolves to come up with a way to thank him. He doesn't understand how his brother doesn't love music like he does, but he can appreciate that Davin would spend a whole evening with him doing something he finds boring.

Colin retreats to his room to turn on soundproofing and work on the melody he started composing in Virtual Rome. He's calling it "Waltz for Katrin" since she's the primary inspiration for the song. He wants to somehow convey everything he thinks and feels around her in music. It's his language, the one he speaks most fluently. Even in his heart language, though, he feels he comes up short. She's impossible to capture in music. But he works on it anyway, unable to stop.

The evening concert can't come fast enough, and Colin stands in the sitting room ready to leave long before Davin emerges from his own room. When his brother does come out, Lance stops him in the hallway, apparently telling him a few things before he goes. Colin can't hear what they are talking about, but he asks TIRA for the time and determines that they won't be late if they leave in under five minutes.

"You ready?" Davin asks from the hall, hands in pockets, as though Colin hasn't already been ready for a half hour.

"I am." Colin responds politely anyway, catching up with his brother's quick gait and stepping onto the lift. When they are alone, he asks, "What did your dad want?"

"Nothing."

Colin is quiet until the doors open in the lobby. He follows Davin to the maglev and takes a seat beside him. To his surprise, Davin adjusts his wrist display so they can both watch a video on the route to the city center.

The maglev eases to a stop, and Davin quickly stands to his feet. Colin looks up, eyes adjusting from the holo to the real world beyond the glass. The night is lit up in bright lights, sporadic Victorian lanterns circling the main streets where foot traffic is heavy. Holo advertisements serve as window dressing while more high-end stores have real wooden signage.

Colin tries and fails to focus on one thing. Out of the corner of his eye, he sees Davin's blue coat as he walks past the platform to the street. He catches up, then cranes his neck to take in the sights. Bridges crisscross above them. Buildings soar into the darkness. He bumps into a shoulder and turns to apologize. The man holds a stack of papers rolled into scrolls and tied with red ribbon. He thrusts one of the advertisements in Colin's direction. "Please, take one. New show being announced. Come to the premiere."

Colin nods distractedly, taking the scroll to be polite and shoving it into his coat pocket. Then he jogs for a moment to catch up with Davin.

"Are we going to make it?" he asks, nearly out of breath after a few minutes of Davin's pace. He's walking fast, like they might be late for the concert.

Davin just speeds up. "Come on."

He weaves through the crowd. Colin wordlessly trails behind. Two women block his way. Then after they pass, he runs a few steps. The familiar blue coat is gone. He spins around, looking for any possible turn Davin could have made. *How?* How did he disappear that quickly?

Colin quickens his pace in case he simply fell behind. Davin is still nowhere in sight. His eyes scan the pedestrians frantically. Then he slows to a stop. Maybe once his brother realizes that he is gone, he'll circle back.

Waiting on the sidewalk alone feels strange, so Colin backs closer to a lantern. As he watches the passing crowds, he realizes that he looks nothing like the people in this part of the city. They are all upper class, dressed in suits, hats, and jewels that Colin hasn't seen since the palace. A few of them even spare him questioning glances, pointing him out and leaning to whisper.

A holo ad beside him bursts to life, a swirling illustration like a wave breaking over the building. He jumps in surprise at the sudden noise, then spins away from the bright light. He briefly closes his eyes, trying to make a decision. *I can find my way home from here. I can't wait all night, and I left TIRA at home. I can't contact Davin and find him.*

He'll have to call this trip a failure. He didn't make it to the concert. He couldn't even stay with Davin. But then he remembers the look on Katrin's face when she said, *"You should give it a try."*

Has he really tried? Has he let himself try?

No. I haven't.

He opens his eyes, a new determination settling in his mind. He looks at the street in front of him and makes a quick calculation. He spins around and runs to the station. The maglev has just stopped. The platform empties of passengers as Colin jogs up to the holo floating between wooden benches. His eyes fly across the map display, locating the nearby theater and assessing the route. He tries to block out the noise as he repeats street names and landmarks under his breath. Then he jumps into action, diving back into the fray.

His eyes stay fixed on his path and the nearby buildings. A holo sign above his head displays street names. Music and light and shouts compete for his attention, but he ignores it all and desperately keeps running. His breathing is ragged by the time he spots a set of red banners floating in the wind. *The theater.* The front steps are bookended with stone columns, and the banners advertise a New Year's show with performers from every domed city. Colin crosses the street and looks up at the tall building he's dreamed of visiting for so many years. Relief begins to calm him down, and he slows to a jog.

Climbing the steps to the door feels like crossing the finish line of a race. Colin takes a deep breath and begins to prepare his words for the man at the ticket counter. Surely his brother made reservations. All he has to do is give his name, like at the palace. He assumed that Davin would do the talking, but now he'll have to find his way inside himself.

A flash of blue crosses his vision, going in the opposite direction. Colin spins around on the top step. "Leaving?" he asks, spotting Davin. His brother must have assumed Colin wasn't coming and was giving up. He'd arrived just in time.

Davin turns, eyes focusing on Colin and widening in surprise.

"Come on." Colin motions with a smile, happy to have caught him. "Show's about to start."

Davin's eyes cut to the side. "I...was going to wait here to say that I did. But I thought you'd gotten lost, so—"

"I consulted a map," Colin explains. "I'm here."

Davin's eyebrows leap up. He hesitates for a second on the steps. But he gradually climbs up and meets Colin at the door. "Great," he says, with not much enthusiasm.

The concert turns out to be free for the public, so Colin didn't even need a reservation. Classical concertos are apparently not as popular as Colin had envisioned. The theater is not full, so when they get to the door, they choose seats in the center. Colin sits down, then takes a moment to look around at the building. It's nothing like the one in the VR simulation. It doesn't have any chandeliers or boxes or elegant crown molding. The curtains look like heavy, red velvet, which he likes, and the seats are comfortable. He's content. The music is what's important. If the music is performed well, he'll be happy.

He glances to his left at Davin.

His brother is still studying him with his eyebrows pinched together and a slight frown on his face.

"What?" Colin asks.

Davin just shakes his head slightly and fixes his attention on the stage. Once the curtain parts and he sees the grand piano, Colin forgets everything but the concerto. The pianist skillfully whisks the audience into the music and holds his attention at every note. Just before the last movement, he eyes Davin and realizes that his brother is fast asleep, slumped in his chair. He's baffled but turns back to watch the pianist. When the applause bursts out at the end of the performance, Davin jerks awake, and his boot falls from where he wedged it between the backs of the two seats in front of him. He stretches.

"That was amazing," Colin exclaims, shrugging on his coat.

Davin stands up and rolls his neck. "I think I heard the first song," he mutters, working his way into the line for the door.

"Movement."

"Whatever."

Colin shuffles behind him in line, his mood not clouded in the least. The concerto was competently played, and the ambience of hearing it performed live was not a disappointment. He can't wait to tell Katrin about it.

"Thank you," he tells Davin.

"It wasn't terrible. I had a nice nap."

Colin shakes his head and laughs.

Their ride home is uneventful. Davin slows down to a leisurely stroll. Colin isn't sure why he was in so much of a hurry the first time if he was just going to sleep through the whole concerto. Colin is able to take in more of the sights and sounds without feeling overwhelmed. He even stops for a second to appreciate the wave simulation that caught him off guard earlier in the window of a store. The waves turn into a set of cologne products, which in turn melt into pools of water. Davin stops for him to watch the animation, then leads the way to the maglev. He lets Colin watch his holo display again on the way back, and Colin wonders if it's his way of apologizing for losing him in the crowd before.

Back at home, Colin happily hangs up his coat. He doesn't plan to compose anything tonight, since he wants to let the music he heard loop in his head until he falls asleep. Without soundproofing on, he can hear Lance stopping Davin in the kitchen to ask how the evening went.

Curious how his stepfather will react to him finding the theater on his own, Colin manually opens his door a crack and quietly watches with a smile.

"You lost him?" Lance is questioning, facing the kitchen counter.

Davin throws his coat over the closest chair, looking back at the hallway. The floor lights are harsh against the side of his face. "Of course I lost him. It's not like it's hard."

Colin's smile quickly disappears.

"So, what happened?"

Davin looks away. "He found the theater on his own, found a map. The station map, I assume."

"Why were you still *there*?" Lance demands.

Davin holds up his hands. "If I'd come back home, it might have looked like I didn't intend to go in the first place! I had to wait for a minute. He found me right as I was leaving." He pauses, then looks up at his dad for the first time. "Earlier you made it sound like you wanted to see how he'd do on his own. If he'd figure it out. Now it just seems like you're mad he *didn't* get lost."

Lance doesn't respond to this. He looks down at his wrist display. "You've got a portfolio to work on."

Davin sighs audibly and shoves the kitchen stool out of the way so he can go to his room. Colin shuts the door to his room as silently as possible and retreats to sit on the edge of his bed. So, his brother had abandoned him on purpose.

Colin tries to process it all, unbuttoning his shirt with quick, agitated movements. Maybe Lance is trying to speed up the process of him signing the papers. Maybe Lance just wants him to be less independent, so that Colin will be safe at home—and he won't have to worry. It doesn't matter what the answer truly is. It still hurts. He throws his waistcoat over a chair and sits back down, another thought shouldering its way to the front of his mind.

Lance wanted me to think I couldn't do anything on my own.
But I did.

Despite everything he's overheard, a shadow of Colin's smile forms. Now he just has to see what happens on New Year's Eve.

CHAPTER SEVENTEEN

TOWER FIREWORKS

Kaelum is a constellation of light. The lower tangle of streets and apartments are filled with fireworks, one of the most ancient traditions of mankind. Trails of smoke rise to the upper levels of the city, where advanced holos and beams of light are enhanced by the haze.

Liden Tower, the exact center of the domed city, stands ten meters taller than the highest spire of the palace. The holographic show will project onto the night sky and revolve around the tower. Traveling there in a separate maglev compartment, Katrin holds her father's hand and peers out at the ongoing celebrations past the glass.

"You look extra beautiful tonight," the king compliments, tilting his head to look at her curls. "How does this even work?" She can feel him touching one of the hundreds of lab-grown amethysts in her hair.

She grins. "It's a special glue that washes out. They catch them in a bowl when they rinse my hair later. It's a whole thing."

He shakes his head slightly. Katrin assumes he can't imagine having to spend so much time on one outfit for one night. He doesn't know the half of it.

"Will your musician friend be here tonight?" he asks, lowering his voice now. He only seems to be half-joking, since he knows a little about Colin. She keeps telling him that they need to meet. She even got permission from Colin to tell him about his compositions, but Katrin hasn't scheduled that conversation with her father yet.

"Probably not. He doesn't go out in public very often."

"Well, everyone will be out tonight."

You don't know Colin, she thinks. But, then again, he's changed a lot in one month. He used to be quieter, worry over his words more, and approach everything warily. Now, she's seen him talk breathlessly about the music he's creating and laugh with easy abandon. He asks her questions about the palace and her mischievous friends—*lots* of questions.

"Maybe," she says after a few seconds tick by, her heart racing for some reason.

He squeezes her hand. "Well, I hope you have fun. Don't go falling off of this tower."

"Dad." Katrin groans in embarrassment. She hadn't even talked to him about that Labyrinth stadium incident and had hoped he didn't know. So much for that.

The maglev stops in a circular lobby underneath the tower. A blue mosaic bursts from the ground and turns into a sloping sculpture that wraps the building. Suspended walkways lead from the train to the private lift they'll take to the top floor. Katrin waits for the doors, then follows their security escorts to the elegant glass box.

People in the lobby crowd close to the walkways to catch a glimpse of her. Katrin hears girls gushing in amazement as she passes them. She briefly considers that the android version of her could convincingly pull off this short walk to the lift with the profile angle, harsh lighting, and crowds in the way of everybody's line of sight. They wouldn't be able to tell the difference.

Distressed by this thought, Katrin spins and looks directly at the people crammed together underneath the walkway. "Hi!" She grins and waves. "Happy New Year, everyone!"

A little girl, watching from her mother's arms, waves back. She's wearing tiny, white gloves and a matching frock coat. The closest adults all just stare for a moment, spellbound.

Katrin turns around and leans over the other rail, waving. "Happy New Year!" This group shouts well wishes back at her, having recovered enough from their surprise to respond. She tries to make eye contact with as many of them as possible. Surprisingly, she enjoys herself, even though her intention was merely to seem more real to them.

A smile creasing her face, she steps into the lift and adjusts the ruched arms of her purple gloves. Stock-still in the corner, Macy eyes her with a curious expression until Katrin glances over and says, "What?"

"We have a list of suggestions prepared if you would like to address the public, Your Highness."

"I just get excited before light shows." Katrin waves her hands around as though giddy from all the activity. She catches her father frowning in Macy's direction. Katrin turns around to face the long glass wall and presses close. Heights don't bother her, so she contentedly watches the levels of the city streak away from her feet and turn into little pinpricks of light.

When the doors finally open, she turns around and straightens back into perfect posture. She takes the key necklace and smooths it out over the front of her dress. It's a deep purple to match her outfit but has streaks of white in starburst patterns. The stylists did the same design last year with a different color. Katrin often wishes they were more creative.

The guests on the open-air balcony form an aisle for her and her father to walk down as they are announced, then they eventually bleed back into their respective groups. Katrin looks around at the tables and simulated candlelight. She loves this night. For once, the spectacle is bigger than her, and she can just blend into the onlookers like everyone else.

The music of a string quartet travels across the large balcony, and Katrin's attention is instantly pulled in their direction. They are playing a classic Kaelumian theme but slowed down and modified for the ensemble. She watches them for a few minutes, then walks along the outer railing of the tower.

"Katrin!" Adelaide's high voice demands her notice, so Katrin reluctantly stops. "Your Highness." Addie curtsies prettily while showing off her new dress. It's blindingly silver, arrayed in metallic lace on the edges. It's not particularly Victorian, but Katrin likes it.

"I'm worried your dress might outshine the light show," she comments, since her friend is expecting it.

"Yes, thank you," Addie says dismissively. Then she comes closer, almost uncomfortably leaning into Katrin's space. "Look"—she smiles conspiratorially—"if Percival comes by, tell him you haven't seen me. My sources have told me that he's brought a present for me and is going to ask to court me, so I have to hide for a little while. Can't make it too easy for him, can I?"

Katrin can't help a quizzical eyebrow arching upward. "Wait, Addie.

You—are you actually interested in him?" She hasn't heard a thing about this, which isn't terribly surprising. Still, she feels it only reasonable to ask.

"I certainly *can* be." Adelaide winks, then prances away. Her platinum hair bounces behind her, impossible to miss in a crowd.

Katrin just shakes her head, then keeps walking with one arm extended to brush the vines twined about the railing with her gloved fingers. The railing is wrapped with lights too. Clusters of white flowers mingle with them, the thin petals catching the light with a warm glow.

The invitation list for Liden Tower is an exceptionally small pool of the most powerful and influential people alive, so among this crowd Katrin ranks relatively low—a blessing. She can enjoy the night in peace.

She finally spots the person she's been looking for—standing at an empty section of the balcony, of course. Roland has never liked small talk. He has a drink in one hand and is staring listlessly at the skyline.

"Good evening," she says casually, standing next to him and resting her gloves atop the greenery. She opens her mouth to say something else.

"Five minutes," he says.

"What?" A frown overtakes her features. His face is of no assistance, impassive as always. The day Roland says something polite, a friendly salutation, she'll know *he's* been replaced by an android.

He finally turns, just enough to look at her dress and then her hands. "You just arrived, I see. It's five minutes until the show starts."

She nods. "Right." He knows that they can't talk until the holographic display begins, kicking off other firework shows throughout the city. If they talk about anything they don't want overheard, their best chance is while their surroundings are loud. In the meantime, she tries not to move her arms too much, since the sides of her dress dotted with crystals are uncomfortable if she twists at all. She also resists the urge to unfasten her shoes and kick them over the balcony. If it were culturally acceptable for her to walk around in stockings all the time, she would. The dress she'd keep.

Colin never seems to mind, but these people would be appalled.

After exactly five minutes tick by, a massive explosion of blue bursts from the top of the tower, lights projected from the dome's panels. Katrin tips her head back to watch. Distant cheers break out from the city below as the show begins. The blue streaks of light fall until they turn into raindrops, then form ripples as though touching a surface of water. She follows the light show as the next shapes dance across the sky, then looks around the balcony. Most of the guests have moved to the other side to face downtown, where a lively collection of real fireworks has started in time with the holographic show.

Roland finally looks down at her, raising his voice just loud enough for her to hear. "Well, what did you think of my department?"

"I'm as disturbed as you hoped I would be, I assume. Are there android replacements for everyone? They couldn't possibly—"

"Of course not. It's much worse than that." She struggles to hear him over the cheers, music, and constant popping of fireworks beneath them. Roland stares out at the display but doesn't react to it. "The Genetics branch hasn't cleared it with the High Council yet, but they're planning on phasing out naturally born humans with no genetic upgrades. Androids *can* fulfill the roles of that part of the population: Underwater Level jobs, crafting, artists, musicians, and all that. They're pitching it to the Council as the most cost-effective path for the empire. And if the rest of us who are genetically enhanced are given android upgrades and essentially become immortal..." He tilts his head and shrugs. "Then we'd have to cut down the excess population."

Katrin's ears ring, either from the noise around her or something in her own head. Her breathing hitches. "But—what if they're wrong? What if it doesn't work? Transferring our consciousness?"

Roland's face stays hard. "They're betting it all on the success of the transfer."

"How in the world do they plan on quietly eliminating that much of the population? There's no way that would work!" This isn't a joke, but she could almost believe it's just one big story to create drama. Nobody would really consider this plan. Then she remembers Colin's straight face as he tells her about his biological father working in Underwater Level. *"You wouldn't hear about it."*

"It might be easier than you think." He finally frowns.

A cheer breaks out across from them. A trail of purple light traces the skyline of the city and explodes into blue on top of the palace. Roland raises his voice to compete with the noise. "Genetic enhancements have always been expensive. How do you think the public would react if we claimed we had an enhancement we'd give them for free, provided by our department? How do you think the part of the population we keep would figure it all out? Hmm? Liden technology controls every eye display, wrist display, remote holo, and home holo in Kaelum." He steps closer, lowering his voice now that he's speaking into her ear. "And guess who Lance Meador and his bankers spend the treasury of the empire on to keep the attention of the entire world?"

A shiver travels up Katrin's spine. She closes her eyes, briefly blocking out the dizzying trails of light in front of her. They still spread in purple afterimage under her eyelids. *It's me. I'm the distraction. I've always been the distraction.* "Why are you telling me this?" Her voice shakes. "You don't want this to happen?" Roland, of all people, wouldn't feel dread. Even now, he doesn't react to her obvious distress.

"I told you. A lot of decisions were made generations before me, but what we're doing now is progressing too quickly. I think we've overlooked possibilities. What if people like Colin exist for a reason? What if we're not acting in the best interest of the future of humanity?"

She nods, feeling distant from her own body. If Roland meets Colin, surely, he'll understand that the world does need people like him. It *definitely* needs fewer people who think it's a good idea to eliminate parts of the population they find unnecessary. As her heart thunders, she remembers what her dad told her: *"All empires benefit someone."*

"And—and why are you telling *me*?"

Roland wraps his fingers around the stem of his glass and looks away. "You are the show, Katrin. You've always been the show. All eyes are on you. If anyone has a way to catch everyone's attention, it would be you."

A pang of terror spreads through her chest. "Me? What am I supposed to do?" Her mind races. She once led a girl through all the secret passages of the palace, and not a soul found out about it. The girl's live video wasn't really live. Everything was edited and programmed to perfection. What can she possibly do?

"Not sure. I suggest you think of a plan. I don't know when they'll be ready for the upgrade. I don't have access to all my parents' correspondences. But the High Council's vote will be in a week." There's no panic in his voice. "In the meantime, I'll schedule a VR meeting with your boyfriend and see what I learn."

"I can't get live holos onto a Column even if I wanted to," she worries aloud. Then, processing his last sentence, protests, "And he's not my boyfriend."

"You hesitated *far* too long." His eyes glint with mischief like they do when Percy gets defensive about something. "You've clocked in too many VR hours to deny it."

"What, are you spying on us somehow?" Katrin can feel the heat on her face and is glad it's dark at the edge of the balcony.

Roland sniffs and empties his glass. "Why would I care about watching you and your melodramas like everyone else?" She doesn't look away, eyes still locked on him suspiciously, so he sighs. "I get time logs, that's it."

Katrin crosses her arms over a section of railing, vines tickling her skin. "I don't even know if he loves...like..."

"Ask him. Ask him, and he'll tell you." Roland props his forehead up with one arm. "Why does everyone seem to complicate these things?"

"Sorry, I forgot who I was talking to." Katrin rolls her eyes. Roland's made it clear many times that he believes the indelicate approach is best for every possible subject. Katrin isn't so sure.

Roland leans closer. "Make a plan. And until then, keep your melodramas away from me." A server approaches them from behind, so Roland stops talking, but he takes his empty glass and shoves it at the man without a word before disappearing into the crowd.

Katrin watches Roland go, missing her window of time to apologize on behalf of her perpetually rude friend. She studies the server's face to determine if he's even human, then looks around for a place to escape. She doesn't want to stand at the back of the tower alone, but she doesn't feel like engaging in lighthearted conversation. Really, she just wants to find her dad, bury her head in his chest, and cry. Then she wants to find a member of the Kaelumian Council up here and demand to know the truth. Roland isn't prone to join the lies and manipulation of palace dramas. He hates it. But dread spreads through her mind like a thick fog at the idea that he might be telling the truth.

"You look like you need a slice of cake," someone says laughingly just behind her.

Katrin whirls around, hoping a second later that the gems in her hair didn't get strewn across the shadowy balcony. She already has a fake smile in place before she sees the stranger and holds out a hand for a porcelain plate. Her first thought when she sees the mound of pink frosting and decorative slices of strawberry is: *disgusting.* Who decided that fruit and cake go together? But her second thought is: *Colin would love this.* So she takes the strawberry cake and looks over the stranger she now has to engage in small talk.

He's her age, perfect, as everyone on the invitation list would be. She can tell right away that he's an athlete from his shoulders and arms, and after she focuses on his black-and-gold eyes for a moment, she recognizes him. "We met at my birthday, didn't we?"

"We did. Though, I have a twin, so I'll save you the trouble in case you met him as well. I'm Josiah."

"Of course." She had no idea about the family connection last time they met, but now she knows all of their names: *Colin, Josiah, Davin.* She met nearly one hundred guests at her party, mostly trying to help people forget she ever spoke to Colin. She knows it's time that she downplays her knowledge of Colin. "I didn't have the pleasure of meeting your twin that night, but I did meet your other brother." His smile wavers. "He was listening to Vivaldi, so I complimented him on his musical taste. He left soon after that. He seemed like he was in a hurry."

She watches the gradual relief spill over Josiah's face. He's not as practiced as some of her friends are at hiding his emotions. She chalks it up to the amount of time he's spent in Labyrinth rather than networking amongst his peers. If Colin's right and their father's influence continues to grow, she'll be seeing a lot more of these boys in the future. Davin will likely inherit the financial position while Josiah already has his career of choice in Roland's sphere. She wonders how much Josiah already knows about the natural population phaseout.

He finally reestablishes his casual smile. "Colin's not really my brother. We just take care of him now that his mom's gone."

She just nods instead of correcting him. "I understand. So, are you the athlete of the family?"

He straightens a little with pride. "I like to think so, though I'll have to work harder to stay active now that I'm in a permanent research assignment. I guess I don't have to ask if you're the artist of your family. Your art is exquisite."

"Thank you," she says, for perhaps the millionth time, fake smile perfectly intact. She imagines teasing Colin about it later. *"Why don't you ever call my art exquisite?"* she'll ask. He'll probably just deadpan, *"Because it's not,"* though he'll find his own unique way to compliment it. Just thinking about the scenario causes her fake smile to widen to a real one.

Josiah takes this reaction as encouragement. "Really, it's brilliant. I love the landscape you did of the coastline and the rocks. I could never do something like that."

"Thank you," Katrin repeats. Then, feeling the need to shake things up, she adds, "My favorite painting so far is a pipe organ waterfall, based on a song I really love."

He tries his best to hide his recognition. "Interesting. I don't...exactly listen to music much."

It occurs to Katrin now that Josiah might be directly involved with the natural population phaseout partially due to his disgust for Colin. It's a horrible idea, but she strongly suspects it's true.

A chorus of delighted gasps snags Josiah's attention. They both look at the railing as a blue whale made of lights floats seamlessly past the balcony. Katrin uses the moment as an excuse to escape. "I should keep making my rounds. Thanks for the cake."

He smiles broadly and gives a quick bow as Katrin turns and shuffles back into the gathered spectators. Bright flashes sweep across the space, making it hard to see where she is walking. The guests around her are mostly still, mesmerized by the show. The sky washes yellow with an explosion of holographic wildflowers, then turns blindingly blue with ships that surge across the horizon with full sails. Katrin tries her best to concentrate on each step since she's holding a porcelain plate in one hand. Lights strung between the tables guide her to the tower's wall, and she finds a glass door a second later.

Her free hand fumbles for a handle, but the door slides open when she steps closer. She leans over a shadowy railing and peers over. She's discovered the emergency stairwell. She can't imagine having to climb down the entirety of Liden Tower in an emergency, so she hopes no serious firework-related accidents happen tonight.

She just needs to breathe, to think. Everything Roland told her is on a recursive loop in her head, no escape route presenting itself yet. Insecurity is clawing its way into the picture instead. *I can't fix any of this. I'm just a pretty distraction on people's holos. I've never truly been able to escape their watch or their reach before.* Macy is smarter than her, and her entire security team knows every trick she could ever pull. She rests her elbow on the rail, propping up her hand holding the cake, and stares into the black stairwell. Her breathing gradually slows to a reasonable rate.

"Sorry, is this the secret dessert eating corner—?"

Katrin gasps in the dark, spinning around. She hears the telltale shattering of the plate on the polished floor. The cake is smashed along her left arm and against the person behind her. Her surprise melts to relief when she recognizes the familiar baritone laugh.

"I'm sorry," Colin says again, the top of his suit and the side of his face covered in strawberry cake clumps and frosting. He was a lot closer when he spoke than she realized, and she'd slammed into him, plate and arm first. His sentence dissolves into laughter, then he tries again. "I thought I was alone back here."

It's surreal to see him in person after all the weeks they've spent only meeting virtually. He's wearing a real suit and waistcoat this time, by a designer that Katrin knows would be horrified to witness what's just become of his handiwork. She can hardly believe Colin's here. She's not a curious fan meeting a stranger anymore. She's run into her best friend. A grin bursts across her face at how ridiculous they both look. "You came!"

She holds her cake-covered arm away but uses the other to hug him excitedly. He hugs her back this time, still shaking with laughter. As she looks up at his face, he's starting to use a finger to wipe pink frosting off his cheek.

"I'm so sorry." She shakes her head pitifully. "I kept that cake for you, actually, in case you were here. It's strawberry."

He tastes it. "Mm. That's really good. Thanks."

She hides her face under her hand. She shouldn't laugh. She ruined his nice outfit. Still, *he's* laughing. She thought she'd spend the rest of the night with her dread and anxious thoughts. She needed this.

"How did you know?" he adds.

"When you came to the palace, remember? You took home a few strawberries. Well, more than a few." Katrin looks down for the napkin that came with the plate. She dropped that too, but she finds it between two broken pieces on the ground. She tries to use it to wipe off most of the cake from Colin's shoulder. He finishes the streak on his face, eating the rest of the frosting. She wants to be mortified that he's eating the cake off of his outfit instead of eating it from the plate because she flung it on him, but he's so calm about it that she lets it go. She folds the napkin in half and tries to wipe down her left arm with the last usable space. They'll have to venture back out into the party to find more napkins to fix the rest of it. Hopefully, the show will still be distracting everyone. Katrin looks at the door just as a row of white lights shine through and dance across the floor before disappearing. A wave of applause breaks out from the balcony.

"Did I miss anything on my face?" Colin asks. His suit coat is still a mess, but she reaches up with her pink-stained arm and wipes a streak of frosting from his jawline.

"I think that's all of it," she says, studying his face until he briefly makes eye contact again. She looks down at the napkin in her hand and knows that her own face is suddenly the color of strawberries. She can't tell in the dark, and neither can he, but she can feel it.

Everyone on this tower would glance at Colin for a mere second before determining what she did when they met. He has no enhancements whatsoever, not even special contacts. But if anyone looked at him a second longer, they'd notice what she did now. He's the son of an actress known primarily for her rare natural beauty despite not being genetically advanced.

I'm completely and utterly toast. "So, what are you doing back here?" She asks the first question that comes to her mind.

Colin eventually breaks eye contact, although she notices that he held her gaze longer than he ever has. "We had been here for one hour and fourteen minutes, so I found this door and stepped inside to take a break," he explains.

"These lights are pretty intense," she says in understanding. "If you're ready to go back out, I think I know where we can find some more napkins." She doesn't want to call for someone and make a scene, especially not Macy.

"I'm ready."

Katrin steps to the door again, getting it to automatically slide open for them to sneak back out. The light show is becoming more elaborate, her surroundings flashing with a kaleidoscope of color. She looks up at a bad time, a streak of white forming a jellyfish passing her vision. She looks down, blinking. The afterimage is still blocking her path.

"Over here." Colin is doing a better job of averting his eyes from the display. He reaches for her hand. Katrin still feels frosting edging her thumb and cringes at the thought of getting more of the cake on him, but she doesn't say a word as he leads her behind the motionless crowd. She blinks a few more times and sees upturned faces admiring the sky, blissfully unaware of them passing by.

Colin looks back only once after he'd slipped his hand into hers without hesitation. Now, in the light, she can tell that his face is *definitely* the color of strawberry frosting when he sees her watching. The unexpected sight causes Katrin to reconsider what she started to tell Roland. Maybe Colin's just embarrassed.

Or maybe, just maybe, he can feel the same attraction.

He brings her to a table stocked with water, ice, extra glasses, and most importantly: stacks of white serviettes. They do their best to clean up as quickly as possible. By the time a server has circled back with a tray of glasses, they've escaped in separate directions. They share a brief smile, then slip into the crowd. Katrin's dress and arm have come out unscathed, his suit decidedly less so. She tries to stand still and watch the rest of the show, but she keeps peering through the crowds to where he's stationed himself at the railing, hands in pockets and head tilted back. He appears to be mesmerized by a set of holographic ice skaters that leave trails of frost blue light behind their skates. It's a look of inspiration. She knows that expression now. This light show will somehow make its way into a song.

Eventually, Katrin turns her mind back to the problem at hand. Elegant Victorian script writes a "Happy New Year" message across the sky to her left. *Bonne Année.* It must finally be midnight. As a finale of sparks shower over the tower and into the city below to widespread cheers, she tries her best to think of an idea. The fear creeps back into her mind again as she nervously runs her fingers across the arm she coated with strawberry icing just minutes ago. Every eye on the balcony is tilted to the sky, so she doesn't make an effort to tame her anxious face. Either she comes up with a PR strategy worthy of her role as the most expensive distraction in the world, or people like Colin may start to disappear. Somehow, that scares her more than anything.

Chapter Eighteen

Tea With Frenemies

At 2am, Colin's brain is processing the world around him at slower and slower speeds. All he wants is to fall asleep on his bed, a couch, or even an empty section of floorboards somewhere. He's not picky at this hour. Luckily, the lift doors slide open and reveal their apartment just as he considers falling asleep standing up for the first time.

Lance has been arguing with someone via holo for the last fifteen minutes, but now he ends the call, muttering under his breath. It's definitely too late for business calls. Colin is incapable of imagining what can't possibly wait until morning. Davin, previously slumped against the back wall, takes off with renewed energy into the hallway at the prospect of being able to go to bed.

"What happened to your suit?" Lance finally looks at Colin long enough to see the wet spots and pink streak prominently covering his waistcoat and shirt.

Colin steps off the lift, too exhausted to explain. "Strawberry cake," he says simply.

"Sorry, cake?" He holds a hand up. "Do not tell me you ran into someone."

"...alright," Colin replies slowly.

"Did you run into someone?" Lance's voice gets louder, more aggravated.

"Yes."

Now, Davin whirls around, at the door to his room. His eyes are wide. "Wait, was the person you ran into wearing purple by chance?"

"...yes."

He gapes. "Was the person you ran into the *Princess of Kaelum* by chance? Josiah said he gave her a slice of strawberry cake."

Colin hesitates. It was funny in the moment, but now he realizes that this outfit he's wearing is probably too expensive for Lance to find it funny. "Yes."

"Colin, you oaf, you can't just run into royalty!" Davin exclaims. "What did she say?"

"She said sorry."

He shakes his head. "You got lucky. It's a good thing you ran into Miss Sugary Sweet and not anyone else on that tower."

Beside him, Lance is running a hand over his eyes. He looks too tired for this discussion. "He's right. I gave you a chance, but this kind of incident is unacceptable for the level of status we need to represent. Do you have any idea how much that suit you're wearing is worth?"

"A lot?" Colin offers halfheartedly. It's too late at night for his brain to come up with anything useful to say.

Lance frowns, typing quickly on a holo display he brings up. He flips it around, nearly in Colin's face. Colin steps back, then waits for his eyes to focus on the images and description. They widen in horror. "Is that in thousands?"

The display vanishes. "Yes. It is." Lance says sternly. "And I bought it for you because when you go out among the most powerful leaders in our government, you *are* the reputation of this family. Both of you." He glances at Davin as well, whose stony expression doesn't change.

Colin knows he shouldn't say that he stepped away from the party because he was getting overwhelmed and just needed a moment to regroup. He definitely shouldn't say that Katrin was the one who ran into *him*.

Lance pauses for a second, then walks away, toward his room. "I can tell that none of this is getting through to you. We'll talk later about what public events you'll be able to attend in the future or not, once we've all slept for more than four hours. And, Colin, look at me."

Colin looks up, fighting away the frustration of being treated like a child yet again. He's still shaken at the actual price of his outfit. He didn't know how expensive clothes could be. Nobody's ever told him.

"If that coat and waistcoat are actually stained, you will be paying me back somehow." Lance walks into his room, and the door hisses shut behind him.

Colin doesn't realize until he gets to his door at the end of the hallway that Davin hasn't shut his after all.

"Hey," his stepbrother whispers. Colin turns reluctantly. "Did she really say sorry?"

"Mhmm."

"What else did she say?"

Colin quickly closes his bedroom door behind him, but he catches his brother's expression. It looks dangerously like suspicion.

In the backstage VR room, Colin sorts through a virtual stack of pictures Katrin brought for their walls. Colin asked for an image of the ice skater lights and one of the ships he'd missed while he was giving his eyes a break, and it looks like Katrin found everything he wanted. He finds the ancient ship in the stack and holds it up to admire the glowing sails.

Despite how the night ended at the apartment, Colin loved getting to see Katrin on the tower. He loved the lights, as overwhelming as they occasionally were. He loved the fact that nobody was looking at him. Everybody was focused on the sky. He had been able to relax a little and enjoy the show. He is glad that he summoned the courage to ask Lance to attend. It was exactly like he imagined. Even if he has to spend the next couple of years paying Lance back for the ridiculously expensive suit.

Colin decorates wordlessly for several minutes, not minding the silence. Katrin places a few of the virtual images on the walls in open spaces, then eventually stops. She stands motionless near the piano and watches him. He carefully arranges three more pictures and makes extra sure that they're even. When he turns around to look at Katrin's reaction, she is not smiling. He doesn't know what her expression means, but she looks far away, like she's thinking about something that's not in this room.

"Is something wrong?" he asks. He wonders if she is still upset about seeing the android of herself or if this is a different problem entirely.

She tries to smile, but it vanishes again. "There's something I have to tell you."

He leaves the rest of the images on the floor and walks closer to her. Whatever she's upset about, he wants to be near her. He *always* wants to be near her, and he hates to see her worried. "Is it...about the androids?"

"It is," she says sadly. She looks down at the floor, at her pink stockings. "Roland told me more. He told me what's about to happen."

He listens as she pours out the story of Kaelum's plan for the androids and the remainder of the population. Isolating and uploading consciousness into android bodies. She isn't sure exactly how Genetics will reduce the natural born population over time, but it sounds ominous.

As Katrin finishes, she looks up at him with wide eyes and stammers, "They know nothing, Colin. They don't—you are all worth as much as any person with any ridiculous aesthetic enhancements, or mental, medical, whatever. It doesn't matter. This is wrong. And I *have* to find a way to tell everyone before it's too late. I don't know when the final vote is. But it's soon."

Colin can't think of anything to say. His breath hitches as he struggles to form words. His thoughts are too preoccupied reviewing all the terrible news she's just revealed. *So this is what happens when men become gods,* he ponders mournfully. They don't think his life is worth protecting. Neither his nor any other natural humans' now. His whole body feels heavy with grief. At least Katrin is so passionately against this evil. He doesn't know what to do, but he reaches for Katrin's hands and applies just enough pressure to hopefully communicate support. *Is this the right response?*

"Can...your father help?" he finally murmurs.

She sighs, squeezing his hands back and looking down at them. "He is good with tech. He doesn't talk to me about it much, but he used to be an AI specialist. He has more freedom of movement than me, but his communication is watched and filtered even more than mine because of the amount of confidential information he has access to." She swings their joined hands back and forth in a nervous sort of motion. "Also, he'll be in the Singapore dome for three days. He won't get back until Friday. I don't know how long we can wait."

Her eyes dart up to the side. She releases one of his hands in order to swipe at something in the corner of her view that Colin can't see. He knows what that means now.

"You have to go?" His heart races. He knows he has to stay in the VR room for now. He has another visitor coming.

She squeezes his right hand one more time with a faint smile. "We can meet here later. I know we can figure something out."

He simply nods, not sure if she means that or if she is trying to sound confident. He pulls her closer with one hand and gives her a hug. It might not make any difference, but he wants her to know that she won't be alone in this. He can feel her release a long breath as she leans her head against his collar.

After a few seconds, she looks up, blue-gold eyes intently focused on his. "Don't let him intimidate you," she says firmly.

He nods. The closer he sees her eyes, the more exponential amount of detail the gold fragments have. "I'll try." That's all he can promise.

She disappears, the VR wiping her image from the room from left to right.

With nothing else to do, Colin sits down at the upright piano. This *may* help his nerves as he waits. He works his way through *Cotton Candy*

Dance. He's already figured out the melody, and now he's gradually layering in extra accompaniment with his left hand. He has no concept of time but periodically looks over his shoulder in case he's not alone. He's worried about meeting Roland. Katrin has tried her best to describe him, but she's even admitted that she's not sure about his motives. Colin would have warned her that he's not good at determining intention, but she seems to trust him to decide for himself. Colin appreciates her confidence in him.

When his virtual guest finally comes into view, Colin is repeating a series of chords with one hand, trying to find the perfect combination. He stops playing and turns around on the piano bench. Roland stares at him with electric blue eyes; his presence is unsettling for some reason. The man's arms are crossed, and he's wearing polished equestrian clothing. His waistcoat and trousers are black, only a few shades darker than his skin, which has warm undertones from the golden lights strung across the walls. Roland takes in his surroundings for a moment, seemingly unimpressed. "So," he says. "Decorating, are we?"

"Yes," Colin says warily, glancing at their new posters, pictures that Katrin had added from the light show the other night. They didn't decorate much this time because of their conversation.

Colin still believes that the Genetics branch can't accomplish their goal of replacing humans, but he's still concerned about anyone naturally born in the empire. The plan is unthinkably evil.

Now he's meeting the heir to the Genetics kingdom.

"What is your purpose here?" Colin asks him, ready to get straight to the point.

Roland's mouth tugs in the direction of a smile. "I like your style. Yes, let's remove the introductions and pleasantries. You know my name, and

I know yours. My purpose here is to try to restore some goodwill. I know you have a solely negative view of geneticists like me."

Colin looks at the wall. "My mom didn't want your department using me as a—whatever you call it. Lab rat. But after she died, my stepdad was more open to it. I don't even remember what any of the tests were. I just remember machines that would scan my head and my eyes. They made noise. I didn't like them." His eyes shift back to Roland, still standing motionless in the center of the room. "Did you discover anything interesting inside my head?"

"Well, you were ten at the time; I was only eleven. I wasn't exactly an expert at that age. But whoever was working back then tried to fill me in the other day. There was nothing particularly unusual that they discovered, or any cause for concern. And, seeing you now, you look—pretty normal."

"Maybe I am," Colin replies noncommittally, defeated. *Normal* is a very subjective term to him. He doesn't see any sense in arguing with Roland about the definition. "If I tell you what I told Katrin, what do you plan to do with the information?"

Roland maintains his focused eye contact. "I'm concerned that eliminating more and more naturally occurring human traits and temperaments could cause problems."

"So, you're saying you'd advocate for my right to exist." He swallows hard. How can it have come to this? That his existence is even in question? If the rest of the population of Kaelum heard about this, they would feel worthless. Less than nothing. It hurts to even think about.

Roland shrugs. "That's about the whole of it."

Colin debates with himself for a few seconds. He knows that there is a long pause in the conversation and that he should fill the silence, but he wants to think about his answer. If he has to tell Roland his secret in order to help others like him, he should do it, right?

"Okay, I'll show you." He stands up from the bench and walks to the corner of the room, pulling out his virtual violin from the case stashed in the shadows. It's nicer than his own and has a good sound. He doesn't play it much because he'd rather use the limited time he has in the VR room playing an instrument that he doesn't have access to in the real world. The digital keyboard on his tablet is useful, but not as fun as an upright piano.

Roland watches, moving to take his place on the piano bench as Colin decides what song he's going to play. He settles on *Pipe Organ Waterfall* and begins the quick series of notes in the theme. His stone-faced spectator doesn't betray a single thought as he plays. After the final downbow, Colin lowers the instrument and waits. It wasn't his best performance, but he wants to see what Roland will say. It's usually challenging for him to read faces, but this man is impossible. A blank slate.

It takes a few moments for Roland to speak. "That's your song?" he asks.

Colin nods. "I've written—quite a few more as well."

Roland's eyebrows leap up. "I see. So, you're the anonymous composer that Katrin won't shut up about."

"I am." They stare at each other for a moment, then Colin looks down at the violin.

Roland stands abruptly. "I guess I have my answer. She was right. You know, you should consider writing under your own name. Give everyone a shock. It could be interesting." Colin doesn't reply, so he adds, "You're a lucky guy according to the Columns. There are a couple million people who wish the princess had fallen for them instead."

Colin's eyes grow round. Roland clearly has a tendency to make unexpected comments. *She has? Is he joking? I can't tell.* Roland's expression hasn't changed. It's surely against some Kaelumian law to fall in love with a princess, so he doesn't say anything about that. He has something else he has to tell Roland before he loses his nerve. "It doesn't matter if I can compose music or if I can't. I deserve to have a chance to live. All the naturally born deserve to live."

"I'll work on the Genetics branch, see how far I can get," he finishes as Colin stands silently with the violin in his hand. "Nice to meet you, Mr. Composer."

Colin nods slightly, hoping he's correct in trusting Roland. "Mr. Geneticist."

Katrin feels like she's stuck in a dream. If she wakes up to find herself back in her plush, violet blankets, she won't be surprised. The afternoon is a complete waste of everyone's time, but the process is taken so seriously. First, the table is perfectly staged—teacups, trays, and doilies arranged in a matching color palette. Then the guests are arranged around the table, their dresses matching their place settings. Katrin's crown is silver with crushed sapphire today, and her dress, gloves, and shoes match exquisitely. Now that she knows the full extent of her purpose, the event feels even more hollow and meaningless.

Holo displays all over the world are already feeding the tea party footage to their millions of eager audience members. Most of the girls surrounding Katrin are actresses. Their genetic enhancements are more eye-catching and outlandish than hers, featuring many bright color combinations. They are already chatting, covering some of the subjects listed in the invitation Katrin glanced over earlier. Even their conversations have been pre-planned.

"Back when this city was called Paris, it was considered the fashion center of the world," one of the actresses with shimmering black hair and blue lipstick remarks to the table. "We are continuing that tradition with the fashion we create now."

"The Mirror collection was such a lovely nod to 1860s Parisian fashion," another actress comments with a soft smile.

Katrin looks down at her plate, debating whether to cause trouble. She drops a sugar cube into her tea with a golden spoon, then decides she's bored enough she might as well give her viewers something interesting to watch. "What about creativity, though?" Nine perfect faces swivel in her direction with polite interest. "The Victorian Renaissance started because everyone longed for creativity and the beauty of handmade, unique pieces of clothing. Clothing wasn't just mass produced. It was an art form and meticulously sewn, embroidered, designed by individuals. Should we merely look back to old fashion and designs and do our best to mimic them, or should we try our hand at something new instead? How many times should we nod back at time periods before taking a step forward?"

"And what exactly do you think we should be creating?" a redhead to her left responds, in a tone that makes Katrin think she wants her to come up empty-handed. "Any ideas?"

She knew the question might come right back to her, so Katrin tries her best to think of something they haven't done. She tries to think like Colin, who is constantly taking inspiration from things around him. It's harder for her, but her eyes land on an assistant standing by the door of the room scrolling silently on a holo display. She quickly answers, "Well—what if we were to use dresses like a template, where we have a solid color and use holo technology to project different designs and patterns onto the fabric? One dress could become many."

The redhead opens her mouth with a skeptical expression, probably about to argue against the idea, but an actress across the table has already leapt in. "Or! It could change throughout a performance, adjusting colors or patterns with the backdrop and setting. It'd be like a quick change during a scene!"

The other actresses quickly pounce, expanding the concept and trying to add their own ideas. Katrin sits back for a while, drinking her tea and listening to all of their brainstorming. A lot of them actually have really fun ideas once they get going. She hopes after the footage of this party makes its rounds that the Lidens will pick up the concept and decide to make something of it. She has a brief moment of satisfaction knowing that her little epiphany could become a reality, but she quickly realizes that it won't change anything. A fashion trend is just a fashion trend, creative or not, but what she really needs to say would be edited right out of this party if she said it. She's no closer to achieving anything of value.

Just to test the theory, she looks back at the redhead at her side and asks, "So, if there were to be designs created and projected onto dresses, do you think humans should be responsible for coming up with designs, or would androids be better tasked with that?"

The other girls stop their side conversations to eavesdrop. The redhead casts aspen-colored eyes across the room, realizing she's the center of attention again. She smiles sweetly. "Androids would probably do it faster."

"You don't think humans bring something to the table that AI can't?"

"Now that we have so many designs already created by humans, androids can synthesize and make designs faster. We don't really need artists to come up with anything new."

Before Katrin can keep the debate going, the assistants at the peripherals of the room begin typing in sync. They send holo messages to each woman that are invisible to all in the room besides the set of eyes paired to their message. Katrin glances down at her own when curiosity gets the better of her.

> *(2:45-2:55) The upcoming release of the Starry and Sage Wonder collection.*

The conversation turns on a dime, swiftly turning to the teacup collection that will be released in two days following a new movie co-starring two of the actresses at the table. It feels like the normal flow of conversation, but it's essentially a commercial for the porcelain teacups. Katrin lifts her own teacup, studying the sage green pattern. It's a vintage 1880s design pulled straight from a digital collection of scans to delight collectors everywhere.

Katrin sits back, holding her head perfectly in place so her crown doesn't shift. *I want out,* she thinks for the fifth time. The conversation ebbs and flows according to the time slots constantly lobbed to them from the producers. Then it finally ends. Katrin bids every actress goodbye with her best manners, then flees to her rooms to review the video of the afternoon. On the Column, she pulls up the "live" event and taps on the frame to play the scene back. Her conversation starter about the unusual holo dress made it onto the feed. Comments from women all over the world are already flooding in within chats, clamoring for the idea. She moves her finger back and forth on the video, moving to different topics of conversation, but she can't find her question about the androids. It's simply gone, seamlessly.

Answers that question. She sits on her bed, pulling her crown from her hair. A gem gets caught on a few strands and tugs hard against her head. Annoyed, she detangles the hair and drops the crown onto her blanket. There has to be another way to get the news out. There *has* to be.

Chapter Nineteen

When Colin finds the princess, she is hunched over a black dress spread out on the ground. From the moment he arrives in the VR room, the scene is jarringly different. The backstage theater room is gone, and he materializes in a new room. It has dark wood floors, high windows, and paint supplies cluttering the space. An askew shelf, a stool, and half-used paint tubes surround the central easel. Dozens of canvases line the walls, ranging from a hand's breadth to nearly two meters in length. The room is cluttered, a little anxiety-inducing, but he admires the line of paintings, occasionally moving a canvas aside to see another hidden behind it.

"I wanted to show you my studio," Katrin comments after a minute. She changes positions, crossing her stockinged feet and bending closer to the skirt of the dress still spread across the wooden panels. She holds a holo display over a section of the garment and a bluish painting projects onto the dark fabric.

"This is what your real studio looks like at the palace," Colin says, knowing she'll correct him if he's guessed wrong. "It is messy."

She laughs. "Yes, it is."

"I like this one."

She grabs a handful of her hair with one hand and holds it back from her face, peering over at the side of the room he's wandered off to. "Oh. Thank you. That's a recent one. I was trying to paint that bakery we saw in Rome."

"You're getting better," he says. It's true. Her comments on her own art have ranged from discouraged to hopeful with glimmers of passion in between, but she's steadily improving the longer she spends painting.

She sits a little straighter, and a wide smile flashes across her face. "Thank you. I've been halving my time between painting and watching videos of some other artists I've found with public Columns. Sometimes they show their materials, or they show steps of their process."

He steps behind her, looking over her shoulder at the plain black dress. "What's this for?"

"I'm going to try to paint on it."

"Paint on a dress? Does that work?"

"I think so. I've been trying to research it. I want to paint a dress that glows in the dark. I have a lot of glow-in-the-dark paints from my birthday that I haven't used yet, and I thought it might be cool to make a dress that's similar to the light show we saw the other night."

"The kind you can only see in the dark?"

"Exactly. I don't know if it works, but I'm practicing some designs in here where I can't mess anything up. Then I'll try it on a real dress eventually." He sits down beside her on the floor and silently watches her project her various paintings onto the fabric, sizing them differently, then discarding them one by one. She says she's not very smart or a very good artist, but he thinks she's mistaken. She's creative. She has good ideas. She's good with people and has a wonderful smile. The more time he spends with her, the more things he collects to appreciate about her. He wonders if Roland was telling the truth when he said that Katrin likes him because of his music.

"Truthfully," she adds, adjusting a sketch of silhouetted flowers on the black material, "I'm hoping that if I do this for a while, it might shake loose a good idea for spreading the word about the android replacements."

Colin spins his music note bead with his opposite hand. "Who controls the holo technology? All of it."

"The Lidens." Katrin sighs. "Maybe I can bribe Percy with art."

Colin doesn't understand, but he offers, "If he's a fan of my music as well, maybe I can give him an unreleased song? Would he like that?"

Katrin looks up from her display, blue light glowing on the side of her face. "Skies, you're right. He might. I saw him with the entire Candy Opera on his display the other day. Would you really do that? Do you have anything in the works right now?"

He doesn't mention the special waltz he's writing for her, but he always has more than one song tumbling around his head. "I have been trying to write a song based on the ice designs from the ice-skating animation the other night. I started humming something during the show, and I need to write some variations for the theme."

"I knew you would write a song about that," she says right away. She switches the sketch of the flowers on the projection to a sketch of scattered stars and diamonds. The picture tilts and stretches as she adjusts it over the dress.

He decides to ask her the question that's on his mind before he can talk himself out of it. "I have a question. I know you really like my music. That's why you invited me to the palace after your birthday. But is that the only reason you like to spend time with me now? Sometimes when we meet, you don't even ask me to play you any songs."

Her gaze cuts to his, and her smile vanishes. "I love to hear you play, and I do love your songs. But all of the people in my forced social circle always have a reason to want to spend time with me. They always want something. I promise, I don't want to do that to you. If you had never picked up a violin when you were younger or discovered you could write songs in your head, I would still want to talk to you. I would rather sit with you and do absolutely anything or nothing at all than go to the fancy balls and eat the best food in the world with my fake friends. I feel like a real person when I'm with you and not a fashion advertisement." Then she adds, quieter, "And I hope you feel like you can be yourself around me too."

He nods. "I do."

He doesn't just feel like himself around her. She inspires him to try things, to become an even better version of himself. He hopes he influences her as well. He wants her to believe that she wasn't just designed to look beautiful by geneticists to showcase their breakthroughs in the field, but created by a God who loves her.

Colin looks back down at the dress. "I like this one," he says, now distracted by the sketch she's projected of different diamonds and stars. The design starts out larger at the hem of the dress and turns into smaller diamonds higher on the skirt.

Katrin shifts her attention back to the floor. "I do too. I think I'll try to paint this one first." She hums quietly to stay focused as she adds new details, and Colin watches for a few minutes before rising to explore the rest of the studio. He rearranges all the virtual paintings into categories of subject matter and color.

Eventually, he hears Katrin say, "Colin...you know, if we can find a way to get a message out on holo, maybe at some big event at the palace, it might be better if you told everyone and not me."

Panic floods his chest. He doesn't face her, not wanting her to notice. He knows he can't hide such expressions. "Why me?"

"I'm always the center of crazy gossip of some kind. A lot of it is, unfortunately, untrue or misleading. I'm worried that it could be spun as some kind of stunt. But if the message came from someone naturally born, who would be affected by the replacement...they might take you more seriously." She hesitates for a long moment, and Colin eventually turns out of curiosity. She's pressing her lips tightly together and staring at the floor. Finally, she draws a deep breath and adds, "Especially if you tell them who you are."

Colin shakes his head. "I can't—I *don't*. I don't tell people who I am."

"I know you don't. I know your anonymity is important to you." Her eyes widen. "And if you don't want to do it, that's fine. *Of course.* I promise I won't ask you about it again. But, if you think about it and you're willing to try...maybe you can let me know?"

He sorts through his thoughts, tapping one of the painting's frames with his fingers. Katrin has been very considerate so far and has kept his secret. She asked his permission to tell her father about him, and she's asking again now. He knows this is important, maybe more important than anything they'll ever do—but is she right? Will anyone believe him, especially if he tells the entire empire who he really is? There are already people in the government who think naturally born citizens aren't worth protecting, much less Colin specifically: the one genetic anomaly. *I don't even know if I can speak in public without losing my train of thought or stumbling over every word.*

These various scenarios tumble through his head, but eventually he settles on something to tell her. "If you can find a way to broadcast the message, I will think about it."

It's not a yes, and she doesn't press the subject. He meanders back in her direction and sits next to her with his arms crossed over his knees. He watches her design process in silence for a few minutes, then shifts his gaze to her face as she asks, "If...when this all blows over, will you take me to the opera?"

The memory flashes back into his mind of The Nutcracker, watching the performance with her and digitally removing the audience. "Sure," he says. He'd never turn down an opportunity to listen to music. "Which one should we listen to?"

She nudges his shoulder playfully. "Yours, of course."

I hadn't even thought of that. Of course if the VR room could download the music for The Nutcracker, it should be able to download his orchestration for Candy Opera from Katrin's account. "Sounds good to me," he says.

Katrin just scoots closer to him. "And where will you be?" she asks with a broad grin. "Sitting with me or conducting the orchestra?"

This forces a laugh out of him as he pictures himself in a tailcoat with a baton. Katrin might not know if he conducted a virtual orchestra improperly, but he's never tried it before. "I'll have to practice." He tries to respond with a serious expression.

She just leans against his shoulder again, winking. "You'll have to hurry then." She gathers her long hair with one hand and tosses it back. Then she bends down to work on her pattern. He watches until she reluctantly announces that she has an appointment with her stylist.

"I'll try to finish the ice skaters' song for your friend Percy so he might help us," he says.

"Thank you." Katrin opens her VR settings. "Although he's not exactly a friend. More like an annoying coworker."

Colin nods and makes the correction. "I'll try to finish the song for your annoying coworker so he might help us." That is one thing he knows he can do.

She grins.

"I will also pray about it," he adds.

"I'll take it."

Colin paces the empty apartment, desperately asking TIRA questions. It's late in the afternoon, warm pockets of light striping the floor of the living area. Davin and Lance are at Lance's office at the palace so he can train his son to operate some sort of financial holo programs.

It's been nearly three days since Katrin told him about the population phaseout.

Whether to help her or not had been eating him alive. It weighed on his shoulders, and the more he prayed about it, the more an undeniable *yes* welled up in his spirit—he should be the one to do it.

So, he told Katrin in their last VR session that he'd help her tell the truth to the world, but he doesn't feel ready *at all.* Their plan is hardly even a plan, but his mind is now on a completely different problem. After Katrin told Colin about her coworker, Percy, he tried to find the purchase on his admin page and found nothing. If Percy bought his opera, it *should* show on his sales. "TIRA, expand search to the release date of Candy Opera."

"No purchase by the name Percival or Liden found."

"Show all opera purchases so far." Katrin's name had been different. Her location appeared as Court 50. Maybe Percy has another identifier as well.

"Twelve opera purchases. All with verified addresses, shown on the left tab."

Colin looks them over and shakes his head. None of these are Percy. He's not sure if the palace is hiding the personal information of certain high-profile individuals or if something's wrong with his display, but it looks like Percy's purchase of his opera hasn't even gone through.

Colin finds the address listed for the company selling his music at the bottom of the page. "Soren," he whispers under his breath, eyes scanning the address and customer service information. He takes a deep breath, trying to mentally prepare himself to talk to someone over the holo. He will probably stammer all over the place trying to explain. He taps the call icon. A blue sphere turns on the holo, over and over again. It's not connecting.

The tension in his chest releases only slightly at not being met with an answered call. "Why is it not connecting, TIRA?" Frustration chips at him.

"I cannot access the studio," she says unhelpfully.

Colin squints at the address one more time. He thinks he has it memorized now, but he is not taking any chances. His heart races as he grabs his coat from his room. "TIRA, we're going to the city to visit Soren Soundwave." He scoops up the tablet. Surely, he has plenty of time before his family comes home. They may even eat out and return late.

Colin rides down to the lobby and rushes onto the maglev with a large crowd on the platform. He finds a seat in the middle of the compartment and looks back down at his tablet. TIRA is silent, but he's told her what he's trying to accomplish. She will try to help him if he gets lost.

He never would have made a decision like this a month ago. Lance had told him to inform him if he ever wanted to ride the maglev, but this trip isn't just to wander around the city on the train. He has a destination. He has a purpose. He shrugs off the guilt. Lance was concerned about him getting lost, but Colin has planned his route ahead of time. When he gets home with the admin page's problem solved, Lance will be convinced that he is responsible. He's capable of doing things on his own if he tries.

The doors open, and the passengers begin to pour out of the compartments. Colin jumps up, tablet clutched in one arm, and joins the steady stream. He hums as he walks, determined to succeed. The financial center of the city isn't nearly as colorful or whimsical as other parts of Kaelum. There are no waterfalls here or hanging gardens. The skyscrapers are crowded together, bridges suspended between them for the maglevs. Holo signage dominates the remainder of the airspace. The three-dimensional aspect of the advertisements makes it challenging for Colin to stay focused on his path, as brightly lit objects seem to constantly be hurtling toward his face. He instinctively ducks an image of a watch when it seems to fly just over his head, and he hears laughter behind him. He ignores it and surges forward.

Businessmen in brown and gray suits and long coats stride purposefully through the lobby of the first building he enters. Colin is the only one looking around questioningly at his surroundings. He hurries toward a white holo menu suspended in the center of the traffic and touches the display. A list of options appears, a slightly fuzzy rendering to his natural eyes. He taps *Soren Soundwave Studios*. A blue line appears on a map, illuminating his path to the right lift. There is a matching blue box that appears at the top of the menu with an option to take the route. Colin ticks the box. The map vanishes, leaving the holo display on its default menu again. He weaves through the crowd to get to the lift at the wall, then stands at the back when the door opens, not wanting to take up too much space or draw too much attention to himself as others enter.

He peers over the shoulder of a man in front of him and reads the holo on the wall once the lift begins to move. His selection has already been entered into the list of stops.

When a cheery, disembodied voice announces his floor, Colin is the only remaining occupant. The music studio is located on the highest floor of the building. He steps out alone, fidgeting with his bracelet, and glances around. There is only one hallway: black marble with little music signatures and eighth notes carved in white across the ground. The front desk has a single figure sitting behind it, so Colin summons his courage and starts walking. With every step, he mentally rehearses his words. *Hello, my name is Colin. I might be having an issue with my music store's admin page.*

His feet stop at the desk. He is the only guest. To his surprise, the woman sitting in front of him is a human and not an android. The fact that this company can pay a human to monitor the desk at all times says a lot about its status. The girl is young like him, though he's not good at estimating age. She has straight chestnut hair that falls to her jawline and advanced silver-green eyes that acknowledge his presence unblinkingly. Behind her is a set of black-and-white doors. He can hear muffled talking and laughing in the offices past the walls.

"Can I help you?" the girl asks. "This is Soren Soundwave. Are you looking for Celia's studio? It's just a floor beneath us."

"No. No, thank you," Colin says, pulling his tablet from his coat pocket. The rolled-up scroll advertisement he was handed at the concert falls to the floor. He quickly bends to pick it up. The red ribbon is coming loose. He sets the paper on the desk, then places the tablet down with his other hand. The girl is staring silently. His cheeks heat, but he swallows and tries to remember his opening line.

"I might be having an issue with my music store's admin page. I was hoping someone could look at it."

"Alright," she says, sitting back and opening a display above the desk with two fingers. As she scrolls the invisible screen, Colin realizes which part of his opening he missed: his name. *Of course I did.* "Do you have your admin display available so I can read the pin?"

"TIRA, open the store, please."

Setting the tablet where she can easily see it, he waits as she types and scrolls, the small sounds echoing through the marble hall. After a few moments that feel like an eternity, she looks up. "This is one of our anonymous accounts?"

"Yes. I think there might be a transaction that didn't show up on my end."

"Well, it does seem like the page is functioning, but I can send you back to the customer service department to take a look at the other admin account too if you have access, and you can tell them exactly what's going on." Her expression remains placid. "Most customers usually message or call about these kinds of issues before coming here. Was there a problem when you tried contacting us?"

"Um—yes. I don't know what the problem was." He frowns, not following her already. "But I'm the owner of the account. I know my password." He recites it to her, along with his name this time and his stepfather's name in case he's in the data somewhere as well. He doesn't want to be passed on to another department to have to explain everything again. He's also uneasy about the way this girl stares at him without smiling either. He isn't sure what to think. *Does she hate working here? Is my waistcoat buttoned sideways?*

Her silver-green eyes finally look away from him and back at her holo. She types something else. "Oh," she says softly. She clears her throat, then keeps scrolling. "Sorry, you said you are the owner of this account?"

She's finally making some kind of expression, but it looks like she doesn't believe him. Colin nods, flustered. "Yes. I am. It's my music."

Her eyes quickly flick back to the display, and she presses her lips together. She looks flustered too. "Um, sorry, it might take a minute to check on the transaction history, especially if we have to access the international database." She smooths her hair over her shoulder with one hand.

"Okay..." Why would it take more than a few seconds? There were only five purchases, and Percy should be one of them. "I'm looking for a transaction with the last name *Liden*," he clarifies anyway.

The girl's eyes widen at the name.

Maybe he shouldn't have come here. He shouldn't have worried about the discrepancy. He'd been praying about the android situation when he discovered it and had felt a strong urge to come, but maybe he shouldn't have brought up the Lidens.

"I'm so sorry," she tries again, her responses more and more apologetic. Colin doesn't understand why. "The first account you showed me is set up as a management account, usually used for reps from other countries who only manage a portion of a larger account for their city or district. It's set up to show only"—she looks closer at the screen and recites slowly—"0.000001% of a month's sales."

"And the other account?" His heart races. *What is this? What's going on?*

"Well, the remainder is filtered into one admin page." She takes the display and swivels it around the desk for him to see, doing her best to center it in front of him. There's a number on the screen that he's never seen before.

5,109,328 units sold.

CHAPTER TWENTY

IDENTITY CRISIS

"Five million," Colin says out loud, since he's having trouble trusting his eyes.

"Yes, sir," the receptionist confirms.

He peeks at her face, brows drawn. Nobody has ever called him *sir* in his life. Then he refocuses his attention on her holo display. 5,109,328 songs sold this month so far. Over three million just of Candy Opera songs, according to a box labeled "Opera Release." Struggling to keep his hand steady, he searches Percy's name. The sale pops up immediately. Not only does Percival Liden have the opera, but he also has all of Colin's songs ever written.

Colin flips the display back around, trying to stay calm. Disbelief and panic are crowding into his head. "Can—can I get the second admin page this information? I need it to be the same, to show it all. Thank you." He moves his arm back down from the counter and accidentally knocks over the paper scroll. The ribbon lands on top of his boots and the paper unfolds itself on the ground. He distractedly bends to pick it up. He blinks at the inside of the advertisement and hears his heartbeat pounding in his ears.

It's not possible.

He wants to love it, to be awestruck that his opera is going to be performed on stage. But he knows what is happening, and it *can't* be happening. It is too wrong. Too terrible. How could he have not known for this long that he is famous? All of his memories now fit into this picture. They've belonged all along.

The way Lance locks him out of his tablet's functions, but never his music software.

The way he lets Colin write as much as possible, especially on the maglev when he might look out the window. He always made a point to warn Colin against looking out the window.

The way that woman in the lobby of their apartment was wearing a dress with glowing crystals like candlelit rain.

The way the orchestra at Katrin's birthday could play his songs so perfectly the first time. It wasn't their first time.

Katrin had *asked* him to take her to his opera. This opera, at the Palais Garnier.

Everyone knew but him.

And no one had known his identity before Katrin except his family. Except Lance, who told him he hadn't even been placed in musical performance in his school results, who is trying to get Colin to sign documents that will give him ownership of Colin and everything he'll ever own or create.

"I adjusted the settings on the two admin pages, sir. They're identical now. Are—you alright?"

Colin looks up. Blinks at the receptionist. He doesn't have words. His mind is too full. His fingers are clutching the beads of his bracelet, pressing them into his palm almost painfully. "I need to go. Thank you," he finally blurts out, shoving the paper scroll and loose ribbon into his pocket. He scoops up his tablet with his other hand and presses it against his chest, as if it'll hold him together somehow.

He takes the lift, standing in the corner and doing his best to breathe steadily. More people shuffle in front of him, but they ignore him. New thoughts keep crashing in like waves as he squeezes his eyes shut. Now he knows why he felt the urge to come here and check on his account in person. It's a heartbreaking truth. He didn't even suspect that Lance would do something like this to him. It hurts. It's hard for him to even imagine a person being capable of lying so well for so long.

At the lobby, he sprints back to the maglev and rides it past the financial center. He rides it past the apartment's stop. He rides it past the stadium and downtown.

"TIRA, show me my aptitude results from your report." He leans over his tablet, fighting to keep his voice calm. He changes the master passwords on his store accounts with shaking fingers, confirming with biometric security confirmation.

"Unauthorized."

"What do you mean unauthorized? They're my aptitude results." He's getting louder now, more agitated. Fortunately, the people around him are paired to their own Column streams.

"I am not authorized to show you the results. They were sent directly to the parent account for review."

"I know they were sent to Lance. How can—how can I see my results?" TIRA isn't usually this hard to work with. She clearly has more restrictions than he knew about.

"I compiled them. That's my job. There is no outside entity involved. The academic programs were loaded onto my system, and I collected data until the programs were completed."

Colin steeples his fingers and tries to think. His mind is fuzzy. "So...you're saying that there's only one person in the world who can see my graduation results."

"I am sorry. That is correct."

Colin powers off the tablet and buries his head in his hands, rubbing his temples. Then a bright chime snaps him back to attention. Now at the busiest station in the city, he runs past the platform and onto a sleek, suspended walkway. A flurry of activity surrounds him from wealthy children chasing exotic butterflies in glass botanical gardens to androids spinning and posing the latest high fashion outfits inside store windows. He keeps running. Heads turn at his frantic pace, but he finds a wooden spiral staircase and skips steps to the lower level.

He's following a dome in the distance. Nothing can distract him. His thoughts are spiraling, unable to take in new stimuli. If he stops to look at anything, he might lose his mind. He dashes across a stone patio with white tables dotting the space. People holding cups of tea aloft watch him with baffled expressions, heads swiveling. He jumps across a narrow, manmade river cutting through the patio, then runs across the rest of the street to the opera house, the famous Palais Garnier.

He stands in front of the building, staring, pedestrians walking around him. The sight nearly causes him to drop to the ground and cover his eyes so he can recover from the shock. Four banners flutter in the wind outside the opera house, two small near the entrance and two massive ones in front. They are royal purple with colorful images of candy crowding the edges. *His* opera, opening in two weeks.

There they are, in bold, mesmerizing colors. Now he can't look away. Each banner, at the very top, says: *The Composer Anonymous*. It is more than a default label he chose when Lance suggested he should hide his identity. It's a title, displayed proudly from the walls of the opera house.

He finally starts to notice the people flowing through the street around him. He looks at faces, most blank since their ears are paired to blogs or Newsstands. Finally, a young boy passes him and stops to look at the banners.

"Excuse me!" Colin calls. He's never approached a person on the street before, but this little boy doesn't scare him much. The stranger's head swivels around curiously.

"Do you know who that is?" Colin points to the banners. "Do you know who Composer Anonymous is?"

The little boy smiles and cocks his head. "Do you know Mozart?" He laughs. "Do you know Josephine Mirror or King Harlan?"

Colin nods slightly, though he doesn't recognize the second name. He doesn't know any celebrities or actors. "I know who Mozart is," he finally answers.

The boy just rolls his eyes. "Yes, Composer Anonymous music is everywhere. And my family's going to the new opera thing in February. If you want tickets, you're too late. They're sold out." He walks away, taking a few skipping steps to catch up to an older boy who hasn't slowed down to wait for him.

Colin remains planted in the street. His opera is *sold out? Also, did I just hear a kid categorize me with Mozart?* He wants to be happy, but all he feels is anger and betrayal. He turns away from the banners and retraces his steps back to the maglev.

He has someone to talk to.

A soothing virtual orchestra playing Debussy greets Katrin as she arrives at the foyer. The Lidens' home is practically a museum, so her eyes are occupied studying all the ancient artifacts from the 1800s that line the walls. Marigold Liden owns the largest collection of Victorian art, including hundreds of clocks. Katrin can watch the seconds go by from every corner of the room.

The doors at the end of the foyer are thrown open, and Katrin whirls in Percy's direction. "My favorite princess!" She smiles placatingly. Percy's used that joke for years, since she's clearly the only princess he knows. She gathers her emerald skirts and moves to follow him. "They didn't keep you waiting long, did they?" he asks politely.

"No, they didn't."

"You hardly ever visit me in my humble abode. Something must be up." Percy walks at a fast clip into the drawing room, the space packed with more Renaissance paintings in elaborate golden frames. He opens another door for her, then catches up again. This room is cozier, an actual living space rather than a museum gallery. There are soft rugs on the floor, plush couches, and a dollhouse nearly Katrin's height.

Percy kneels and knocks on the side of the dollhouse. The narrow window has wooden shutters and a pink flower box with real flowers planted inside. "Apolline, I have a guest. Go to your room a minute."

A pixie head with black curls pokes out the pink window of the house. The little girl's amber-green eyes, identical to Percy's, widen dramatically. Her ruffled dress bursts out of the door. She nearly trips over the edge of the rug, then rushes to Katrin. "You didn't tell me the princess was coming over!"

Percy groans. "Look, she didn't come to play with you. Just let us have a minute, okay?"

Katrin hasn't seen Apolline for nearly two years. She was barely five the last time she visited and was highly demanding. She remembers squeezing into Apo's dollhouse to play, much to the girl's delight.

"Your friends never want to play with me, and I want to have a tea party!" Apolline won't give up. "The other girl says it'll ruin her fancy dress."

Percy flushes, probably because he didn't intend for Adelaide to be brought up in conversation. "Look at her dress. It doesn't look fancy to you? Just go play with that android bird mum bought you." He glances at Katrin, frowning. "Sorry."

Katrin steps in, looking down at the little girl. "I'll come and knock on your door when I'm ready, and I'll attend your tea party," she promises her. "We'll be very careful of our dresses like proper ladies, won't we?"

Apo beams, satisfied. "I'll get the tea set ready." She runs to her room, the door shutting automatically behind her. Rummaging sounds follow.

Percy collapses on the couch, propping his feet up and arranging pillows behind his back. "You don't have to. I'll distract her so you can leave." Katrin's never known him to be anything but annoyed with his sister. She is very spoiled, so she can understand, but she rarely gets any attention from any of her family members.

Katrin remains standing on the rug. "No, it's okay. I'll play with her for a few minutes."

Percy lets it go, clearly eager to change subjects. "You look like you're about to pitch me some business proposal." He waves her to the other velvet armchair, and she reluctantly sits, smoothing her skirt.

After a moment, Katrin decides to lay it out for him as quickly as possible. If he doesn't go for the idea, she'll know right away. Impulsive as he is, he doesn't think over things for long. She takes a deep breath and starts, "I have a request. It's very specific, but I know you can do it." Percy quirks a brow, but she continues. "If you do this for me, I'll get you an unreleased song by Composer Anonymous."

Percy springs up from the couch, his relaxed posture transforming into pure kinetic excitement instantaneously. He punctuates his words with large hand movements as he exclaims, "You *know* who Composer Anonymous is?" When Katrin just sits, motionless, not denying it, he begins pacing. He laces his fingers behind his head, then starts waving his arms around again. "Katrin, how do you know? Not even my dad knows who it is. Not even the Treasurer, the World Bank guy who runs the composer's account, knows who he's working for. How do you know? Who is it?" He stops in his tracks. "Is it you?"

The short laugh that bursts out of her isn't ladylike. "Me? Percy, have you ever seen me with a musical instrument? I wouldn't even know how to hold it." She smiles at his assumption that the Treasurer doesn't know who Composer Anonymous is, as if Colin's not his own son. It's a clever setup really, worthy of Colin's unique mind. "Do you want it or not? Will you help me?"

Percy runs up to her chair and kneels in front of her in typical dramatic fashion. "I will give you anything you want. I'll give you the Musée du Louvre. Will you tell me who it is too?"

"I told you what Composer Anonymous is willing to give you. Of course, entering into a mutually beneficial relationship with the composer, with myself as the intermediary, can only improve your chances of finding out."

"Done," Percy says without hesitation. He stands. "I don't care what the favor is. Consider it done."

Katrin tries not to let her smile creep too far. Percy is the only one of her companions who would make such a deal without knowing the terms. The rest are too distrusting, as they should be. Still, she doesn't think this favor will be too impossible for him, or too damaging. If he does it properly, no one will even trace it back to him.

She stands up as well, holding his gaze as though she's holding him to his word. "It's actually less straightforward than the Louvre, but it doesn't cost you anything. I need live footage to be sent to and projected from the palace for one night."

Percy's elation screeches abruptly to a halt. He opens his mouth, then closes it, brow furrowing. Clearly baffled, he tries a second time. "Wait. Live footage as in...?"

"Security doesn't touch it. For one night." She stares him down. "Can you do it?"

His confusion quickly morphs into a distant look of calculation. She lets him think. If he's serious about pulling this off, she wants him to be sure it's possible. After a few seconds, his bright eyes bouncing back and forth in scheming, he looks at her. "I can do it. Name your time and place." He pauses again before narrowing his eyes in interest. "May I ask what this is for? How blind do you want Security to be?"

"As blind as you can manage." Katrin lets her face show her thanks. "I knew you wouldn't let me down. We'll talk details later. For now, if you'll excuse me, I have a tea party to attend."

Percy follows her to Apo's room. He tilts his head back, suddenly a kid again as he begs, "Pleeeeaase. Please tell me who it is!"

Apo opens the door to her room, a silver crown atop her black curls now. The room is decorated with a low white table, pink tea set, and an arrangement of guests. The guests range from android birds, cats, and other pets who occasionally ruffle their feathers or flick their tails, to elegant dolls with detailed ball gowns. Apo flashes Katrin a smile. "Come in, princess." She moves her feet in an awkward but adorable curtsy as Katrin finds her place at the little table. Then her face instantly changes when she sees her brother coming. "No boys allowed."

She shuts the door in Percy's face.

Katrin summons all her self-control to not laugh.

Chapter Twenty-One

The Truth Matters

Katrin quickly scribbles her note on the sheet torn from her sketchbook. Her handwriting is legible when she tries, which she considers a success in a time where most people don't write. She's lucky cursive handwriting came back in vogue with the Renaissance, or she would be deprived of this medium of subterfuge.

She folds the note on her desk, then runs back to her studio to return her calligraphy pen. She positions the inkwell on her shelf. Her hands shake. Talking about taking action is easy enough. But even writing the note to Roland, vague as it is, makes everything real. She didn't even use his name. *We have a plan to get the word out about the population phaseout. I'm going to need your help tonight. Meet me in the studio before Programming this evening.* She mouths the words as she checks it one last time. She bunches her thick curls in her hands and holds them up against her head. Her neck is damp with sweat. She's an awful spy. No composure whatsoever.

Breathing deeply, she looks at the far wall of her studio, all the canvases lined up in a row. She can picture Colin walking through her collection, examining her paintings with quiet interest. He wasn't actually here in the studio, but she hopes that she can bring him sometime. The longer she goes about her strict schedule of meetings, lunches, and prearranged gossip, the more she finds herself constantly wishing she were with him instead. Everyone she knows would treat him with such disdain if they saw him here, and that fact stirs anger in her belly. He's probably kinder than everyone in the palace combined, including her, and he doesn't even seem to care that he's wealthier than any of her companions. She envisions attending Candy Opera at his premiere and seeing him there in his element. If he reveals his identity, soon everyone will be able to see him at one of his own shows. And Katrin will be applauding the loudest. This vision of the future keeps her steady—for now.

She occupies herself for a few minutes by arranging her finished canvases and cleaning her workspace, playing *Cotton Candy Dance* from the holo on her shelf. After she's satisfied with the relative organization of the studio, she retraces her steps to the bedroom to hide her note for Roland to pick up later. She stops at her desk and frowns at the typical mess. Ribbons, rings, earrings, and perfume bottles. An empty tin of colored pencils. A sugarplum candle. But no note. She digs for a few moments, flustered, but she knows exactly where she left the folded paper.

"Sorry, Your Highness."

Katrin whirls around, lace on her long skirt catching on the desk's leg. Her heart races in panic, and she knows she didn't hide the fear on her face quickly enough. Macy stands in her doorway, two of her young assistants behind her. Blond-haired, pixie-faced Cécile, who always cleans and decorates the tower rooms, and stoic Tara, a future producer. Katrin didn't think about Cécile in the adjacent room earlier. It was such a common occurrence that it didn't enter her mind.

Macy holds up her note in one hand, expression grave.

Katrin grips the edge of the desk tightly behind her back. She thought this would be safer than a digital footprint. *Macy's people go through my things?* She should've kept the note on her person until the moment she hid it for Roland to find.

She really is a terrible spy.

"This note seems to indicate your intention to reveal highly confidential information," Macy says, her tone severe but even. "I don't need to tell you that this would be a very serious offense." She waves a hand vaguely at the other two girls, and they make their hasty departure from the room.

Katrin struggles to keep her voice steady. "This would be—more serious than murder?"

"You have no idea what you're talking about." Macy lowers the note, folding her hands calmly next to her holo display. "Which is one of the many reasons why confidential work remains confidential. This would be a gross misrepresentation of the reality of the situation. Now"—she glowers at the spot where Cécile had been standing—"we would know who this was being sent to if *someone* had enough common sense to leave the note in place so we could follow it. But since you've noticed its absence, I suppose I'll have to ask: who's your source?"

Katrin steps away from the desk, more angry than scared now. "What *reality*? That only some humans are worthy of existing? That it'd be easier to replace some people with androids?"

Macy steps closer to her, clasping her hands behind her back now, eerily calm. "I can think of someone who would be very easy to replace with an android."

Katrin stares at Macy, studying her for longer than she's ever taken the time to before. Macy has advanced aesthetic enhancements, but they're all subtle. She was made to blend into the background. Short, straight hair, unassuming height, and simple clothing. For once, Katrin sees a young woman barely older than her, trained to manage every aspect of the palace. A woman who is good at her job. Katrin may have all the pretty dresses in the kingdom, but Macy has all the keys. And she clearly relishes that power.

"Are you threatening me?" Katrin asks, her tone sharp.

"Who was the intended recipient of your note?"

"I can't tell you that."

Macy straightens, which seems impossible to Katrin, because she already has such impeccable posture. She acts like she was trained by someone from the Kaelumian military. "Very well. Since we're revealing our hands today, I'll have you know that I'm removing your Level 1 access. You will now have Level 2 access, which will essentially limit your movements to doorways in Court 50." She allows herself a slight smile. "I have what's called Level 0 access, or All Access. You didn't even know that existed until today, I'm sure. I'll also have you know that out of all the areas I manage at the palace, the spoiled princess I have to babysit is the most tedious. I really could manage to have you replaced with a lovely android who follows directions and smiles and waves when told and hardly anybody would notice. I'm afraid this note by itself doesn't exactly qualify, but if you did something really catastrophic, I'd be grateful for your cooperation in having yourself replaced. The only reason you're still here is because the king has some limited power in our government, and he has a number of loyal personal supporters. But not even he could protect you if you did something disastrous enough. So, consider your next move wisely."

Katrin gapes at her, and her breathing hitches. "What—what is wrong with you? What did I ever do to you?"

Macy lifts an eyebrow. "You make my job difficult." Her lips curve up in a grin devoid of sentiment. "There's nothing special about you. An android could paint better than you can and would have a steadier hand. An android would do everything you do; it would just do it better."

It stings like a slap to her cheek, like a knife in her back. "Then the same would be true of you, wouldn't it?" she manages to rasp as Macy turns to leave.

Macy barely glances over her shoulder. "Exactly, princess. That's why we follow protocol and don't leak confidential information." She steps out of the room, fingers already flying across her holo screen. The door slides shut behind her.

Katrin slumps to the floor, her skirt billowing around her. She curls her fingers into her hair, burying them in her frizzy curls. Her face is afire with anger and shock at Macy's words. Her mind is blank, until a thought finally strikes with frightening clarity, and she opens her holo display. The light snaps on as she tries to open her communications window with her father. The window is blank. Somehow, Macy has already cut her holo access to the king.

Katrin curls her arms around her knees as tears blur her vision. What can she do? Is Macy right? Is there really nothing special about her? If it all really is that simple, then why did Katrin start the conversation with so much righteous indignation at the idea of the Genetics branch replacing the humans in Underwater Level? If they matter, they *all* matter.

What would Colin tell her right now? She wipes her hands down her face, blinking quickly as tears continue to gather in her eyes. She takes a deep, deliberate breath. She has to calm down. She has to think. "I have worth," she recites, voice shaking. She swallows. Tries again. "I have worth. I am created." She stands up, palms on the desktop to keep her from tripping on her thick skirts. She paces the room, rubbing away a tear at her chin. She whispers, "Colin, you seemed so sure." She laughs, in a strange despairing vortex of emotions. She's talking to him almost like he's here. This reminds her suddenly of her father, praying over her on the rare nights they were together.

Desperate, she fights to recall anything he used to whisper in those raw, heart-mending prayers, but it's too foggy. Fresh tears well in her eyes. She hasn't been allowed enough time with her father to have proper memories of her childhood. After a second, she paces back across her bedroom and tries to make up her own words.

"God, I just want to know the truth. I just want to do the right thing. Please, help me, if you can. Colin seems to think that you made all of us humans and love us, which somehow makes us worth something. And he's the nicest person I know, so I want to believe him. I don't feel worth anything right now. I can't even do the one thing Roland asked me to do." She blinks again, refocusing on the empty holo display. A sudden thought crosses her mind. She touches the menu, her calendar flashing on the screen instead. The colors are blurry through her watery eyes.

She has a programming meeting in one hour. There's a party planned for the palace courtyard tomorrow night, likely a location she'll be escorted to now that she doesn't have access to leave the palace on her own.

The whisper leaves her lips as the only solution settles once again in her mind. "God, I need a miracle. The people of Kaelum need a miracle. This may not seem important, but...I need my party requests to be granted."

Colin walks past the kitchen with intention. Davin looks up from his holo, eyes following him across the apartment until his face scrunches up in confusion. "What's wrong?" he asks.

Not stopping, Colin checks the living area and the front hallway. Then he paces back through the kitchen, his breathing audible in the silent space.

Davin leans over the counter. *"What's wrong?"*

He can't explain. It's too much. Colin takes off his coat and lays it over a chair. *Where is he?* Voices echo, distant but audible—a soundproofing malfunction that tends to happen with larger video streams. He stands next to his stepfather's door and strains to hear. There's a conversation happening between several speakers, a holo meeting. He hears Katrin's voice and presses closer, surprised.

"Composer Anonymous," she is saying. "It's the greatest mystery of our time. No one knows who is writing these songs. It could be anybody, from any country, right? So, I propose for the next party we're streaming, we add a competition. It'll double, maybe even triple our viewership if we do it leading up to midnight."

He leans his head against the door curiously. This is the final stage of their ploy to tell the world about the natural population phaseout.

That's why she wants a large viewership.

"Of course, it'll be unlikely we'll have the real composer stream in, but we'll frame it as a chance to prove his or her skill. Anyone can stream into the party on our holo screen and play covers of the composer's most popular songs. Then I can be the competition's judge and reject contestants that I don't believe are convincing."

"It's a good idea for marketing," a woman's voice that Colin doesn't recognize chimes in. "But would it really be satisfying if all the contestants are rejected in the end?"

"For the sake of the competition, I can still pick my favorite performer. I'll be wrong, of course, but the rumors and speculation are the point of it. It'll only fuel the mystery, and I'll get to listen to some of my favorite songs all night. I think it'll be fun."

The room seems to turn in her favor, several other voices joining the conversation and arguing different points about the competition and the party planning in general. They eventually defer to Lance when the cost of actual items or décor gets mentioned. He quotes price points but doesn't seem opposed to Katrin's plan.

Because he knows I'm cut off from all news and social platforms, Colin thinks, agitated.

After a few more minutes, the meeting wraps up. Colin backs away instantly.

Lance walks through his door the moment Colin is out of the way. It shuts swiftly behind him. He peers over his work holo and notices Colin waiting by the kitchen. He lifts his head slightly and asks, "What is it? Are you sick again?"

"No." Colin is breathing fast already. His mind is too full to be afraid. He's just still in disbelief. He steps closer, into the hallway in front of their bedrooms. "I just want to know why you did it."

"Did what?" Lance asks immediately.

Colin holds up his tablet that's been dangling in his right hand. He enlarges the display with his left hand, spreading his fingers so the music shop is as big as it can be viewed in the air between them. The numbers are eight centimeters tall now, bold and obvious. The true success of his music is listed in staggering columns. "Don't lie to me again. I know the truth now. I know I'm not making five sales per month. I know I was only seeing point zero zero something percent of my own sales and revenue. How long have I been world famous?"

For a split second, Lance's expression morphs into anger. Then all the emotion on his face simply vanishes. "Since you were twelve."

Colin closes the holo so he can see Lance clearly again. His heart still thunders, and his breathing is uneven. "Why? Why didn't you tell me? You lied to me!" Anger isn't one of his default settings. He tends to fall into silent discouragement or even recursive loops of negative thoughts. But rarely external anger. It feels new and terrible.

"Colin, you're a composer. You have a specific talent for a specific thing," Lance answers evenly. "Fame is a completely different world. You wouldn't want it, and you aren't capable of dealing with it. Fame comes with public pressure, public appearances, constant scrutiny, expectations, critique, and long-term memory in the public consciousness if you're ever subjected to embarrassment. Believe me, I understand that whole world. You don't."

"But—" He can't get past two glaring thoughts circling around his mind. "I could have stayed anonymous. I could have always been anonymous. But you didn't even let me see that I was doing well, that people love what I create. I thought only five people had bought my songs this month. Do you know how many times I've almost quit making music because I didn't know if it was worth it anymore? But I kept going because I loved doing it. What about my academic results? You said I wasn't placed in music performance. Where was I actually placed?"

"It doesn't matter," Lance snaps.

"Of course the truth matters!" Colin exclaims. He sees Davin stand up from his chair at the island in the kitchen out of the corner of his eye. He'd forgotten he was still there. "You always say you're trying to protect me. But then why did you need to take my money?"

"Colin, why in the world would I let a twelve-year-old have access to bank accounts like that? What would you have possibly used it for?"

"What do *you* use it for?!"

When he raises his voice, Lance steps closer. Colin can't help himself and takes a step back, closer to his door.

"Don't talk to me like that! I am your father, and you will speak to me with respect. Now, how did you find out about this? Did you hear one of the songs when you were at the palace that one night? Josiah said you saw the princess. Did you talk to her about your music?"

Colin doesn't try to lie, even now. His anger is already melting away to sadness. Lance won't even answer him. He won't even try to engage with him. He still thinks Colin can't understand. "I talked to the princess. I talk to her a lot actually. She's lovely."

"Lovely? Colin, what are you talking about?" Lance suddenly seems rattled. Clearly, Colin speaking to anyone is a threat to him and his secrets.

Colin takes a deep breath and steadies himself. Then he looks his stepfather in the eye and says, "You know Katrin's announcement about the contest?"

"I just got out of a programming meeting about that two minutes ago. How could you even know about that?" He looks down at Colin's tablet as though TIRA might be the culprit somehow. "TIRA, is my soundproofing enabled?"

TIRA doesn't help him in the slightest. *"Soundproofing has experienced a minor technical error and is currently rebooting."*

Colin presses forward. "She said anyone can send the palace live footage of themselves playing the violin, and she decides who the 'real' Composer Anonymous is. It's supposed to be a fun night of her watching people attempt to play my songs. I'm sure some people *can* actually play them competently, but I am going to make my own video. I want everyone to know who I am."

"You are *not* going to do that." Lance points a finger at his face. "Besides, you know exactly why you can't tell anyone what you are!"

"I don't want to be afraid anymore. I was made like this for a reason. I can do this incredible thing, and I don't want to waste it. I want everyone else to know they were made for a purpose, that they were created too."

"I don't know where you got that idea from. This creation stuff is nonsense. But you clearly don't understand what's at stake here."

"You mean your reputation?" Colin wants to understand, but he is running out of excuses for Lance. The truth is simple, and he's always known it. He just never wanted to think about it.

Lance doesn't like him. He may even despise him. He hates that his beautiful wife is gone and that he's stuck with Colin. He used to say he shared their faith too. Clearly, he stopped pretending the first moment he could.

Lance had always pushed Colin toward his passion for writing songs, and Colin had felt just a *little* warmth toward him for that reason. Now he understands why.

"I said *no*," Lance responds intensely. He reaches out and snatches the tablet from Colin's hand. "You're not making any videos."

Colin isn't prepared, so he easily loses his grip on the tablet. Frustrated, he answers, "You should have talked me into signing those documents before I found out. I am *not* going to sign anything."

"You will come to your senses, if you have any," Lance snaps. He presses a palm against Colin's shoulder, shoving him through his doorway. Thrust off balance, Colin trips on one of his shoes lying next to his bed. He throws a hand behind him and catches himself on the bedframe.

Lance strides back into the hall. "TIRA, close door A4."

"No, wait—" Colin panics. He's losing his chance, his one window that Katrin gave him. He has to stream in live to Composer Anonymous night. He didn't even want to do it before. He was sick to his stomach at the thought of being seen by so many people. Of having to talk to that many people. But he has to do it. He can't miss it.

In his bedroom, he has a bathroom *and* access to the Shelf. His stepfather can keep him trapped in here for as long as he wants. Without TIRA and his tablet.

"Override accepted. Closing door A4."

"Wait! Please!" As the door hisses shut, he pushes off the bed and runs back without thinking, desperately reaching out a hand. He doesn't know if he can stop the door from closing, but he knows they have sensors. The sunlit hallway is disappearing into a crack on the left, but Colin's left hand slips in first.

Bang. The automatic door still hits the narrow frame. Colin hears the thud even as pain travels up his arm like lightning. The door's sensors kick in just enough for it to edge back a few centimeters before reengaging. Freeing his hand in the split second before the door locks shut completely, Colin pulls it against his chest and drops to the ground with a gasp. He squeezes his eyes closed, biting back a scream.

For an indeterminate amount of time, he rocks slowly on his knees. He has no thoughts. Just searing, agonizing pain. When he gradually opens his eyes and regains enough space in his mind to think, all he can think is: *That was a horrible idea. Why did I stick my hand in an automatic door?* His last glimpse of Lance showed disbelief written across his face, like that was the last thing he'd expected Colin to do.

He sits with his back against the side of the bed and holds out his hand, mind still spinning in agony. It's red, but he can't tell if he broke any of his fingers. He tries to bend them but sucks in a fresh breath and presses his head to his knees at the feeling. It's impossible.

His eyes snap open again, and he looks around his room. He sees his violin case propped up against the wall, and the thought hits him: *I can't play it.* He casts his left hand a miserable look. The fingering on his songs is difficult as it is. He can't play his violin in this condition even if he could find a way to send in the video.

He doesn't know why he holds out hope that Lance will eventually open the locked door or check on him. The soundproofing in *his* room is functioning perfectly now, and Colin can't disable it while TIRA has override settings running on the security system. Before the 2300s, the medical field was still primitive enough that bones took a long time to heal. *When Lance chooses to, this could be fixed in twenty-four hours,* Colin considers glumly. All he'd have to do was take Colin to the right hospital, which could mean Lance wants him to sit here all night and reconsider his earlier refusal.

Lying across the foot of his bed, Colin remains perfectly still for what feels like hours. A prayer plays on loop in his head, a prayer for a way out of this mess. He rests his hands across his chest. The pain doesn't lessen but persists, throbbing. With no other distractions, he rehearses what would have been his speech to the palace in his head. He rearranges sections of it, erases some altogether. *This is pointless,* he thinks miserably. What if Lance is right? He can do one specific thing: he can compose. But talking in front of people, putting the truth out there for everyone to see? They would probably just laugh at him. Reject him. It would make sense.

The Shelf clicks mechanically. He sits up, looking at the slot in his wall adjacent to the hallway. He reluctantly stands and walks over to it, expecting some kind of food. Instead, the compartment is empty. Just a small tray at the bottom and a wrist display sitting in the shadows. Colin fishes out the device with his right hand and opens a small window of light with a single line of text in the message box.

How do I hack into TIRA and disable the system?

Chapter Twenty-Two

Royal Hacker

Colin blinks in utter confusion at the words emanating from the wrist holo on the Shelf. Then it occurs to him: *Davin.* He was outside watching. He must be trying to help. A small window of relief opens inside Colin's blurry mind. His thoughts are sputtering like a candle in the rain, but he tries to think. Davin must not have seen what he did to his fingers, which makes sense, but he must be trying to get around TIRA's override protocols. He could send the tablet through the Shelf, but Colin's fingerprints and voice commands would likely be disabled.

He spies the time stamp at the top corner of the display. *10pm.* Oh! He taps the reply box. "*Give me a few minutes.*" Then he adds, "*Thank you,*" and sets the wrist holo back on the Shelf tray, returning it.

He grabs the VR device from its hiding place and runs back to his bed, struggling to fit it onto his face properly with only one hand. When he finally settles it in place, he lays back and lets his brain escape the room.

Fear bleeds into each thought as the device scans his eyes and admits him into the virtual waiting room. He was so worried about this meeting before. He almost told Katrin he couldn't. But it's too late now. This might be his only way to talk to someone outside the apartment.

He takes a steadying breath, then opens his eyes in the backstage room. Shock strikes him as he takes in the scene. There's already a person standing in the middle of the room, waiting for Colin's arrival while silently examining the posters and photographs on the walls. Colin tries not to not let his nervousness snuff out his resolve.

It's the king. He looks younger than Colin thought he would, but it makes sense. He has the most advanced enhancements the city could buy. His face is completely different from Katrin's, long and narrow, featuring bright, teal-colored eyes that appear almost iridescent. Colin wouldn't have been sure this was her father based on appearance alone, but he sees that the king is wandering around the VR room in socks. They're definitely related.

"Your Majesty." Colin bows slightly.

The king doesn't react as quickly or negatively to his bowing as Katrin did. He turns to face Colin fully, hands in pockets. "You must be Colin," he says with a smile. "Katrin talks about you every time I see her."

He nods. Katrin says she doesn't get to see her dad much. "Yes, Your Majesty."

"Since it's VR, I suppose I can forgo my own title in here. Besides, only one of us is considered the first classical-style genius composer in centuries."

Colin blinks, processing that statement. That's going to take some getting used to. "I...suppose so."

His grin widens. "And you have no enhancements? None?" Colin shakes his head, so the king adds, "Incredible. Sorry, it just seems to confirm something I've always thought. We conduct experimentation and enhancements on humans almost like we're taking the reins of evolution. But I've always felt that if we tamper too much, if we ignore that we're made with intention, then we might forget that what we *are* could be for a reason. We can't take apart, rearrange, and discard too much without consequences."

Colin listens, surprised. He remembers what Katrin said about her father, but it's still crazy to be talking to another believer. He's never met one in his life, besides his mom. "You mean, you think God is making some kind of point with me?"

He laughs almost silently. "Yes, well, I believe everything He makes has a point to it. But He might be trying to say something special through you." He looks back at the walls. "Katrin does meet a lot of celebrities, but she says you're the most humble celebrity she's ever met. And also, the most talented."

Colin reaches for his music note bead instinctually and realizes that he can move his hand. He flexes his fingers, relieved that they don't hurt in here at least. The pain back in reality might be affecting his brain capacity, though, so he tries to concentrate as he talks so he doesn't lose focus. "I didn't—exactly know that I was a celebrity, sir."

The king exhales in what sounds like a laugh, still smiling. "You didn't know?"

"I hardly ever leave the apartment. My stepfather runs all my accounts for me. I didn't think hardly anyone listened to my songs."

The smile disappears. "Katrin didn't tell me that part."

"She assumed I knew. Like you said, she assumed I was just being modest." Colin tells the whole story, words pouring out as the king watches and listens intently. He doesn't interrupt, so Colin keeps talking. He explains everything from beginning to end. He's not good at telling stories. He tends to focus on one part too much or leave things out as he details events non-sequentially. But the king doesn't ask questions. He doesn't say anything until after Colin tells him about the Genetics branch, their android research and plan to replace non-enhanced populations.

"So that is Katrin's plan to get the word to the people?"

Colin nods, disheartened. "I might have accidentally broken my fingers, so I can't play the violin."

The king casts a look down at Colin's hands, but the damage isn't visible in VR. "I'm so sorry. She dropped off this VR room with me last night, but I was wondering why I couldn't reach her today. Palace security might be blocking her communications. They might know what she's trying to do." He looks down for a few moments, worry clouding his features. But when he glances back up, he steps closer and puts a hand on Colin's shoulder. "We'll figure it out. I used to know a lot about AI systems. We'll find a way to fix your TIRA. Don't worry about the violin. There will be a lot of people tomorrow night playing your songs who are proficient with an instrument, but you don't need that to prove you're you." He waits until Colin gives a reluctant nod. "What do your fingers look like now?"

"Um, they're turning kind of blue. The two in the middle. Here and here." He points on his perfectly intact virtual fingers. It feels strange to be able to move them here, but he can tell that time is taking its toll on him. He feels slightly dizzy, even here, and is having trouble keeping track of what the king is saying. He swallows. "I should probably go soon, to get some water from my sink. I might be getting dehydrated."

"You said your brother might help you?" the king asks. Colin nods again. "You don't have H207 or B207 enhancements, so you could realistically have a fracture in either or both. Try to get him to send you some food and medicine if he's still awake. He should be able to research what you need if his holo is still working."

Despite his exhaustion, Colin still tries to joke at the irony. "You still believe I'm better without enhancements?"

"Not all of our medical advances have been for the worst. Just terribly overpriced." He pauses, bright eyes squinting a little. "You could find a comb. If you have a smaller one that would be best. And a handkerchief pocket square, maybe, if you have any of those. You could fashion a makeshift splint for those two fingers that'll hold them still for now." He moves a hand up and down, scrolling a virtual menu Colin can't see. Then he types in the air for a few seconds. "Can you tell me where you are? Your address?"

Colin swallows again, the room a little fuzzy. "You need my address?"

"We're going to come get you, of course." When Colin just stares, speechless, the king finishes, "It would be cruel to leave you there, though not as cruel as what you've had to live through already. I'm sorry it's taken this long for anyone to find out."

"I don't know if I can live on my own. I haven't been able to do a lot of research about homes or finances or anything—"

"We can help you. We'll help you figure everything out and get settled. Until then, I have a fairly large home that I'm sure has a room somewhere you can stay in."

Colin manages a smile, a little overwhelmed.

"You're not alone anymore."

Colin closes his eyes. "Thank you." It's not enough. *Thank you* is not enough. But he doesn't know what else to say. He remembers how eagerly Katrin asked him about his mother and how attentive she was to his answers. She clearly longs to have a mother. Standing here, talking to the king, he wonders if this is what it could be like to have a father. A real one. One who is kind to him, who makes jokes, who tries to fix all his ailments and accidental broken bones, who can encourage him spiritually.

He decides to tell the king about the song he was going to play for the contest, even though his confidence is still wavering. "I think...I may know what to do. I have a song that's set to release at midnight tomorrow night. That's the one Katrin wants to hear. But no one else will know it."

"Ah, a new song. What is it called?"

Colin wills the VR program not to have the capability for his cheeks to blush. "It's called *Waltz for Katrin*."

He waits a second or five before meeting the king's gaze, but when he does, he sees a soft, pleasant look on the man's face. "You know, Colin, I've been praying for years for Katrin to come to the truth. Now I finally see her grappling with ideas, asking questions, and seeking answers to things I always hoped she would. And it wasn't because of me. It was because of you. I can't thank you enough."

"The truth matters," Colin says, suddenly hit with emotion. He's talked about worth with Katrin for how long, and yet he doesn't believe it himself? The truth is that this isn't about him. He's been so worried about what people will think about him, how they'll respond. He asked God to help him tell the truth. He has the God of the universe *in* him, and yet he thinks it isn't enough?

The king gently squeezes Colin's shoulder. "It certainly does. Alright, God willing, I'll see you very soon. You should go order some food so you and your brother can get some sleep."

"Thank you. You have no idea..." Colin isn't sure how he can put into words everything he is thinking, so he doesn't. "Thank you."

The king nods. "Thank *you*. It was an honor to finally meet you."

Colin sits near the shelf, waiting for the wrist holo to be sent back. He's eating cassoulet with his back against the wall, his fingers in the bizarre comb splint and his legs stretched out on the floor, ankles crossed. He's less miserable now that he has food for the first time in ten hours and some unknown liquid medication inside him. It's taken the edge off his pain. Now he's started a halting conversation with Davin through his holo. His brother is slow to reply, but when the Shelf opens, Colin sets down his dish to read the newest message.

The King of Kaelum is sending me instructions to hack an AI program through my holo account. This is the most insane thing that's ever happened to me!

Colin doesn't reply the obvious: *"Is it working?"* even though he's tempted to do so. He doesn't want to distract his brother anymore, so he finishes eating without asking questions. When he had explained why he needed medicine, Davin had replied back in horror, *"Don't tell me Dad did that to you,"* to which Colin simply wrote back, *"I just panicked and reached for the door. It's my fault."* Davin didn't care. *"I still blame him,"* was his only response.

It's nearly midnight now, which means it's exactly twenty-four hours until he has to appear live before the world. He feels queasy thinking about it.

Click. He spins around. With a nearly inaudible sliding sound, the doorway appears, faint lights glowing in the hallway. Davin pokes his head in, looking around for a moment before seeing Colin sitting next to the Shelf slot. "Ah," he whispers. He holds up the larger holo display he brought from his room. "It worked. I'm officially a hacker now. I also disabled the security cameras."

He walks in, and the door shuts soundlessly behind him. Colin finishes the last few beans at the bottom of the dish and sets it down next to his leg. "Go ahead," Davin says, setting his tablet on his lap.

"TIRA," Colin commands, "turn on interior closet lights." A soft warmth illuminates from the edges of the closet doors. "Turn off interior closet lights." The glow vanishes. Colin's impressed. "TIRA seems to be fully functional and responding to my voice commands."

"I am at your service," TIRA intones.

"I've done more than open a door," Davin brags, sitting down on the floor next to the bed, pointing at the tablet. "Ask her to open a search for your opera."

"TIRA, locate Newsstand information about Candy Opera."

A separate window opens up beside his face, a trending story about Candy Opera, using the same images and designs from the Palais Garnier. He reads the article, still in disbelief that he's a household subject of conversation. "Skies," he whispers in surprise. Davin has disabled whatever was blocking the internet on the system.

Davin smiles a little, but he sobers and quietly adds, "I also was able to access your academic information. Dad didn't lie when he said you didn't get placed into the performance category that you wanted. But look." He moves closer to open up a new window and enlarge the assessment page. He eyes Colin.

Colin squints at the report. Reads for a few seconds. "I wasn't placed in performance." He exhales slowly. "I was placed in composition."

"Naturally. A much smaller, elite category. Harder to get into. I sent a copy of this back to the palace. The king said he'd created a message box that evaded some kind of security firewalls that usually intercept stuff. I didn't know he was a tech guru, but today was the first time we'd ever had a conversation, so…" He shrugs. When Colin just stares at him, he shifts positions, like he's trying to get comfortable on the wood floor. "Look, Dad always fed us the same lines he gave you today. I believed him because it was easier. And I thought it made sense. We were all younger when it first started, all of the conversations about Composer Anonymous everywhere. At school, everywhere. He said you couldn't handle all the attention. He wanted you to have as much of a normal life as possible, simplified, where you'd be happier. I thought you were happier here, by yourself, just writing without anybody bothering you. So, I kept the secret like he asked us to. But what you said today… You're right. He lied to you with that distorted store front. He's been training me in finance, using mostly his own accounts to explain. He's not just setting aside your money for you because you were too young. He's spending it. Also, depending on the way he's set your accounts up"—he shakes his head—"it might be difficult for you to get them back."

"I don't care about money. But I do care about the truth."

"I'm sorry," Davin says. It's something Colin never thought he'd hear from his brother. "It shouldn't have taken so long for me to stop taking him at his word. You're an international phenomenon. You didn't get lost when I tried to lose you at the concert. Sorry about that, by the way. Also, I'm pretty sure you're secretly seeing the princess." He narrows his eyes at Colin questioningly, and Colin tries not to make an expression of any kind. He fails. "Anyway, I think it's all actually very simple. He told you that you couldn't do anything so that you wouldn't. But—you can."

"I mean, I'm still me, but..."

"You're what you're meant to be," Davin interjects. "Isn't that what you believe?"

Colin isn't positive if it's his own perception or the medicine in his body tricking his brain, but for once Davin doesn't look completely closed off to the subject. He brought it up, but not dismissively. He doesn't seem condescending. He seems lost.

"It is," Colin says. "But my faith is both about being and...becoming. Being made new."

They sit together in silence for a moment. Colin holds his tablet and closes the extra holo displays in the air. Davin eventually stands up, yawning. "Well, do you need anything else, besides working fingers?"

Colin glances down at the handkerchief tied carefully around his fingers. They're still a nasty blue color. "No. Thank you."

Colin opens the music software on his tablet and looks at the score on the screen. *Waltz for Katrin.* He reluctantly closes the program and hands Davin the tablet. He may not feel ready, but it doesn't matter what he feels. It's time to say goodbye to anonymity.

Chapter Twenty-Three

The Imperfect Replica

When Colin wakes up, his mind is immediately consumed with the problem of leaving and the looming midnight hour of the competition. *I don't have a suitcase, for starters.* For a moment, he sits on the edge of his bed and wonders if he dreamed up his conversation with the king. But then he looks down at his homemade finger splint, fresh pulses of pain beating throughout his body now that the medicine has worn off. *It was all real.*

He hears something in the hall and throws off his blanket with his free hand. He presses close to the door. TIRA's soundproofing is disabled for the time being, so he can hear footsteps in the hallway.

Davin must already be in the kitchen because Colin hears Lance talking to him. "You're dressed up today. I assume you plan to come with me?"

"You said it would help me gain experience in managing the palace accounts." Davin's voice sounds normal. Calm.

"Alright. Stay quiet in these sessions. Some of these men don't like to be delayed. Or interrupted. And I don't have time for a lot of questions today."

"Of course." He hears a chair being pushed across the floor. Then a few shuffling sounds.

"I'm going to stop by to see Josiah later. It won't take long."

"Why?"

"I told you I don't have time for questions. Meet me at the lift. Bring that newspaper on the counter—and that tablet while you're at it."

Colin hears a door shut but doesn't leave his spot by the wall. *He must be talking about my tablet,* he realizes. He's taking TIRA. Probably to destroy the tablet. He wishes there was a way he could have kept the device with him, but he'd left it with Davin so that Lance wouldn't be suspicious of its disappearance. Now he'll probably never see it again. *It's okay,* he tries to tell himself. TIRA is a program that is the same on any academic tablet. Besides, he wants to make human friends one day. Real friends.

The worst loss would be his musical scores, but he suspects Lance keeps a backup of those on the Composer Anonymous account. Which Colin now has full access to.

He prays silently that Lance will leave without checking the shop even once. Colin changed the passwords on impulse the other day, and if Lance tries to get in now, he'll be locked out. Colin can't imagine anything that could make him angrier.

More sounds of shuffling across the apartment. Lance's distant voice. "Also, bring Colin breakfast through the Shelf before the lift gets here. I need him compliant. I don't need him getting sick."

"I've got it here."

Colin steps back from the door, hearing the familiar sound of a small box being delivered. He kneels silently and opens the shelf. There's a messily written note torn from the corner of an old newspaper on top of his breakfast box. *He's up to something, visiting Josiah. Something to do with his lab? I'll tell you what I find out.* Colin reads the note again. He never told Davin the entire story about the phaseout of naturally born humans. Of course, maybe Lance just plans to donate Colin to Josiah's lab to study. Nothing would make Josiah happier.

He shudders. Help better arrive soon.

Across the hallway, Colin hears Lance's holo window make a sound. His stepfather makes a sound of surprise. Colin holds his breath, briefly closing his eyes. Not the shop. Not the shop.

"They moved the vote up. Finally," Lance says instead. The lift chimes faintly, having reached their floor. The doors slide open. Colin slowly lets out a breath as the doors shut and the mechanical purr of the lift fades into the distance.

I'm safe. For now.

He pulls out his backpack and begins to pack his few favorite belongings as the minutes tick by. He carefully stashes the VR equipment in the middle. It's slow going with one hand, but he's running out of time. He looks back at his door, still unlocked, and thinks about the last thing Lance said.

They moved the vote up.

He really doesn't have much time. He takes his violin case and sets it carefully atop his bed. Then he waits. The apartment is silent. No people. No TIRA. Colin takes the biodegradable fork that came with the breakfast tray and picks the strawberries out of a bowl of fruit. He sits on the couch to stop pacing, and his leg jogs instead. The moment he eats the second-to-last strawberry, the panel at the lift door glows blue.

He has a visitor.

Colin sits against the couch on the floor of a massive room, breathing silently, as though the entire palace might hear him. The guest room echoes. It has high ceilings with gold panels and crown moulding, far too fancy for him to feel comfortable. He can't even bring himself to sit on the velvet couch, instead sitting on the rug and watching the holo display on the coffee table.

"Are you sure you don't want some tea? Un café? Anything?" He looks over at the man standing by the door. His name is Max, one of the king's men whom he professed to trust. Colin knows he is staring too intently at the holo. A small, decorative menu hovers in the air above the couch with white letters that read:

You are 7th in the queue.

In only a few minutes, he will be next, and the display will be live—to the world.

"It might calm your nerves?" Max adds.

"No, thank you," Colin says. "I don't feel like eating or drinking anything right now. Maybe when it's over." He runs his hand, instead of over his music note bead, over the smooth sides of the new splint on his fingers. The two fingers with small fractures are combined with his pointer finger and completely immobilized now. Thankfully, because of the medicine he's taken, it doesn't hurt as badly anymore. He'd be more disheartened about not being able to play his violin if so much else wasn't happening.

He left his apartment. Max had carried the one bag he'd packed while Colin held his violin case tightly in his right hand. He was nervous about leaving, but Max was already prepared with his lines. "His majesty said to tell you not to worry, that your safety and wellbeing are of the utmost importance."

So far today, Colin's been escorted discreetly through the palace by Max, put up in this large room, had a visit from a human nurse, and has been brought meals that he barely touched. He's too worried to eat much. He has a weightless silver card in his pocket that amounts to a VIP visitor's pass at the palace. According to Max, the king receives a handful of them every year for guests as needed. Once they are in use, they will expire over time. Max seems confused that Colin is entering the Composer Anonymous competition that's in full swing in the palace courtyard with broken fingers, but he doesn't comment. The security guard hasn't even asked why the king seems to be giving this unknown teenager a suite and holo access. The man looks a lot like his employer, tall and slender with bright blue eyes, but has definite signs of aging. Gray hair, plenty of wrinkles around the eyes. He does smile a lot, so he's earned the wrinkles properly. He is the only older person Colin has seen inside the palace. Maybe people dislike being reminded that they still haven't conquered aging.

Colin likes Max. He's not sure why. He's not suspicious of him, so he's comfortable with Max standing guard near the door. What he's not comfortable with is the text on the screen that keeps changing, causing his heart to skip a beat each time.

You are 5th in the queue.

Utterly terrifying. He crosses his ankles and tries not to stare at the screen. He lays his head back against the velvet couch and counts patterns on the ceiling.

"You know," Max says in his pleasant yet raspy voice, "I've never seen someone non-enhanced before, not in-person anyway."

"Really? It is probably because most of them are relegated to specific parts of the city for their professions. My mother didn't have genetic enhancements either." He lost his count, so after he restarts counting the triangle pattern and finishes at the corner of the room with seventy-two, he asks Max, "Do you like music?"

"Very much so."

"Do you prefer digitally created music or live performances?"

"Oh, I think it would have to be live performances. There's nothing quite like it."

"Why is that? What's the difference?"

Max seems to give this a moment's thought. Then he answers, "Well, I suppose it feels more real that way. There's also something about how it..."

Colin picks up his head from the couch and looks over to see Max making motions with his hands. "How it fills the air?" Colin finishes for him.

"Yes. How it takes up space." Max looks over at Colin's holo above the coffee table. "But I'm sure whatever you plan to play from your tablet for the competition will be wonderful."

Colin didn't realize that the subject could be taken that way, as if he was worried for his impending performance and needed assurance that his digital playback wouldn't be so bad.

He knows it won't be as good. He looks at the oversized clock on the wall, taking a second to register the time in his brief brain lapse. *11:42pm.*

A small animation spawns on the corner of the holo display, a ribbon of light circling the box of text in the center.

> *You are 3rd in the queue.*

Third? That fast? Someone must have gotten cold feet, whatever that means. Colin knows what it signifies now—that he could be live any minute. He sits up straight and taps his tablet on the table, TIRA ready with the program.

He's glad he didn't eat anything.

The display changes. Colin gets a live view of the party in the courtyard, which is probably the sight that prompted many hopeful contenders to exit the queue. He can barely hear the hum outside his window in the palace, but he can see it clearly now. There are thousands of lights strung across white arches. Mosaics across stone. Hundreds of high society guests eating and dancing and watching the giant holo dwarfing the courtyard below.

His eyes land on a beautifully decorated dais, where Katrin is seated and watching the show. He squints at the display, his mind suddenly overwhelmed as it tries to process what he suspects he's seeing. He studies her intently for nearly a minute, then twists to look at Max.

"Max, that's not the princess. That's not her."

"What?" The man leaves his post at the door and comes closer, crouching by the holo.

"Look," Colin points. "Look, the—" He sputters for a second, trying to force his mouth to move as he's running through all the implications and possible next steps he should take. "She's not moving her ankles like she usually does, and those don't look like comfortable shoes. She's also not adjusting the key necklace or pressing her finger on the key chain like she does when she's watching a holo. The image is not close enough to see her eyes, but that's not Katrin. I can tell."

Max murmurs something under his breath in surprise as he tries to study the small figure at the top of the holo.

"You have to tell the king and get him to find her. Genetics has an android replica of her they're trying to use."

"I'll contact him right now." Max's normally smiling face turns grave as he opens his wrist display. "They might have taken her Level 1 access. That would keep her in Court 50."

Colin digs into his pocket and pulls out the silver VIP card. "If you can find her, give her this."

Max takes the card and hurries out the door. Colin hears him jogging down the hall. After he leaves, the room is eerily silent.

You are 2nd in the queue.

The display grabs Colin's attention. *No, no, no.* If he goes live right now, there is no telling how the android will be programmed to respond to him.

Beep. A holo call from his tablet cuts through the noise in his brain. Colin hesitates to answer since the display in the middle of the table could send him live to the courtyard without warning, but it's Davin. *Why is Davin calling me?* It must be important, so his finger hovers over the button, then taps it.

"Hello? Hello? You there?" The program is doing a good job of blocking out most of the ambient noise, but Colin can tell his stepbrother is in a crowd.

"I'm here," Colin says. "Where are you? What's wrong?"

"I'm at the party! Hey, everyone's distracted by the videos and bets and stuff, but I already know none of these thespians are the real deal so—you know how I told you that dad's been training me to do his work with some of his accounts?"

"Yes, I remember." Colin closes his eyes to concentrate.

"Well, he didn't give me the entire palace budget to look at, obviously, only parts. But the palace security staff and mainly that team always following the princess around—that's not even on the palace budget. It's a different private account. He pays them all personally, overpays them to be honest. Not strictly legal, if I had to guess, but you better not be anywhere near the palace or this courtyard. You told him what you were planning to do; Security would be all over you." Colin must hesitate for too long, sitting with his arms frozen on the coffee table and trying to determine what to do, because Davin says, "Hey, earth to Colin. Did you hear me? Are you here? Tell me you're not here."

"Um—"

"Do you mind? Just pick one, seriously. There's chocolate and there's caramel. It's not that hard. You're holding up the line."

Colin makes a face, lost. Then he realizes his brother is arguing with someone at the buffet. He drops his head to his arm across the table and taps his finger splint anxiously. He knows he can trust Max, because if the guard was working for his stepfather, he never would have brought him here. But he also knows that if his stepfather owns Katrin's security team, then he's probably not safe here. He looks at the door, which is unguarded now. "I am somewhat...nearby."

Davin mutters something inaudible. Then Colin can hear him chewing. He tries to continue talking with his mouth full, and Colin struggles to understand. "Look, you better watch your back." Crunching sounds. "You don't want to end up getting detained by those guys."

"I will. What did Lance talk to Josiah about today?" he asks curiously, side-eyeing the display screen again in case he has to end the conversation suddenly. His mind is splintered into a dozen shards.

"Some project they're working on? I don't know. Dad asked if Josiah was escorting the princess to the palace tonight, which doesn't make any sense."

It does. Colin lays his head back against the couch. If Max gets back before he goes live, he has a far-fetched idea he has to tell him. In the edges of his vision, he sees the display change and focuses on the words.

You are 1st in the queue.

"I have to go." Colin ends the call.

Only one performer left. He stares at the feed of the courtyard, the people milling around, some of them clearly laughing at something. The musician ahead of Colin must not be winning over the crowd. He scans the rest of the party. The dais is empty now. He moves closer, trying to see what's happening. His pulse skyrockets again. The android is gone.

Katrin can hear the distant sounds of the party fifty stories beneath her window. *Her* party that she's not invited to. The programmed lights in her room are off except for the fake candles' flickering since they can sense her movement. She's been pacing. Frantically. The violin music has occasionally been audible if she stands under the window, so she's been listening for Colin. She hears his songs played over a dozen times, but none of the musicians sound like him. Sometimes she hears voices as they introduce themselves, men and women, young and old. They all claim to be the famed composer. Both surprising and unsurprising that so many people are willing to lie. It's in jest, of course, since it's a game to most. Also, because none of them would have access to Colin's accounts and they know it. No one can prove they're the real composer. But all the guests outside showed up just in case the real one decides to announce himself.

It's nearly midnight. Her plans have all but crumbled. Even if Percy came through and disabled the security firewalls, he can't exactly disable her android imposter. Katrin still doesn't understand what happened after the party programming meeting. At first, everyone seemed to like her idea for Composer Anonymous night. Even Macy bought the pitch. She even assigned Katrin a security escort for the night to bring her downstairs. Then, without warning, Katrin was left here. Locked inside her room. Alone. No one came for her. Even worse: she can hear the crowd of oblivious guests downstairs completely accepting the android's performance. They can't even tell the difference. Nobody seems to know or care that she's trapped here.

Macy's cruel comments still play in her ear. *You would be easy to replace. There's nothing special about you.*

The door to her room opens with a click, new lights snapping on. Katrin whirls around from the window. The door shuts behind Roland.

He immediately stalks into her room without explanation, disappearing into her closet.

Katrin opens her mouth to greet him, then stops as he walks past her. "Rol—what—" She runs after him into her adjacent room, a closet and vanity table nearly as large as her bedroom. A bundle of fabric is unceremoniously tossed at her face, a blue gown and matching petticoats. "What are you doing?"

A silver card hits her hand next and drops to the floor. She sighs and picks it up with two fingers. It's one of the VIP cards. She's seen these a few times, years ago. It can get her through almost any door in the palace. "Where did you get this?"

"We don't have a lot of time for questions." He rummages around her wardrobe and shelves, tossing a pair of shoes in her direction. "Colin sent the card. I sent myself when I saw your double outside. Pretty convincing, I must say. But the fact that they're keeping everyone at a distance from the dais was enough evidence for anyone who knows about the android. It's strange that they chose tonight to bring it out in public."

Her mind races. Colin gave her this card? *How is that possible?* "Is there any way this could have something to do with Colin? How would they know?"

"Who have you told? Where did you talk about it? Out in the open like we're doing right now?" He finds a pearl necklace in a box and takes it out, tossing the box.

"No." She throws the dress onto her bed. "No, only in the VR room. Only to him. Percy doesn't have enough information to piece anything together."

"Did Colin tell someone? His family?"

"I don't—I don't know. His stepfather was in our meeting yesterday. Do you think he—?

"Meador?" He throws the necklace to Katrin, and she sets it down next to the dress.

"Yes."

Roland pokes his head out of the closet, frowning. "You better hope *he* doesn't know. He owns your staff and probably you too if you think about it in a certain light. He even has a son in Genetics. I met him the other day. He's new to his department, but he might have the ability to get that android here to the palace."

Katrin bristles at the thought of Colin's family conspiring against them, but there are more pressing questions on her mind. "Roland, what are you doing?"

"Really? I thought you were mildly intelligent."

"Roland."

He emerges from the closet with blue satin gloves and tosses them onto the bed on top of the dress. "This is what the android is wearing. They must have remade this outfit from footage at some point. Put it on and meet me in the hall. I've been doing some investigation on my own. The android has voice commands."

Katrin hesitates for the barest second. "You're really going to help me?"

"If Colin manages to come to the competition tonight, it'll force the empire to stall the phaseout of naturally born humans and let me do some more research as a byproduct. Trust me. I'm trying to help. But you have to hurry."

"Alright. I'm hurrying."

Roland walks out, and Katrin throws the outfit on as well as she can without the many hands usually assisting her. She hides some of the buttons she's unable to fasten by brushing her curls down her back. Then she pulls on the gloves and hurries to the mirror. She looks like she feels: harried. Face flushed. Hair slightly frizzed. Shoes probably fastened crooked. She tries to freshen up with makeup and perfume from her vanity, but she has no idea what color *anything* the android is wearing on her eyes or lips. Roland didn't mention it.

Still praying all is not lost, she walks to the door and tucks the silver card into the top of her glove. The door slides open without a problem, likely sending a small notification pinging somewhere that a VIP Level 1 access has opened her door once again. Security better be too distracted with the party tonight to notice.

Katrin takes three steps for each of Roland's single large strides down the halls. He quietly relays information about the android as fast as he can. She tries to steady her breathing as she listens, so she won't appear out of breath once she goes outside. The light fades to rows of flickering candles, then a silver lift that leads to the courtyard and gardens. She looks across her shoulder at Roland, but his face betrays no emotion. She won't get any encouragement from him for what she's about to do. She isn't even sure about his stated motivations in all this. Her fears may turn out to be completely true. She's not all that special to Kaelum. What then? *Do I matter despite all that?*

A single chime. She steps out of the lift after Roland and clasps her gloved hands together. The sound of music grows louder now, a shrill violin sound that's causing a few outbursts of laughter from the crowd. She and Roland walk down a shadowy rock hallway, ending at an archway. They're still hidden from the courtyard party. There are no candles, only curved windows in the rock with hanging ivy blocking most of the light.

Katrin slows down as it becomes darker. Past the arch, she can see the raised platform where lights and flowers line the mosaic tiles. The distant android is sitting perfectly still, facing the projection at the opposite end of the courtyard.

Katrin balls her hands tightly. Her foot kicks something in the dark, and she spins around, heart leaping. It sounds like an empty flower pot. As the alarm passes, she turns back around to face the light in the distance. The fake princess is so perfect, wearing her blue dress and occasionally moving her fingers against her throne's arms. Her hair is perfectly placed, each curl swirling in an identical spiral. Another round of laughter breaks out in the audience, and the android raises a hand to her lips as if trying to cover a smile.

Katrin hates watching. Roland walks confidently to the archway and stands behind the android. The two security men seem to exchange a glance, but Katrin can't tell if they say anything from her angle. A third man turns around curiously, and she instantly recognizes the twin she met at the party. *Josiah.* Roland was right. He *was* working in Genetics, and he must have set this up. None of them dare to stop Roland, who is much farther up the food chain. Roland bends to say something to the android, and she stands up elegantly and begins walking. Confused, the rest of the security team closes in. Katrin backs up, further into the dark.

"Just a precaution," she can hear him tell them. "The lossless compression. Take it from someone who's worked on this generation model. It has to recalibrate its eyes, mouth, and hand sensors every three hours or the performance will lag."

Katrin wonders if Roland made all this up. Sounds like it. The security team lets the android walk away on her own as Roland continues to chatter about nonsense, her small steps coming closer. Katrin finally steps out from the shadows so the replica's sensors will pick up on her presence. Sure enough, the android comes to a stop in front of Katrin. She tries to study the outfit in the dark. They are identical in almost every way. Blue-gold eyes stare unseeingly and unblinkingly at Katrin's face. Her lips are shiny with gloss like her own. Pearl necklace. Satin gloves.

"Good evening, Katrin." The android's voice is her own. The exact intonation and timbre. It causes chills to travel up her arms.

Katrin stares back, suddenly unintimidated by this soulless machine. The android will never know how much she loves her father. She will never feel a phantom ache for a mother she never had. She will never shed a tear over how a performance of music moves her inexplicably. She will never know the little jump of her heart in her chest when she looks up at Colin's grinning face and realizes she wants to kiss him.

The android could never.

Katrin steps closer and stands eye-to-eye with the replica's face. "It is now time to say farewell, Your Royal Highness," she whispers.

At the passphrase, the android repeats in the exact same voice, "Farewell." The eyes close, and her body becomes perfectly still, though perfectly balanced. Katrin looks down at the blue beaded dress. *My mistake. One difference in the outfit.* She reaches around the motionless android's neck and unclasps the key necklace, putting it around her own neck. Then she takes a deep breath and steps around the android.

As she walks into the light, the security team glances in her direction. She can only see them with her peripherals because she stares straight ahead. She sits as elegantly as possible on her throne and places her hands on the arms, tapping her fingers slowly, one by one. She looks ahead at the giant holo, covering her view of the entire night sky. She does not blink. She breathes in shallow breaths. Behind her, Roland is probably retreating to the shadowy walkway to help walk the android home. After all, it is owned by his family—in a way. To her left, a shadow falls over her. She resists the urge to turn and see who it is, but she can feel her pulse quickening. She can see just enough out of the corner of her vision to recognize Macy's familiar, dreaded presence. She can sense the woman studying her face.

The performance in front of her ends, and only a few hundred in the courtyard with their drinks and plates of desserts turn to look at her reaction. They seem to know she'll reject the last competitor already. There is a man standing in the projection, the view of a second-story window behind him. He's holding the neck of a white violin in one hand expectantly.

Katrin shifts her gaze just slightly, seeing two hovering boxes over a pillar in front of her throne. One is black and the other is golden. She lifts one hand and touches the black box with one finger. Every light in the courtyard flickers off then back on again as the crowd laughs again, a few scattered boos near the buffet. Katrin swallows. Maybe she missed Colin. She has no idea who has already gone and who has not. The android could have already rejected him the moment he appeared minutes ago while she was in the lift at the palace. Just as the fear begins to invade her mind, the holo across the courtyard flashes a new competitor on the display across the sky. She tries not to react, but her eyes probably widen. Her glove is clenching the key against her chest.

Colin's face appears. He's sitting with his tablet on a table in front of him, right hand hovering over the screen and left arm at his side and vanishing out of frame. He's motionless for a moment, then clearly faces her, squinting slightly as though trying to decide if she's real as well. Katrin smiles up at the projection and a similar smile of relief replaces his look of concern. He knows. He can tell the difference.

In the background of the room, next to a velvet couch, a candle-lit silhouette of a man crosses the floor briefly, sipping from a cup of tea. A small laugh bursts out of Katrin as tears gather in her eyes. It's her father, which a few in the crowd seem to notice. A buzz begins in the courtyard, every eye fixed on the holo above as they whisper about the likelihood that their eyes deceive them—that they just saw the king sipping tea in this teenager's room.

Katrin can't stop grinning. *This is about to be the greatest video this city has ever seen.*

Chapter Twenty-Four

Stakeholders of the Future

"I'm sure you have all heard of me." Colin can hear the words coming out of his own mouth, almost as though part of his brain is witnessing this happen from far away. His heart is pounding in his ears. Hundreds of faces stare up at him. His right hand moves across the tablet, starting to play the digital song he composed. He doubts anyone has started a performance quite like this by tapping buttons instead of playing a violin. Their confusion is obvious. The guests share glances on his screen. They don't recognize the song.

"For—for some of you, the first time you heard about me was when the news spread of a single genetic anomaly being born after hundreds of years." This causes an immediate hum across the gathered audience that Colin tries to ignore as he continues. "I was born with traits that our empire no longer considered necessary, that were not considered the best of humanity. According to most of our geneticists…I should not exist."

At the dais below, all but one of the security detail surrounding Katrin check wrist displays and disperse into the shadows behind the garden. They were likely sent to find him and shut down his holo connection. One of the figures even vaguely looks like his stepbrother. Katrin looks over her shoulder but quickly turns to face him again.

Colin swallows, feeling strength come over him. "The next time you heard about me, I'd already been playing the violin and writing songs for a few years. My mom gave me my violin. She saw potential in me when everyone else just saw failure. The Renaissance had just taken over the world, and I loved what was being rediscovered and enjoyed after artificial sounds had made up the majority of our music for so many years. People wanted to experience music performed live again, music written for the orchestra again." He watched the colorful bars of his tablet's score scroll by as the second verse began to play. "AI music is not the same as live music, and we all feel it. We can feel it in the air. We can experience it in the nuances of each individual performance when a person plays it with their own expression and passion. We almost *want* to experience something a little flawed, something that's not perfect and the same every time. Why do we want that? Because we want things to be real. We long for reality, whether we admit it or not. Why did we have a Renaissance? Because we admired the authenticity of it, of human hands crafting human things. Of real expression. That's what art truly is. If you lose the human expression, you lose art. We can't connect with artificial sounds the same way." The melody begins to emerge, a bright pleasant sound of a digital violin. Perfect notes, all identical. The crowd in the courtyard seems to be listening both to the song and his words, but he can't determine their response. They definitely don't believe he's the real

Composer Anonymous yet.

"Which leads me to ask: what gives a person worth? That they can contribute a skill that's considered useful? That they look a certain way? That they're talented? That they're wanted? What if you happened to be born with traits that our empire no longer considers necessary, that are not considered the best of humanity? As most of our geneticists believe, what if you should not exist anymore if you don't have genetic enhancements? You could be replaced by an android who could do your job." Colin can tell that his words are creating a stir in the party below him. A few guests cast looks at the android servers that are all around them holding trays. "The truth is this: you are valuable. We all are. Not because of our status or enhancements, but because of Who made us." The song on his tablet repeats the melody, then transitions to a series of harmonics. The digital clock in the corner of the screen reads: *11:58*.

"If no one has told you, you were created by a God who loves you. You are valuable because He places value on every person He creates. This message is coming to you from Composer Anonymous, who from now on will be known as Colin Burke. This song that I am playing is called *Waltz for Katrin*. It is written for a princess who is my best friend, whom I also happen to love very much. In two minutes, after the song ends, you will be able to access my personal recording of this piece on violin."

The door behind him slides open, dragging him briefly back to the room. The king and Max had stepped into the adjacent sitting room to give him some space for his speech, but suddenly he finds himself surrounded by members of Katrin's security team. He quickly turns the holo display with one hand to face the door and the cluster of frowning security men, Josiah among them. A severe-looking brunette is at their helm, and as she approaches, she speaks softly into her wrist holo.

"Jarred, cut live video access to the courtyard now." Colin has heard about this woman from Katrin several times: Macy.

Colin touches the corner of the display to cut off his view window. He doesn't look behind him to see if anything on the screen changes. He stands to his feet and backs away from the coffee table and couch. Once he's standing by the door, Macy steps closer to him. "So, the princess has pulled you into her schemes to leak confidential information. Are you her source or just her messenger?"

"What do you think I said?" Colin asks after a second, unsure of how to respond. He knows he framed everything about the empire as a hypothetical. "And how did you find me so quickly?"

The woman points to his tablet. "We tracked that tablet through the account login."

Colin's login. *Lance can track that.* "I know who gave you that information," he says.

Davin is probably right about palace security. Lance runs them all himself. Josiah must have procured the android for tonight to stand in for the princess. They could have even instructed the android to reject every musician. Colin understands what's happening now. Lance is using any power at his disposal to try to cover up Colin's existence and protect his assets.

"I'm asking the questions," the security woman snaps. "The population phaseout. Who told you about this?"

"So...you're admitting that this is the truth? That Genetics is planning on phasing out naturally born humans?"

The sound on the screen from the courtyard below them is loud enough now that Colin can even hear it from the window, hundreds of voices in a frenzied dissonance. Josiah suddenly pushes around Colin's shoulder, looking closer at the holo projection on the table. He taps the bottom corner, enlarging the display again. The video is still live. He whirls on the brunette angrily. "Did the video access not get cut?"

Macy just stares with round eyes at the display, at the upturned faces of the guests looking back at her. Her severe face goes completely blank, and she's suddenly speechless. The other men keep asking her questions in growing panic, then they rapidly exit the room and get out of the frame. Macy still stares like a glitching program at the view of the courtyard.

Katrin's annoying coworker Percy came through after all. He stopped them from being able to block the live feed.

Colin steps closer to Macy and reassures her calmly, "I know my stepfather Lance pays you to do this, but you could be doing so many better things with your life. You don't have to work for him."

The woman is startled out of her apparent trance by his words. She flashes a look like bafflement at him, then flees the room after the other security members.

Josiah simply reaches for the holo window from the side and ends the feed. The blue glow between them vanishes. The room is now empty. "What is this?" Josiah moves forward, seething. When Colin steps back, his stepbrother grabs his arm. "Who is helping you? You're not smart enough to come up with all this on your own!"

"You should go." Colin barely recognizes his own voice. He's calm. He just wants Josiah to stop before he gets himself into any more trouble. This is already going to look bad for him.

Josiah only yanks him closer. "Nobody is going to believe you're Composer Anonymous. Now tell me who let you in here!" Josiah's voice echoes distantly from the courtyard, the faint sound coming from the window. He stops suddenly, eyes fixed on something across the room.

Colin turns, craning his neck as best as he can. The king is standing at the doorway to the adjacent room, leaning against the frame. A holo window is poised in the air above his hand, aimed at the two of them. Colin can see the courtyard party feed in the mirrored reflection of the holo. The king's solemn expression is fixed on Josiah as his hand holds the live feed in place. Colin realizes that he must have hacked the queue to jump to the first video slot after Colin's ended, essentially picking the footage back up where it left off.

More truth to show.

Josiah lets Colin loose as if he's been burnt. He clearly can't think of any words to utter that would change the look of displeasure he sees on the king's face. So he leaves as well, following Katrin's so-called security team out of the suite.

The king wordlessly motions Colin to come to his holo feed with one hand behind the display. Colin walks forward. He can see that the party is in chaos, everyone talking at once about the drama they've just seen unfold. He hopes the feed is loud enough that they will still hear him.

"Well, now you know the truth. But we are not androids. We are human. We can love. We can create. We have value that cannot be taken away from us." He runs his fingers over the splint on his hand. He wasn't able to hide it from the feed, not when it switched to the king's viewpoint. Everyone in the courtyard has seen him now: his entire worn outfit and jacket, his broken fingers. Him. Exactly as he is. The noise dies down for a moment. All Colin can hear now is the distant echo of his own voice from outside the walls. "I also hope you can see me as Colin, the person, and not just a genetic anomaly. Even if you would rather not, I still know who I am. But, if you enjoy my music—it's the stroke of midnight, and *Waltz for Katrin* is now available from the artist formerly known as Composer Anonymous. Goodnight!" He waves with his good hand and taps to end the video. Then he runs to the closest window that looks out over the lights and the courtyards below.

Katrin has pressed the button on the holo beside her throne, and the lights disappear.

The night turns black, then explodes with golden light to signify that he won. Lights appear in the trees, in the gardens. Golden confetti bursts from behind the mosaic walls, covering the air above the guests. Cheers and shouts of amazement sweep the crowd as more and more glows of holo displays confirm the new song in his store. He can hear echoes of the song in synchronous violin melodies as person after person proves that he is the real composer for themselves.

Colin takes a deep breath. Exhaustion is finally claiming his senses. And he's finally hungry too. He lifts his right hand and can see the shakiness now. In the moment, it was like all his apprehension vanished. He hadn't stumbled over many of his words or paused for too long. His prayers were answered. He spoke clearly. He told the truth. He knows many people will still be disappointed to find out who he is, but he can't change that.

Colin hears footsteps behind him and turns. The king stands beside him at the window, watching the golden confetti fall to the ground. He smiles, putting an arm around Colin's shoulder. "You did it," he says softly, as though he knows all this excitement and noise has been hard on him. "That was incredible."

"It wasn't me." Colin shakes his head, still amazed that the last ten minutes even happened. Did he even say somewhere in the middle of the speech that he *loved* Katrin?

"Well, I was praying for you the whole time."

"I could tell." Colin smiles.

Max appears on his left. Surprise lines his face. "How does it feel to be famous, young man? I can hardly believe it. I've been listening to your music for years. Quite a talent, you have."

"It's—daunting, I guess." Colin looks at the older man, happy that at least one of his fans didn't bat an eye at him revealing his identity.

The king pats his shoulder. "Don't worry. I'll guard you from your crazed fans until we can revamp security around here."

Katrin sits on the virtual piano bench, silently scanning the collage of her and Colin's backstage walls. She came alone, so the VR world is silent. It's only been a week since Composer Anonymous announced his identity to the world. She and Colin have added even more photos from their combined holos, turning it into a developing timeline of their relationship as it grows. There are virtual tickets from concerts, patterns from Katrin's new dress designs. She didn't magically gain mastery of art overnight, so when the designers asked if they could "tweak the designs" a bit, she consented. There are first draft scores of Colin's new songs on the wall, all signed *Colin Burke* for the first time instead of *Composer Anonymous*. She smiles at the digital copy of *Waltz for Katrin*, which—regardless of it being named for her or not—is truly a wonderful song.

The second figure appears in the room on her left, and she looks to her side without standing from the bench. Davin casts his black eyes around the room, taking in all the organized clutter and virtual instruments. His gaze lands on the large poster printed and framed at the top of the wall, the central focus of the space. A single line of text on white paper.

God is our refuge and strength, a very present help in trouble.

He takes a second to slowly spin in a circle and study everything, then remarks, "I'd say this room has Colin's style all over it, but he's way more organized than this."

Katrin shrugs and jokes, "It's me. I'm the messy one. I would let him organize my studio, but then I probably couldn't find anything."

Ever since Colin told her about his stepbrother helping him get to the palace, she's been eager to interrogate him. Trust is painstakingly earned, and her level of clearance is still higher than most people's. Colin's kindness and trust are some of his best qualities. They make him who he is. But she'd determined to make sure that Davin is acting in good faith.

Davin watches her for a moment, not speaking. Katrin lets the silence stretch. Then he smiles a little and looks away, back at the collage on the wall. "You two really are in love, aren't you?" When Katrin's expression doesn't change, he adds, "Sorry."

She ignores his question. "Look, I just wanted to talk to you because I don't know you yet. I don't know what you want. I don't know what you're after. I don't know if you just had something against your father. Or if you're hoping to befriend Colin all of the sudden because now that you've helped him regain his incomprehensible wealth, you can benefit." Davin's brow furrows at this comment, so she finishes, "If that's not the case, prove me wrong. Help me understand. Because if you have any intentions to manipulate Colin, just be aware that I *will* find out."

His frown deepens, but Katrin notices that he doesn't cross his arms or assume a defensive posture. "To the first option, yes. Yes, I technically saw my father as an obstacle and knew I could remove that obstacle." Then he quickly adds, "But tell me you wouldn't, if you were being trained by someone to cheat the system like them and you didn't want to."

"Also, now you don't have to wait to take over."

"Yes," he says warily, clearly unsure if this is the response she wants.

"Well, at least you're honest. I think." She crosses her ankles. He glances at her feet, likely confused that she's not wearing shoes. "Is there a reason you've bullied Colin his entire life and now conveniently decided to stop?"

"It's kind of hard to explain." He finally adopts a defensive posture, shifting his weight and looking down as he folds his arms.

"Oh, is it?" Not about to let him off the hook, she waits for him to elaborate.

A shallow sigh. "Here's the truth. It's not pretty. I'm not trying to excuse anything, but this is the truth. I always wanted to be the next treasurer, I wanted to do what my dad did, but I was a terrible student. Especially at first. He didn't think I could handle it. He kept telling me to try something else, but I wouldn't have it. I told myself that I would impress him in every possible way, and he would change his mind. I would be a model student, have better academic scores, never disappoint him. All that."

"What does this have to do with—?"

"I'm getting there. After Léa, Colin's mom, was gone, Colin was completely inconsolable. He would shut himself in his room all the time. It became...more obvious that Dad didn't like having him around and would get angry at anything he did. So, since I was trying to be my dad's favorite around that same time, I just kept my distance. One day, probably a year or so after she died, Josiah and I took Colin's violin out of his room—I guess because we were bored and curious—and Josiah tried to play it. It sounded like a dying cat. But when Colin saw us with it, he freaked out. Dad was on a call in the kitchen or somewhere nearby instead of his room. When the noise disrupted his meeting, he came in and took out all his anger on Colin instead of either of us. Colin ended up locked in his room, and Josiah still had the violin in his hand. He didn't even take it away." Davin's gaze drops to his feet. "Like I said, it's not pretty, but it's the truth. As a ten-year-old, when you find out that you can get away with anything..." He leaves the sentence hanging when their eyes meet again.

Katrin knows he can't possibly mistake the pained look on her face. She'd expected him to make promises, to deflect, to deny involvement. She wasn't expecting him to be *this* honest.

"I hadn't really spent time with Colin in years. But I finally got what I wanted. I got the opportunity to work toward the career I wanted, and Dad agreed to train me to do it. When I found out more about the accounts he supposedly maintained for Colin, all the pieces really came together. All the stuff he would let Colin do or not do, the places he'd let him go, things he'd let him see on holos—it was all about the money. It wasn't about what he was capable of accomplishing or about protecting him. I took Colin to a concert to make sure, and it confirmed all my suspicions."

"He told me he chased you down."

"Pretty much."

They look at each other for a second. Katrin wants to be angry, but she can't. She needs him to be defensive, to deny his involvement in some way, but he seems genuinely ashamed.

Finally, she says, "He told me he forgave you."

He shifts his weight again. "Yeah."

"And?"

"I don't know how to take it," he admits.

She stands, smoothing out her skirt. "He didn't have any stipulations or anything?" she asks, only half-jokingly.

"Well, he didn't have any stipulations per se, but he did ask me to read this one book he likes as a favor." He taps his VR display, scrolling through a few small windows in the air in front of them before landing on a digital book.

"Wow, that actually *is* a big stipulation." She cracks a smile.

"Why?"

"Well, the Bible is kind of long."

He looks closer at the display, opening up a bar at the bottom that shows the page count. "Oh. Wow. I guess I should get started then."

She manages to hold back her laugh. She can't exactly tease Davin about this. She hasn't read Colin's favorite book yet either. Now that she's chosen faith herself, she has a seemingly insatiable appetite to read and discover more. She's put her current painting project on hold and tracks down her dad every free moment he has on his schedule to ask him questions. When he's not available, she asks Colin. He answers everything he can.

"I guess if Colin can forgive you, I can too," she says, serious again. Davin's tense expression softens with relief. "But that doesn't mean I'm not watching you."

He bows, unironically—at least, she hopes it's unironic. "Of course, Your Highness," he says. "Tell Colin a package should be coming for him today. When I left the apartment, I found a waistcoat he left behind. I figured he'd want it. He says he likes the way it feels. He hates buying new clothes, you know?"

"I do." She tilts her head, still finding it hard to remember that, whether Davin was a good brother to Colin before or not, he's still known him longer. "I will."

Davin smiles. "Are you going to see him today?"

"Confidential information, I'm afraid." She pulls up her virtual menu and exits the room, closing down the simulation and waking back up in reality.

Chapter Twenty-Five

By Colin Burke

"The High-ish Council has come to order," Adelaide announces.

Across the table, Percy groans. "Please don't call it that, sweetheart."

Roland sits back, fingers laced together in front of him and a smug smile on his face. The name for the council has stuck with Adelaide, unfortunately. Adelaide doesn't apologize. She's already moved on to Item 1—who is sitting to Katrin's left and watching the odd proceedings politely.

Katrin watches Colin out of the corner of her eye, gauging his reactions to her companions. If any of them dares say a mean word to him, she's ready to go to battle.

"First, we're voting on adding Colin as a member of the...council. As a cultural stakeholder." Addie avoids the name altogether now. Percy has insisted that they vote on the official name today.

Percy, Addie, Katrin, and Roland vote yes. Phoebe simply declines to vote, but they all know how she feels about Colin. She still believes he reflects badly on all of them—the upper crust of society and the ones with genetic enhancements. She sits at the end of the table in stony silence.

Percy received the promised, unreleased song. It's called *Ice Dancer Prelude*, and he's still ecstatic about it. Katrin knows that Roland still considers Colin a curiosity to be studied. Adelaide is an avid fan—she already has her own box seats ready for Candy Opera—so she's a non-issue today.

"Alright," Addie moves on. She dips fruit slices in a porcelain bowl of chocolate sauce she brought with her. Of course she's eating while trying to talk. "Vote to add Davin Meador as future treasurer."

They all vote in the affirmative, including Katrin. Colin, of course, is all positivity and easy forgiveness when it comes to Davin, but Katrin has only had one short conversation with him. She crosses her arms over the table and hopes they haven't made a mistake. So far, Davin has been nothing but helpful.

"You wanted to show us something?" Addie motions to Davin's holo display. It's minimized to a glowing line in the air.

"Yes, if I can. Thank you for adding me to this...council." He refuses to meet Percy's eye, instead opening the holo with a flick of his hand. It casts blue light across his black hair. The window opens to a larger display in the center of the table they can all see. "So, we all know the High Council is meeting this morning as well. My father has been summoned by King Harlan. I've been communicating with the king and sharing data from our AI at home. This data will show that he tried to delete Colin's academic records entirely. With other proof of mismanagement, it's likely he'll be forced to step down. Since I've already been trained with the accounts, I'll be able to assume the role, at least for a little while."

Roland awards Davin with a look of approval, to which he nods in acknowledgement. Katrin wonders if it's Roland's way of recognizing how cunning it was of him to take his father down purely to claim his title. The public pressure around the Genetics project now that Composer Anonymous himself was revealed not to have enhancements is enough to set back the android replacement production. Roland can launch everything he's researching with better backing now.

Looking over at Colin, Davin adds, "Also, I thought him wanting legal guardianship must have been tied to a financial issue somewhere, and I was right. Because of the way he set up your music account when you were a kid, a 739A account, there *is* a legal way you could get it back now that you're eighteen. Isn't that right?" He moves the display so he can make eye contact with Phoebe. He stares her down, not letting up until she sighs and sits back.

"Yes," she reluctantly admits. "Legally, they would be his."

Katrin blinks in surprise. *That was unexpected.* Taking his father's job, that she could understand. But it sounds like Davin is doing extra research that solely benefits Colin.

"Thank you," Colin says. He told Katrin that he doesn't care about the money, but she knows he'll appreciate the security that comes with it. He's starting a whole new life now. "Maybe we can meet later, and you can walk me through it?" he asks his stepbrother.

"Of course," Davin confirms. He minimizes the large holo display. "I'm going to look over the palace budget when I get the go-ahead, but it'll be an—undertaking. But don't worry, princess, we won't forget to assign you a new security personnel."

Adelaide sighs dramatically. "Will we have to get a new publicist and producer too? We were having so much fun."

Percy turns, looking affronted on Katrin's behalf. "They locked her up and tried to replace her with an android!"

"I know," she pouts, clearly not as concerned about it. She glances at Katrin. "But surely, you'd want to keep your double around. I mean, you hate some marketing meetings, right?"

"I wouldn't want to trick people like that," Katrin answers. "I'm going to request that we give the android a *slight* makeover, so it won't look exactly like me, and reassign it to be an office assistant."

"So boring," Adelaide sighs again.

Katrin doesn't argue with her. She'll have to put up with Katrin slowly working to regain some control of her own life.

With what little security footage he could find, Roland proved that Josiah removed the android from the department without proper authorization. He's moved Michael—Katrin's tour guide from her trip to the Genetics building—into that role instead. Katrin only discovered yesterday that Michael has two adopted sisters who are not enhanced, a rarity in the upper class. Hopefully, he'll be a better balance for the department.

"I actually have a question for Colin, if I can change the topic here." Percy lifts a hand, though he knows no one will stop him from talking. Colin offers Percy his full attention. "So, I went to the rehearsal for the opera yesterday, which is coming along really great, by the way."

Katrin bites back a remark that no one received Colin's permission to make the opera in the first place. She's not sure where Percy's going with this yet, so she gives him the benefit of the doubt.

"The conductor asked me to pass this along. They want you to conduct the premiere, if you want."

Katrin spins to look at Colin, waiting for his reaction.

"Well," Colin starts slowly. "I'm sure...the conductor who was chosen...he's been preparing a long time for this. I wouldn't want to—"

"No, no. It's just for one night," Percy clarifies. "He can do the rest. He just thought it would be appropriate for you to conduct your premiere."

Katrin can't stop the smile that takes over her face. After Colin sent Percy private access to his *Ice Dancer Prelude* with a letter attached, Percy has been surprisingly friendly toward him. She's dying to know what he said in that letter, but she suspects he was just his typical brilliant, kind self. Percy acts like he'd gift Colin the Louvre now. She only wishes she had known when she'd asked Colin to take her to his opera that he thought she meant another VR outing. His opera is going to be very real.

Colin's gaze meets hers, then darts back across the table. "Then—thank you. I'd be honored."

"You know how to conduct too?" Adelaide asks, distracted from her food for a moment. "Is that like a normal thing all composers know how to do?"

Colin shrugs. "It is a different skill. I have researched it and watched some holos. I will have to practice."

"I didn't know you could look that up." Adelaide looks mystified.

Percy replies with a hint of sarcasm, "That's because you just watch fashion holos."

Katrin presses her lips together to avoid cracking a smile. She's not sure how long those two will last before breaking up melodramatically. She has a bet going with Roland that it'll take two more weeks. He thinks it'll only take four more days. Colin didn't participate, suggesting that they weren't being very nice. She couldn't argue against that.

Davin looks around in the brief, awkward silence, then reluctantly speaks up. "So…I heard that this meeting doesn't have a name yet and we're supposed to vote on one?"

"Yes." Percy sits up eagerly. "Offer up your vote now, everyone, or forever hold your peace."

Roland raises a hand. "I propose *The Present and Future Kaelumian Empire Local Chapter of the Council of Stakeholders Round Table*, or *TPAFKELCOTCOSRT* for short."

Colin's face morphs into an expression of horror following Roland's deadpan delivery.

"He's just trying to annoy Percy," Katrin leans over and whispers to him. He nods understandingly and relaxes.

"I propose *Kaelumian Ministries Council*, because *technically* that's what it should be, and for the sake of my sanity," Phoebe announces from her end of the table, flashing the others a disapproving look.

"I don't know, I kind of liked that *Kaelumian High-ish Council* one," Davin says.

Percy groans. "Can we vote to kick these two out?" He points at Davin and Roland.

"I don't think you can reasonably kick me out of a meeting that has no name." Davin's defense makes almost as little sense as the former statement. Katrin assumes he's had practice with this sort of absurd banter living with his twin all those years.

"Any other proposed names?" Percy asks wearily, looking at Colin, Adelaide, and Katrin.

They choose not to prolong everyone's suffering.

"Alright, everyone in favor of whatever Roland said?" He glares at each person individually, as though daring them to raise a hand. No one budges.

Roland confidently lifts his hand.

"Everyone in favor of *Kaelumian High*-ish *Council*?" Percy emphasizes the word in disdain.

Davin raises a hand with a grin. Adelaide starts to raise her hand as well, then takes one look at Percy's glower and slowly lowers it.

"Everyone in favor of—what was it Phoebe said?"

"*Kaelumian Ministries Council*," Colin says helpfully.

"Yes, that."

Percy, Adelaide, Phoebe, Katrin, and Colin lift their hands, the overwhelming majority. Phoebe looks *almost* grateful, glaring at Colin with only half as much malice as before. If Phoebe would actually give him a chance, Katrin figures that their straightforward, logical approach to many matters might help them become friends over time. They have a few things in common.

"Looks like we have an official council name," Percy announces with satisfaction. "If I hear either of those other alternatives mentioned again, I'll move to eject the culprit with prejudice."

"Who put you in charge?" Roland complains. "Addie, you preside for a while. His grandiose vocabulary is driving me crazy."

"Says the man who proposed to name the council every word in *his* vocabulary."

Phoebe buries her hands in her dark hair and lays her head on the table in defeat as the two of them start up another pointless argument.

A new message pops up on Davin's wrist display, and he expands it slightly to read. A smile creeps over his face, and he tilts the window toward Colin, who squints at the words. With her enhancements, Katrin can see the headline clearly around his shoulder.

CEO OF WORLD BANK STEPS DOWN AMID ALLEGATIONS

OF MISMANAGEMENT

Davin looks almost gleeful at this news, but Colin doesn't seem to be celebrating. She places her hand on his where he's wrapped it around the edge of his chair for a brief second before placing it back on her armrest. Colin is kinder than she's ever considered being, so she's not sure what he thinks. She suspects that he always had an anxious attachment to Lance since he spent most of his life trying to please and placate him.

Across the table, Percy throws his hands up. "I give up. Who has something mildly sensible they want to talk about?"

Colin takes a break from the pile of packages on the rug to sit in front of the window and watch the park below. Paths zigzag through gardens and under waterfalls, and distant figures meander across the city. It's a beautiful view, and it's one that he chose himself.

He's wearing his black suit, tie, and waistcoat, feeling out of place in the messy room. He's thrown his overcoat on the back of the couch, but even without it, the outfit still looks like the wrong attire to be unpacking and organizing in. He wants to be ready to leave, but also can't let the various piles around the apartment sit unattended for long. After a few minutes, he jumps back to his feet and returns to the mess.

Max, his personal bodyguard on loan, is standing by one of the packages Colin's already opened and studying the large black shape curiously. "What's this one?"

Colin opens the latches of the case and holds open the lid. "It's a cello. Isn't it incredible? I've always wanted to try it out for myself." It's a beautiful wood with a rich varnish that caught his eye when he was looking it up. He can't wait to pick up the bow and begin experimenting with the new instrument.

"You can play that?" Max seems to think Colin is capable of anything.

Colin grins while loosening his bothersome tie. "Not yet. But I'll learn how."

Max shakes his head with a short chuckle. "I don't know how you do these things."

"I could teach you how to play something if you want," Colin says, closing the case.

Max declines with a "thank you," as Colin figured he would. But then the older man bends to pick up two of Katrin's canvases propped against the couch. The *Pipe Organ Waterfall* painting and a landscape of ice cream mountains. "Where do these go?"

"I am going to hang them in the music room. I've never hung pictures, but I guess I can learn how to do that too."

"Well, I can help with that."

"You don't have to," Colin assures him. "The king asked you to be my bodyguard, not to help me move in."

"I would love to help, dear boy. I can't watch you run about, working all evening, and sit here idly. Now where did those sawtooth hangers go?" He wanders across the room to the coffee table situated on the plush rug, then takes the paintings to the music room. The double doors open automatically for him.

"Thank you," Colin remembers to say after a few moments. He steps over a smaller package and crosses over to the kitchen, where he set out a plate of strawberries and never started them. He picks up a strawberry and bites into it, surveying the open area of the apartment. It's changed a lot since he moved in. He's been slowly adding essentials and furnishings to the rooms until it's beginning to transform into a space where he can feel at home. He added items similar to ones in the apartment he shared with his mother, but some of the furnishings are very much his own. He has large windows with a view of waterfalls in Bois de Vincennes. Soft couches. Scripture verses displayed proudly wherever he wants. It used to make him nervous for the work-in-progress rooms to be messy, as though Lance might appear behind him and yell at him for not cleaning. Now, he's starting to relax, to give himself time to figure it all out.

The music room especially is his own creation.

A notification from his security system chimes on his wall display. He abandons the strawberries with a broad smile and rushes to the door. It automatically slides open, and Katrin walks in. Her golden-blue eyes are already taking in all the changes he's made since the last time she was here. He enfolds her in a quick hug.

"Hi! It's so good to see you. I talked to your brother today. Remind me to tell you about it later," Katrin says, walking past the kitchen with him on her heels. He watches her with a smile on his face; it remains every second she's around. She's already noticed the cello case on the rug. "It's coming together so well!" She bends next to the instrument. "Do you intend to collect a whole orchestra?" She laughs, then opens it with an "*ahhh*" of appreciation.

"I might." He follows her to the windows. "You look beautiful in blue. It matches your eyes. It's lovely."

She looks up, grinning. "Thank you. Addie helped me pick it out. She does have her moments of brilliance." She glances over his outfit in return. "You look great too. Are you headed to rehearsal soon?"

"Yes. In thirty-four minutes."

"May I come watch?"

"Alright." He puts his hands in his pockets and discovers more of the sawtooth hangers Max was looking for. He pulls them out and sets them on the table so he can hopefully find them later. "Conducting is harder than I expected. One hand can be doing one thing while the other has to be cuing something else entirely. It's been challenging."

"I know you can do it."

Colin peeks over his shoulder when he hears rummaging in the kitchen. Jarred, Katrin's new head of security, apparently trailed her inside in his typical invisible fashion and is opening a cabinet. When Colin catches his eye, Jarred points at the box of strawberries on the counter. "Is it alright if I have some of these?"

"You can have them all if you want," Colin says. "I've got more."

"You're a strawberry addict, Colin." He takes one, then opens another cabinet to search for something else to snack on.

"I am not," he declares, though he knows Jarred is joking. Jarred is one of the first friends Colin has made in his new life. He asks Colin non-stop questions about how he thinks and how he sees the world, but somehow it doesn't come across as condescending. He seems like a genuinely curious person who likes meeting people and learning about them, so Colin happily answers all his questions.

Katrin sits on his couch, then stands back up to look at the cushion. She removes the fabric package sleeve she sat on and tosses it on the rug.

"So, how's the High Council these days?" Colin asks her, kicking the sleeve with one shoe until it lands in the pile of packages.

"Same as always. Sometimes we seem to be making progress and going in the right direction. Other times it seems like we're losing ground. There are still several members who are convinced we'll become immortal one day."

"Well. Humans will be humans."

She shrugs, hopping back up. "Let's not talk about the Council today. Can you show me the music room? Have you added any new instruments to your collection already? Besides the cello, of course."

"I have." He proudly leads the way to the adjacent room. When the door opens, Katrin instantly turns to the far wall. Max has just finished hanging both of her paintings. The guard even has a digital display of a level on the wall; he turns it off as they come inside. Colin is grateful. Max knows how much a slightly crooked frame would bother him. "It's perfect," he compliments when the blue glow disappears and he can see the frames in the natural light. "They're exactly where I would have put them."

"I'll show you how to do it when we get to the ones in the hall. You'll get the hang of it."

Katrin laughs obligingly. Colin does not. "*I* appreciate your puns, Max," she tells him.

"At least someone around here does," he says cheerily, gathering the extra hardware and returning to the hallway.

Once they are alone, Katrin wanders around the room and looks at all the instruments Colin has collected and displayed. His violin is closest to his desk in the corner. There is a viola next to it, a small harp, a dulcimer, flute, English horn, and another wall of even more instruments that struck his curiosity enough for him to bring one home. In the center of the room is a baby grand piano.

"May I hear it?" Katrin asks.

He crosses the room and sits down on the piano bench. "Of course. What would you like me to play for you, Your Highness?"

She tilts her head, which makes her long curls fall across her arm. She looks extra beautiful when she's thinking and has a far off look in her eye. But he thinks that about many of the things she does.

"*Canopy Crown* would sound really nice on the piano, I think."

"Very well." He plays the song, making up some of the accompaniment with his left hand, since he doesn't have the piece figured out on the piano yet. Katrin doesn't seem to notice him improvising the song as he goes. She sways to the music, making up her own dance since the song is a waltz. After he plays through most of the song, trying to watch her, he pulls up a display window by the piano lid. He taps *Canopy Crown* on his list and the violin overtakes the sound of the piano. He stands up as the music continues and asks, "Can you show me how?"

She grins. "To dance?" She reaches for his left hand when he nods and places her other hand on his shoulder. They step back from the piano. "I'll be careful of the fingers."

"They're alright." He looks at her hand around his. "They've healed." Then he puts his other arm around her waist like he's seen couples do while dancing.

"Okay, so—waltz." Her cheeks are slightly flushed. "How much time do we have before we have to be at the opera?"

He glances back at the display over the piano. "Twenty-two minutes."

"Oh, we can make you a professional in twenty-two minutes. No problem."

He laughs, then focuses, following and repeating her instructions until he can slowly perform the steps. Katrin eventually echoes over the music, "Down up up. Down up up," until they complete a few circles around the piano. Then she says proudly, "Yes! Exactly. Easy. Professional. What did I say?"

They dance until the song loops and they're both slightly dizzy. Then she stands in front of her painting of the ice cream mountains, recalibrating her balance, and he stands behind her. He discovered several days ago that if he stands right behind her, he's exactly tall enough that her head fits neatly under his chin. He likes to fold his arms over her shoulders and stand like this as often as he can now.

"What are you thinking about?" Katrin asks after the silence lasts for a while.

"That I'm happy to be me." It's a new thought, one he's not used to, but it's the truth. He believes with his whole heart that he is who he is for a purpose. "Also, is it breaking some sort of Kaelumian law to tell a princess that I'm in love with her?"

She turns around, smile widening. "It is not. I've checked, coincidentally, because I feel the same."

"Excellent." He looks down at her hands, clasped in his. He's elated, heart racing, even as he's completely comfortable and content with her. She's his favorite person in the world. He brushes back a single caramel curl that's dancing around her face. "And do you think I could ask to kiss a princess too?"

"Yes. And also, yes."

"Excellent."

Five minutes before the train arrives for rehearsal, Colin kisses her in the music room, *Canopy Crown* looping in the background. The sunlight turns orange in the window.

And he's inspired to write a new song.

Meet the Author

Christy is a graphic designer/illustrator by day and a writer in the evening in a particular, comfy chair in her room. She writes both fiction (YA sci-fi, romance, adventure, alternative history) and some non-fiction (devotionals, apologetics). Sometimes, she just calls herself a "creative" since she picks up more hobbies than she can ever properly carry. She plays classical piano, sings, and collects things like skeleton keys, pocket watches, and vintage books. She invites you to follow along if you're interested in stories that capture the imagination, are riveting and yet wholesome, and champion a Christian worldview.

Looking for more trustworthy fiction for you and your family?

Follow along on the journey and stay up to date on upcoming releases! With fiction for the whole family including Young Adult, Middle Grade, and Adult fiction, you can rely on Glory Writers Press for wholesome stories for the whole family... without all of the added inappropriate content or anti-Christian worldviews.

Follow us or send us an email! Our authors love hearing from their readers on how our books impacted you!

www.glorywriters.com/shop

@theglorywriterspress

glorywriterspress@gmail.com

THE CHRONICLES OF ELIRA
by Author Victoria Lynn

Non-magical Young Adult/Adult medieval fantasy

With the new regent bleeding the country dry, Violet keeps her head down and her heart quiet. She knows what happens to those who cross the Kingsmen.

But everything changes when she finds one of them wounded and unconscious in the woods. He wakes with no memory, and Violet makes a dangerous choice—she destroys the proof of who he was.

Now, with unrest rising and secrets unraveling, Violet must face the truth: some pasts are harder to bury than others.

Marcus is no stranger to loss. When conflict erupts on the Eliran border, he joins a convoy to offer medical aid—only to encounter horrors beyond his imagination and a woman who will change everything.

Dilara has escaped a brutal life of slavery in Rusalka, but freedom brings its own challenges. Haunted by trauma and thrust into an uncertain future, she must learn to trust again—especially in the man who now stands by her side.

As war looms and secrets surface, can Marcus and Dilara find healing in each other? Or will their pasts keep them chained to pain and sacrifice?

Elira is fractured by war, grief, and betrayal. As the kingdom teeters on the edge of collapse, King Elgon holds on to hope awaiting the return of his most loyal knight.

Malcolm's mission is perilous: rescue a long-lost heir and redeem the mistakes that haunt him. But with enemies closing in and a secret that could change everything, one wrong move could doom them all.

Rosalie has spent her life locked away in a tower. When freedom comes, it drags her into a world of danger, destiny, and a crown she never asked for. The choices she makes will shape the future of a nation.

CHESTNUT ACADEMY

by Author Olivia Lynn

Middle Grade Fiction

Ten-year-old Princess Millie is thousands of miles away from her Royal Family in Europe, attending a fancy horse school for girls in Kentucky! Upon her arrival at Chestnut Academy, Millie overhears her classmates stating what a "Royal pain" it would be to go to school with a Princess. Millie desperately wants the girls to like her, so she chooses to keep her royal identity hidden. But will a bottle of purple hair-dye be enough to keep her secret? What will happen when everyone finds out who she truly is?

Millie is all set for a fun-filled "Galentine's Day" at Chestnut Academy—until her dad asks her to spend the day with her little brother, risking a major club violation: No Boys Allowed!

But when the boys of Craven Hall issue a surprise challenge and invite the girls to their school dance, things take a hilarious turn. Can Millie and the M&M gang outsmart the boys and win the prank war, or will they have to call a truce in the middle of the fun?

Millie and the M&M's are lacing up their hiking boots and saddling up for an overnight camping adventure! The stakes are high as they face off against the oh-so-snooty Amy and Amanda in a survival badge competition!

Badge by badge, challenge by challenge, the M&M's are determined to come out on top! However, as the competition heats up, Millie finds herself torn between racing for victory and disregarding Miss Belle's words of caution. Will Millie risk the safety of herself, her horses, and her teammates to secure the win?

Princess Millie is thrilled to spend her birthday week at Circle D Dude Ranch in the Colorado mountains. With her dream horse, nonstop trail rides, and exciting rodeo competitions, it's shaping up to be her best birthday ever.

But when her best friend Makayla starts spending time with a new boy, Millie feels left out—and more than a little annoyed. Can she win back her friend and the rodeo competition, or will one boy ruin the M&M's friendship for good?

THE COLORS OF RAIN

by Author Abiail Hayven

Young Adult Pro-life, Christian Fiction

Evan made a deathbed promise to his dad to hold their family together and lead them well. In the face of challenges on every side, Evan neglects his studies, and to make up his grade, he must write the story of the girl in his class who always has a palm-sized masterpiece painted on her left hand.

Rain has lived in Ivy Hollow nearly her entire life. The circumstances of her story have never been easy to come to terms with, but they've never been a secret... until now. Her senior year brings two new students to her small-town school, and both turn out to be a threat to the life she's created for herself. Her long buried past is being exposed all over again, and she's terrified of facing it.

Jordan doesn't want anything to do with Ivy Hollow, but her mom's new business has them living there anyway. While she's unpacking boxes, Jordan discovers a dark family secret that will shatter every conception she's ever had—and it just might have something to do with the girl at school who has a unique name and only one hand.

Three stories. One small town. Once they collide, life will never be the same.

www.ingramcontent.com/pod-product-compliance
Lightning Source LLC
Chambersburg PA
CBHW020739310726
48969CB00002B/322